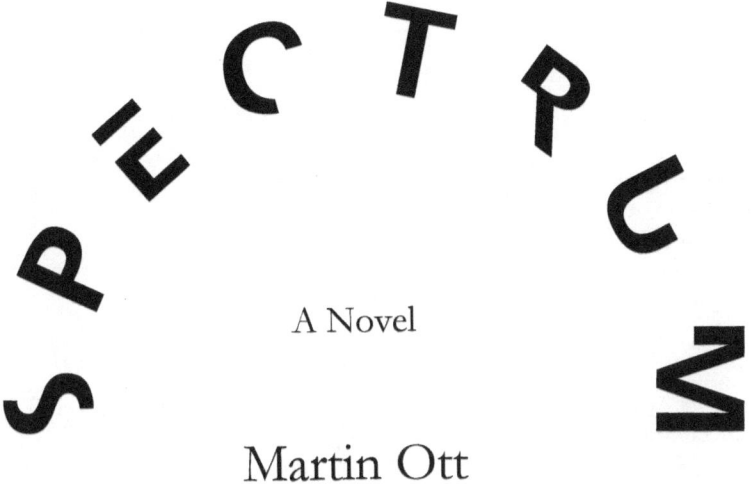

SPECTRUM

A Novel

Martin Ott

C&R Press
Conscious & Responsible

Cover Art "Tumors" by Eugenia Loli
Interior design by Andrew Sullivan
Exterior design by C&R Press

Library of Congress Cataloging-in-Publication Data

ISBN: 978-1-936196-59-3
LCCN: 2016931079

C&R Press
Conscious & Responsible
www.crpress.org

For special discounted bulk purchases please contact:
C&R Press sales@crpress.org

This book is dedicated to Kevin Woodson and the stories we created together and separately over the years.

I wake
and it's not a dream
I see the long coast of the continent
writhing in sleep
this America we thought we dreamed
falling away flake by flake
into the sea
and the sea blackening and burning

—   Philip Levine
The Names of the Lost

CONTENTS

SPECTRUM

INFRARED
Prologue

Greek was well named for someone who named himself, an intruder into all times, places, and stories. He had wandered the globe. Crushed empires. Loved a woman, once.

He lived alone in a sunken cave that had once been the tallest ozonodome in Collings. Isolation was a two-edged sword. He didn't mind the time alone, but lately his thoughts had become scattered. He had fewer and fewer visitors each year. A good sign. It meant his suffering may have been worth it.

"As if you don't enjoy your pain. You need to have had good intentions to be a proper martyr."

I gave up everything.

Greek was also quite mad.

"No, you just gave up."

You don't want to admit I'm the only person strong enough to have used power for the good of others.

Most people who live alone probably digress to conversations with themselves, although Greek doubted anyone could claim his multiple personalities.

"History may not leave you as glowing a review. What makes you think you didn't send humanity on a collision course with extinction?"

Better to die free than...

Greek concentrated and tried to dampen the voices of his ghosts.

"Don't quote nonsense. Wisdom through others' eyes is hardly applicable. Instead of Greek, you should have named yourself Secondhand II, Almighty Ruler of Borrowed Memories."

Shut up.

"Shut up."

Greek shook away the cobwebs and staggered to his feet, the

hardwood in his fire pit crackling and popping from the heat. Outside the jagged entrance to his cave, light bled through low-hanging clouds and fused slowly with the earth, an occurrence that still seemed unnatural after so many decades within the walled city.

Day and night, sun and moon, Greek and his memories: each spent fleeting moments with one another. The longer he lived, the more he was convinced that the universe was a coupling of passionate lovers who spurned one another between illicit encounters. Life didn't allow pain to be joy, or vice versa, but fed on the clashing of opposites.

Greek placed a hand on his belly and ignored the early rumblings of starvation. Winter had only begun in earnest weeks before, but it promised to be especially harsh. He should have replenished his food stores months ago instead of relying on the yearly tithing from New Springs, fifty kilos to the south. It was only fitting he pass away in the dead of winter, a pasty memory fading from time and sun.

Greek tossed a stick into the heart of the fire. The tapered end burst into flames. It was like watching an exhausted swimmer floundering in eddies of a mad and unforgiving ocean. This cave, like the sea, held terrifying mysteries and an almost infinite capacity to generate and sustain life. From life also comes destruction. The twig was quickly consumed, sputtering a wispy gray trail toward the oval skylight above.

He heard a squeak behind him and knew, even before he turned, that his visitor had already departed. Greek smiled at the tiny pile of half-eaten grain. It was stupid of him to be sharing his meager supplies with some unknown creature, but he needed the company. Even invisible company. Animals had suffered more than humans in the cities, engineered to specification and to have no offspring. The patter of feet in his cave above the rubble of what was once Collings City cheered him considerably.

Greek wrapped his robe around his shoulders and strode into the labyrinth of his humble domain. Home was a fallen skyscraper, the ruins of which led down through the layers of earth where he'd once lived. This journey dredged up feelings he'd been trying to bury from having caused the city's destruction. He needed neither light nor hands to guide him through the twisting corridors. Darkness descended. The air grew flat and cool. The walls were smooth, with few rough edges, the remnants of former times. The remnants of fabrications of all kinds.

He gradually wove his way to his secret cubbyhole and fiddled with the controls. He used most of the tiny output of his crude generator to keep this ancient vault sealed. He drummed out the code on his minicomp and ghosted the hatch. A thick slab of steel whirred into nothingness, revealing a chamber hardly wider than he was tall. He tested the air with the flat of his palm. Rich, warm, invigorating, the vials of crisping radiated a dull heat. Its power and addiction inhabited a murky realm just beyond human comprehension: heaven, hell, or both.

Greek couldn't bring himself to pour out the storehouse of fluid. If the crisping invoked memories in him, imagine what it could do to a planet that comprehended the true nature of humanity. Quakes and floods would only be the beginning. While humankind could always use a good thrashing, the Earth had done nothing to deserve being crisped.

Greek had access to more information through the crisping than everyone else on earth combined. His memories were limitless pools of brine and regret. The thousands of brown cylinders were a gateway to humanity's recent trials and rebirth. It also held the fuel for its destruction. A century ago, the crisping was the world's most valuable commodity. Now it was stored in the cave of a mad old hermit.

Of course, Greek indulged habitually.

He fumbled for the nearest beaker and uncapped it, swigging the brackish fluid. He let his mind wander the corridors of the recent past. Impressions gave way to memories. Emotions grew: hopelessness, anger, revenge, love.

He could feel the effects immediately. Blood pumped into his extremities, straining his heart with the flush of exertion. His limbs tingled with an itch that begged to be consummated. He rose and stumbled back to his hearth. The essence of womanhood flooded his mind, threatening to snap his tenuous hold on sanity. A searing white fog clouded his brain. White...the color of hate and lust and light.

He threw himself into the fire and curled into the flames. Blood boiled. Thoughts surged. Energy coursed. Muddiness became clear. Clear grew a hard shell, surrounding the twelve claws of time in a tortoise-like sphere. Memories flew beneath his su-per-charged fingertips. He was scared by how easy it was for him to revert to the computer he'd once been.

What sliver of the past should he access tonight and drive into his hardened skin? The most painful and alluring choice was the story of his lover Florida and the final days of the city they had once called home.

White and black, yin and yang, Greek lost himself in his mem-ories, a machine, a ghost, a human, a tragedy unfolding.

CRIMSON

1

The penthouse of the tallest ozonodome in Collings City throbbed with the palpitations of too many people in too small a space. A party smoldered behind smoky windows, emanating a hazy crimson glow. Inside, a crowd had formed in George Polk's rumpus room, a high-tech entertainment center and gambling den where the president entertained guests, brokered deals, pretty much whatever he wanted.

"I can't see a thing."

"Can someone turn down the lights?"

Polk smiled and traced his pinky nail along miniature nodules on his belt. His impossibly dark skin seemed to devour the muted track lighting as he fidgeted with the controls. The hologram sharpened into focus, expanding the oval racetrack around the rapt audience.

"Come on, Mobius, put some heart into it."

"Again, the whip. Give him the whip."

Polk tapped his buckle and sent an electronic signal coursing through the tiny body of his ten-year-old thoroughbred. Mobius, the reigning champion, spasmed, then gritted his teeth. His alabaster legs churned as he regained the lead on the inside rail. Roars of approval cascaded throughout the cavernous hall. The milling crowd pressed against seated ticket holders, catching flashes of the dozen pale racers thundering into the third lap.

On the opposite end of the oval penthouse, Mere Roosevelt sank deeper into his seat. He was not having a good time. His dress grays clung to his skin: stiff, uncomfortable. The strobe lighting at the well-stocked bar dotted the room with an ephemeral humanity. Aside from the baristas, escorts and caterers, he was the lightest person here. Not that this was much of a surprise. His invitation to Skytown was an obvious mistake. He didn't belong here.

Mere and a few other introverts guzzled liquor and kept a wary watch on the petty nobility in the rumpus room. And their hangers-on. Hologram generators buzzed a shadowy kaleidoscope. Albino racers circled execs with inhuman speed, forcing them to spin swivel-seats in synch with the racers. President Polk revolved in the circle's hub, taking bets from anyone willing to bite on 2-1 odds against his Mobius.

Mere had never understood the allure of gambling. There was no such thing as easy answers. Even hard work only brought more questions followed by even harder work. He smiled for the first time all evening, lost in an imaginary conversation with himself: *hi, how are you? Bored and angry, thank you. I'm either going to crawl under my chair or pitch one of these arrogant asses out the window.*

The alcohol was starting to make him punchy. His exhausted thirty-year-old body was checking out on him as well. Although he'd arrived barely an hour ago, his fascination with the leisure class had waned. There was something unnerving about watching boys drugged into high-speed competition.

Although the people, places, and things surrounding him were big, beautiful, and slightly kinky, it all felt false: life-size sculptures of prewar origin, paintings of forest meadows, urns of unimaginable worth. Everything in the room screamed, "I'm an object, available to the highest bidder," including the people. Mere's temples throbbed and he was overcome by a wave of nausea that he sometimes got while kneeling at Sunday mass before the black-robed apostles.

"You going to go watch the race?" a man asked his companion at the bar.

"Like we don't know who's going to win?"

"Who's going to win?" Mere asked, even though he knew who the favorite was. Any excuse to break the monotony and join into conversation. Laughter erupted around the bar. Mere buried his forehead into his palm and swilled company liquor from a gargantuan stein. Beneath his fingers he gawked at scantily dressed women from a highly respected escort agency who served neurosushi and salmon-lobster bisque. The friendlier ones popped delicacies into salivating mouths with smiles and dead eyes. Mere had spent most of the evening shooing away women and food with names he couldn't pronounce.

It figured. His big break was turning into a break down. Invitation to this party was his crowning achievement, the culmination of years of hard work. So why wasn't he enjoying himself? Was it because he felt like a fraud? He had, after all, just developed a transmission fluid that increased the efficiency of the city's organiputer. So what? Who did it help? Really? Certainly not him or the millions mired hundreds of meters below. Mere realized he would never feel comfortable among those who mattered, jostling with young carnivores and ageless toadies for attention.

He hadn't always been this bitter. There was nothing like corporate life to deaden your nerves and dampen your enthusiasm for just about everything. He knew he should try to shake off his foul mood and rejoin the party, but he just didn't feel like it. Obtaining knowledge and information had been his lifelong pursuit. Now he realized it was the quest itself that had made him happy, the rush of unearthing something off-limits. Since his promotion he had access to more "sanitized" information than he could ever want or use. They were making it way too easy for him to join the ranks of bureaucrats and stop bucking the system.

Cheers and applause rocketed the holohearth. Mobius won, edging out his nearest competition by several meters. Polk's thoroughbred was the brightest ten-year-old of the season, an odds-on favorite to win the triple crown. It was rumored that Mobius was really the president's albino nephew, provided with a private trainer, drug handler, and muscle-graft surgeon since he was old enough to walk. Inebriated officers trickled back into the main hall, leaving an impressive throng settling up with Polk. Mere felt like a caricature of misery. He smiled a skeleton's smile and stared at the backdrop of picture windows. Each was inlaid with state-of-the-art shutter glass. The effect was dizzying. Windowpanes changed shading, angle, refraction, and level of magnification every few seconds.

Collings blared from the windows like Gabriel's trump. A stainless-steel storefront in Hightown shifted to the underside of mushroom domes in Skytown, melting into a ramshackle warehouse in lowtown. The shutter-snap images made even the most familiar parts of the city seem alien, malignant, almost alive. Jagged lightscraper teeth snapped at him from behind the glass, like his wife's chihuahua-chicken Tim did at home. The glassy-eyed execs stumbled about blindly, oblivious, horny. Nighttime painted the penthouse in a cornucopia of pastels and shadow-hues, a smoky reflection of what lay beneath the skin.

"Hey Roosevelt." A hand settled on his shoulder. "Loosen up and take another dimeld."

Mere turned and looked up at Reed Bourne, his supervisor and only acquaintance at the festivities. If partying in Skytown wasn't surreal enough, he had to hang out with the most hated Level 2 in his lab and pretend to like it. It was disconcerting how much Reed looked like his own brother: the same piercing hazel-gray eyes, thick arching eyebrows, supple lips, and round cheeks. Mere had gotten more than his fair share of ribbing at work because of it. Reed fished a white capsule from his coat and dropped it in Mere's palm.

"Thanks. I think. Couldn't hurt. Unless someone tries to talk to me." Mere shrugged and gobbled the synthetic opiate, this month's designer drug, probably developed by a disgruntled Pyramid employee in his spare time.

"What have you got to be glum about? Your research is going to make Pyramid a fortune. Not that we don't already have a monopoly in biocomp."

"I don't know what's wrong with me. I'm a little overwhelmed."

Reed ran his fingers through his curly black hair and looked around the room. "Don't send a man to do a boy's job."

"Meaning what?" Mere choked, fighting back the surge of his legendary temper. At least, in his own mind, it was legendary.

"Meaning relax and enjoy yourself. You know how to relax, don't you?"

"I thought my new promotion made that mandatory."

"That's the spirit. We'll forge you into management material yet. I hear the old man's going to give you free reign in the lab." Reed boyishly tapped his arm with the back of his hand. "Maybe a stipend and a few more assistants."

"All of which I'm sure aren't going to hurt your career any."

"Damn right. I don't care what you do or how you do it as long as I end up looking good."

Mere's ample lips swam apart. "Do I get to be your boss?"

"No one's my boss. Not now, not ever."

A sarcastic remark froze in Mere's throat. President Polk, dressed in a virgin black suit, strode toward them. His skin, darkened by science and a commitment of the leisure class to fashion, made his gray eyes dance with brown specks. Polk was big-boned and muscular, a wide aristocrat's smile swiveling on a burly neck and shoulders.

Mere thrust his stocky frame up from impossibly deep cushions. He did not, under any circumstances, want to speak to his host. He tried ducking out of the room along a row of crystal pyramids spinning on near-invisible wires. The president veered toward him.

"God bless Usa. So you're the Roosevelt I've heard so much about," Polk said in a booming voice that was familiar, hypnotic, frightening as hell.

"God bless Usa. Yes sir, it's good to meet you."

Mere sheepishly extended his hand and got it crushed in Polk's hydraulic grip. The president, even at his advanced age, was still intimidating. Mere tried to hold back his anger as his fingertips throbbed in pain.

"So, son, what do you think of the celebration?"

"I think that if I tell you what I REALLY think, you'll toss me out of here and if I suck up to you, you'll lose respect for me."

Polk chuckled for so long that Mere's thoughts had time to run the gambit from relief to nervousness to fear.

"Maybe people were wrong about you," Polk said.

"Maybe." Mere felt lost by this turn in the conversation.

Polk whirled, catlike. "Hey, Bourne, Roosevelt's practically a ghost. I thought you kept your people more presentable, especially the important ones."

Mere had let his tan deteriorate with recent overtime. Other things had slipped as well, if recent fights with Gail were any indication.

"I don't have an excuse," Mere said.

"No need to explain. I hear you've been making me a lot of money. You don't know it yet, but soon you're going to be busier than you ever thought possible."

"Thanks for the confidence."

Again the laugh. Polk was one creepy guy. Finally, the president wiped tears from his face with a handkerchief, saying, "I don't use tanning booths myself." Polk eyed him from toe to head. "You ever been crisped?"

Mere nodded no, although he once spent six months saving up for a bottom-of-the-barrel crisping in the white-light district. It was the ultimate sexual experience, one people had been known to kill for. Reed winked behind the president's back, warming Mere's face to a bright pink.

"Have a seat and my people will take care of you."

The president's nimble fingers scrolled across his belt. Two bald and naked women, identical in appearance, popped up through the buffered parquet floor. Marble closed around their perfect bodies, leaving no trace of an opening. Each was a mirror image of the other, except one held a bundle of black wires, the other red.

"Ready to jump start?" both asked at once.

One brushed his foot with the wire and Mere almost fell out of his seat. They were real. He'd figured them for holos. The twins looped around him, caressing their nipples with the metallic connectors. "No crowding, room enough for everyone," Reed told the gathering crowd. Mere tried not to let his embarrassment show as the twins fitted electrodes to his temples.

"...a lot about someone's character...." Mere caught a snatch of Polk's conversation with another black-suited board member.

These corporate types were obviously no strangers to the ritual. President Polk was by far the darkest man he'd ever seen, probably the result of three crispings a day.

"Can you believe how...." someone else whispered.

Mere withered beneath the chortles and stares, sinking into his seat. He focused on the wobbling pirouettes of the low-hanging pyramids, the company's official logo. It was also a symbol used by the oldage superstitious in lowtown. Could the founders of Pyramid have once been pagans?

A bar attendant stepped out from behind the glass booth and unbuttoned her shimmering tunic. Crimson flashes danced along translucent material fluttering to the floor. As the busty redhead approached, Mere could tell she was already well into the sex drug's catalyst. Her pupils were dilated. Perspiration welled up through her pores, bathing her body in a reflective froth. She swayed seductively as she bent over him and unbuttoned his shirt.

"Who—" Mere started, but she pressed a forceful finger to his lips. Who was he to argue with a beautiful woman, especially one on an obvious mercy mission from Usa? She yanked his shirt halfway down his arms and brushed his quivering chest with her own. Low-level pulses bathed his brain with a rhythm that tuned itself to his heartbeat. He dug his fingernails into the chair arm. His jaw clenched. He lost the ability to think coherently.

Brown fluid trickled from her nipples, forming a puddle on the valley of his chest. The burning itch was incredible. His penis was aflame. He grunted in primal rhythms, then it hit. Crisping. Heat without light. Burn. Burning. Burnt. He was someone else. Someone else was him. Mere screamed in the convulsive throes of little death.

GARNET

2

The cable spun in wobbling circles as the glass booth descended. A pinkish track light sliced the transport in half, red-washing a dozen seated passengers. No more. No more bodies. No more women in his sights. Usa, how could he still be this horny? Mere pressed his forehead to the glass, away from a dozen maids descending from a day's labor in Skytown. These tired looking women were mostly lightenings (off-whites) and middle-aged, but his erection held no prejudices.

What was going on? And why didn't he remember anything from his crisping? His heart fluttered from the shifting legs and swishing of flesh beneath fabric. If he were able to think past his arousal, he would have noticed the women's skin prematurely wrinkled from sunlight and eyes crowed from years of subservience.

Mere shook with white yearning and barely masked rage, struggling against a bout of palsy. Ever since childhood he'd been wracked with seizures and occasionally violent attacks. No doctor had ever been able to tell him the source of his malady. His affliction was unusual in that he dropped in and out of consciousness like a rock.

A cacophony of images whisked through his mind: endless fantasies where he and these shrewd matrons were trapped in this booth for all eternity. Lust overcame him. His teeth bored into his bottom lip. He covered his groin with his elbow and twisted his garnet wedding ring into his thigh. Sick. Sick. Sick.

He closed his eyes and moaned, fighting to control his body, mind, or both. His skin swelled with an appetite that threatened to swallow the world. The darkness did not, could not help him as he ejaculated, yet again, in the damp folds of his trousers.

***

Relieved whispers followed Mere from his berth like lovesick teenagers.

"Humma himma believe it?"

"Sssss...hssst...ssss...issa...police when you need them?"

Mere bowed his head and stumbled off the shuttle. Women. No women here. Thank Usa. The Bennett Terminal hummed in electric desolation, the air drenched with mustard lights and the flickering of predawn wind. Fiberglass booths and chairs lined the skyway on-ramp. Even though he'd lived in Hightown almost five years it still felt alien, cold. He stepped on the conveyor and merged into the four-lane skywalk that spun spider webs and cloverleafs above the sprawling metropolis of lowtown.

He rubbed his eyes and suppressed a yawn. The dried remains of bodily fluids caked his skin, making walking uncomfortable. Immense hourglass urns, filled with blooming flowers, divided statues and benches on the promenade like matronly chaperones. Like women. All women. Like Gail. He slowed on the conveyor sidewalk, unsure whether he was up to facing his wife. He was sick of arguing with her and even sicker of dreading the arguments to come.

Mere was exhausted, but annoyingly awake, the burnout of recent days intermingling with an adrenal buzz from the crisping. He didn't want to think about what happened at the party or if Gail would considering it cheating on her. The charcoal panels of the skyway hummed tunelessly beneath his feet. The seams buckled and wavered. The skyway's railing knotted in metallic spindles like gigantic spider arms playing with its prey.

He peered at the back of his hand, flexing and unflexing his fingers. He didn't notice any change in pigmentation—he was still plenty light for a Hightowner. A patrolbot whizzed by and pinched a flap of skin from his elbow. He spat at the quickly departing metallic spy and a gust broke his phlegm into spittle, carrying it back into his face. Droids made privacy impossible in the upper quadrants of the city, one of the many prices you had to pay for upward mobility.

Like the ritual he'd been forced into earlier that evening in Skytown. He felt that some core essence had been drained from him by the crisping, a part of himself he wasn't sure he'd ever be able to regain. His fears went deeper than the hypocrisy he felt for hob-nobbing with the corporate elite or public sex with a stranger. He could sense something malignant bubbling up in his body. A cauldron of jumbled emotions and doubts which made him feel alone. Very much alone. He wished things weren't so out of kilter with Gail. Normally, he could count on her to speak her mind and give him perspective, criticism, a shoulder to lean on.

His complex rose in the distance, one hundred cramped and overpriced condos sprawled in a tight arc along the skyway. He didn't want to head home yet, but he couldn't think of any other options. Infrared shift just went on. The only open bars were in Oldtown. He wasn't up for the effort.

Mere gazed up at the mosaic of sky. Stars dotted the Eastern third of the firmament while a cobalt-gray filled the middle strip. He often wondered why there were only stars in the easternmost sky. Most theories revolved around the terra cliffwall, a precipice of unfathomable height and width that filled the western firmament with patches of brown and mottled greens. Clergy explained that the cliffwall was the world's edge and Collings, capital of the Usan empire, guarded its citizens from the winged demons that roosted there. Mere was religiously noncommittal. He did not believe in Usa and the underground vault of heaven. Neither did he have patience for oldage shamans.

Science was his religion. It was as flawed as any other, filled with hierarchies, pettiness, and glossed-over misdeeds. Only now was he beginning to understand how crippling it was to stumble through life with a microscope for glasses. People confused him. He confused himself. Gail confused him most of all. The fragments of the world he understood and reconfigured in his lab kept him from asking who am I? What is reality outside these city walls?

The densely packed lights of Oldtown blurred beneath the handrails as he hopped onto the deceleration strip leading to his complex. He looked the other way, more from his fear of heights than sadness or guilt. Although he hadn't lived in the lowtown borough of Irony for years, the familiar streets still beckoned. He fought off an irrational urge to vault the safety wires, grateful for the vertigo that made jumping unthinkable, regardless of how alluring his childhood fantasies of flight remained.

* * *

Mere curled up into the blanket on his landlady's antique sofa. He bunched the faded fabric around his midsection to hide yet another erection. Everything—light, shadow, silence, conversation—massaged his frayed nerves and aroused a hunger for flesh that threatened to drive him over the brink. He could feel the heat rising from the curves of womanhood beside him. Helena, although old enough to be his mother, was a statue of a woman: unyielding and worthy of worship, classic curves barely nicked by her advancing age. Her apartment had a museum quality as well, beautiful and unreachable in a way that normally made him feel impotent. Not tonight. He wanted to straddle the world and make it his mistress. He felt as virile as time ravaging the future.

The muzzled teeth of dawn spilled in through the window slats. The Cheshire cat wall clock pawed at the numbers on its belly while its tail flicked and eyes roved the room. An hour had passed since he paused at the amber glow streaming from Helena's apartment. His landlady had invited him in and listened, without judgment, to his barely comprehensible tirade about selling out and becoming crisped. She cradled a bottle of rom in her lap and waited for Mere to finish spilling his guts before asking, "You ever consider quitting Pyramid?"

Mere nodded no, although he often wished he could find a job where he didn't have to suck up to management. There were no other real options for a scientist who wanted to do interesting work. "Pyramid has done right by me. I stay busy." Helena's penetrating gaze made him feel the twinges of his impending hangover. "That's the problem with this city. Everyone's hurrying, but no one's going anywhere."

"Hmm," Mere forced a yawn, cupping his hand over his mouth. He didn't want to be impolite, but their conversation was starting to drain him. All except the tiny surge of crisping that kept pricking his genitals.

Helena's mouth upturned in a sly grin. "Just like the cat on the wall. Time has twelve claws. The more you scurry from number to number, the less you see the cage. The cat has us all pinned between appointments and disappointments."

Mere's eyes roamed the cluttered living room as her nonsense patter tugged at his brain. Helena's apartment was an anomaly. He'd never seen anyone more obsessed with out-of-date furniture and appliances. Antiques were rarely seen in Hightown. The people here were obsessed with obscuring the past. The unkempt state of her home added to the feeling of former times: cluttered walkways, dust-covered tables, cobwebbed light fixtures. Even the walkways were coated in gray silt, as if no one lived here. Generally, Hightown had all idiosyncrasies drummed out of it, everything with its own antiseptic function.

"You grew up in an orphanage, right?"

Mere shook his head *yes*. He hadn't remembered telling Helena about it, but she was one of those busybodies who knew more about everything, family and friends included, than you did.

"Then you're probably asking yourself why you aren't happy with a good job, beautiful wife, and a Hightown home.

"I know I should be."

"But you aren't. Doesn't surprise me. You always struck me as the unhappy sort. I don't mean that in a bad way. Contentment, in most ways, is ignorance. Only the depressed and neurotic can pave the road to enlightenment for the rest of us. That '*love yourself, love life*' crap keeps people from seeing the handwriting on the wall. Take you, for example."

Mere fidgeted, fighting dual urges to blush and run screaming from the room. Unlike those kind-hearted listeners who let you mutter half-truths, Helena scraped marrow from bone. He also worried that she knew about the hard-on he was trying to hide.

"You want nothing more than to go home, sleep off your bad mood, and pretend everything isn't falling apart around you. Well, it is. Don't forget it. It's good news. The best. Believe in your dreams. They are as real as anything else in this pisshole of a city."

The dream lady was at it again. Gail consulted her religiously, letting her analyze the smallest details of her mostly erotic nighttime visions. Mere didn't dream...anymore. When his parents died, he willed away all fanciful illusions, fighting his natural tendency to be daring, romantic, adventurous. Even in his deepest sleep, he held back these visions. His childhood fantasies of fighting demons and saving women in distress had been replaced by work, work, and more work.

"Self-loathing, *is* hating everyone," Helena mused, nudging him from his stupor. "Sorry, I was just thinking how the opposite of what I said about love was true."

"No one believes in me. I don't have friends." Even as he said it, Mere felt the release of built-up tension. He couldn't believe he was spilling his guts to this old kook.

Helena shook in laughter. "Even the cat on the wall has friends, as much as it tries to be aloof."

Her hand reached across her service table and settled on his forearm. Mere rose and lurched toward her. Fighting an urge to hold her down and kiss her, he stopped, stumbled, and backpedaled toward the door. He waved goodbye, knowing that if he stayed he would embarrass himself. Still, he had to admit, he felt better than when he first arrived.

When he stumbled through the phasing hatch, Gail was awake and waiting for him. She looked well rested and cooler than the morning winds blasting across the skyway. A trail of brown bangs connected a balled hand to her furrowed brow. Maybe she had already slept and risen—it was unlike her to stay up. Tim, her chihuahua-chicken, bobbed up from her lap and scurried into the kitchen. In five years of uneasy cohabitation, Mere and Tim had come to an understanding, a truce of sorts. Neither recognized the other's existence.

Gail slapped her palms against her padded armrest and shifted her lounger out of rest mode. She stood defiantly, hands on hips, her eyes searing him to the bone. He reached out to comfort her, but she recoiled. Mere was instantly reminded of a recent argument where she'd complained that he touched her too often. The living room swirled with an unreal cleanliness. Mute anger turned in on itself. The messiness of life boxed and put away. The furniture dusted to a canine gleam. Even his compustation reflected his guilty image back.

"Look what the cat dragged in," she said.

"It's not like I even wanted to go to Skytown. Reed invited me. I couldn't say no, could I?"

"Saying no isn't one of your problems, Mere."

"I wish I could say the same about you." He regretted the words the moment they left his lips. He knew that he should apologize, but was too tired and cranky to prolong the unpleasantries. "I'm going to bed."

"You come home smelling like rom and women, insult me, then think you can just walk away? After cheating on me?"

"Getting crisped isn't exactly cheating, Gail."

"You don't get off that easy. You promised me that you

wouldn't get crisped without me. At the very least you're a liar."

Mere cradled his head in his palms. "I couldn't help it."

"Neither can I," she said, turning her back and stomping off to their bedroom.

He wanted her to rant and rave as she had weeks before or to make a definitive statement like tossing his possessions out into the hallway. Anything was better than the silent treatment. What was happening to them? They were going through the motions these days, the love they had for one another fading away even as their own skin became darker to blend in with their surroundings.

* * *

Mere tossed and turned throughout the night. Maybe it was the shock of dreaming, actually dreaming, for the first time in years. Each time he woke and tried to snap himself out of it, he found himself slipping back into the same nightmare. In it, he sat on the boughs of a fossilized tree next to an ancient gardener who pruned leaves with an axe. Mist capped the cityscape below. Far below. His vertigo made him dizzy, but the gardener smiled and patted him on the shoulder. The grandfatherly man flashed a toothless grin and swallowed the hatchet, transforming himself from doddering old age to infancy. Mere looked down at his own hands and they were leathery white mitts, wrinkled and peeling back from bone.

He was changing. Into what, he had no idea.

The gardener's memories rushed into him until he was older than history, omnipotent and impotent both, straddling a pyramid larger than dreams. He'd enslaved the spectrum of light, remade the laws of gravity, and transformed the alphabet, the logos of a former time, into a world flatter than the oldest of myths. Power coursed through him. Egyptian wonders of forgotten times held no candle to his city. Indeed, it would be like comparing an ant to a dinosaur or a single utterance to the history of the universe. No one, future or past, would forget who he was...ever again.

The infant crawled toward him, cooing and spitting up brown fluid. It reached out a tiny hand and shoved him off the branch. Mere's shorn skin acted as a parachute as he descended along the curved city walls. Gargoyles snapped at his feet, tearing greedily at his skin. He flapped his arms frantically and a side draft pushed him beneath the ozonodomes into Hightown. Below, he could see Pyramid employees shimmer in the ecru cadence of revolving skyways. Formaldehyde laced the air with an almost piney freshness.

Mere dropped past the mustard halogens and accelerated toward Oldtown. Blue shifters scurried home past ultraviolet stiffs just coming on. White shirts descended on hoverpods, relieving the tired bludgeoners of lowtown with fresh troops. Banks of neon dimmed but did not blink out, casting a spackled glow on abandoned warehouses and unrepaired streets. Several albinos, drunk and homeless, wound through deserted neighborhoods like stripped wires in a faulty appliance.

Mere's vision narrowed as he descended into an alley behind Boo's Bar in North Irony. His skin detached and fluttered away, leaving his skeleton plummeting toward a vast sea of ancient asphalt. He tried to howl, but had no tongue. His teeth fell out in endless clumps, splattering the streets and rooftops like hail. He accelerated toward a well-dressed man stepping out of the shadows behind a blue shift worker. The men were familiar, almost as familiar as the impending collision of bone and rock. They were both him.

A dark-skinned Mere Roosevelt whipped a handgun out of his jumpsuit. Six shots from a flagette pistol erupted, the impact slamming a lighter-skinned Mere Roosevelt against a street lamp. He has murdered. He has been murdered. Mere crashed through chipped concrete and burrowed beneath the city. He tunneled through gray flesh into the womb of the underground, piercing swollen pink layers, awakening in his Hightown apartment...SCREAMING.

* * *

Mere swatted violently at the air. The sleeper couch filled the den with the whine of a Zero G vacuum. He blinked his eyes in a painful fluttering that matched his heart just moments before. His back spasmed, forcing him to hover sideways to ease the throbbing. He clenched his hands into fists and relished the sensation of skin against skin.

Thank Usa, it was over. His nightmare had felt real, more vivid than being awake was now. All his senses in the dream had been heightened beyond comprehension. Now he felt nauseous, somewhere between wanting to vomit and curl in a fetal ball for all eternity. As a child, recurring nightmares of an ancient gardener watching over the city had haunted him. These dreams had stopped shortly after his parents met their untimely demise during the last major cityquake.

Lingering images of death and decay soon subsided in the sunstrike wafting through the skyglass. Mere examined the back of his hand and noticed a darker pigmentation surrounding the thick circuit of veins curling from knuckles to wrist. Memories of last night's sexual appetite and exhaustion, capped by his strange fight with Gail, flooded his thoughts.

He and his wife needed to spend more time together, that's all that was wrong. His project at work was over and he should be able to get some time off. He reached into his sycron jumpsuit and rearranged himself, loosening his penis from an entanglement of hair. The skin on his stomach and thighs was chapped and painfully sticky.

Mere flipped the gravweb toggle and commanded, "Buckle."

The gravity harness enveloped him, dragging him down to the cushions.

"Release."

The Zero G bubble normalized. The tug of gravity made his head reel, transforming an already strange hangover into a swirl of down, up, and sideways. He rolled clumsily from the cushions and folded the extension behind the sofa. He needed to find a way to make things right with Gail.

"Hey, honey, sorry about last night. I'm an idiot." he called out loudly. "Let's go out for a holofilm today."

His cluttered workstation was the only part of the apartment that suggested a young couple might actually live here. All other signs of life and leisure were absent. Even their collection of holotapes and novelights were alphabetized and catalogued. He lived in a library, no, a museum, a mausoleum of a life. Even the redtipped feathers from Tim's continual shedding were absent. As was the furry squawking bastard himself.

The automated kitchen was spotless and the coffee-tea percolator hadn't been made. Odd. Gail usually woke before him and made him breakfast, even on those mornings, like now, when he didn't deserve it. He wished she would go back to work as the charismatic holophonist he fell for during their less than magical first meeting. Five years ago, she helped him link a call to a team of scientists in faraway Havel. She had been polite, unreachable, and aloof. Uncharacteristically, he'd asked her out on a date, and his life had been changed. She'd dealt with his mood swings and bouts of anger, his manic energy and urge to run from every conflict and fight. She'd made him a better person.

Before Gail, Mere didn't know he had a type. Now every woman resembling his wife filled him with a deep and distrustful physical yearning. He knew their problems stemmed from his inability to commit, to let Gail in to see who he really was. Truth was, he scared himself. He fought a continual urge to fight or flee. His past growing up on the streets of North Irony was always beneath the surface. There he'd learned to do almost anything to survive.

He suffered from their move to Hightown but in many ways it affected Gail worse. Relocation had been awkward for both of them. As new Hightowners, most of the locals considered them beneath notice and their friends from lowtown rarely ran the gambit of skyway police to visit. She spent her days on long walks with Tim or cleaning their home. Battling dust was her way of dealing with the stress of their marriage and unhappiness.

The rest of the apartment checked out empty. Mere approached the last and most likely hiding place: rapping lightly, sliding open the bedroom panel, whispering, "Gail, you asleep?"

Their bedroom was a disaster. The word implode leapt to mind. Gail's hamper had vomited its contents throughout the room, wrapping it mummy fashion from ceiling to floor. He stumbled through the carnage of clothing and displaced objects to their hoverbed.

"Gail," he said, prodding their bunched-up bedding. He growled and booted a bundle of her wardrobe toward the door, exposing a bed of white shag. Then it dawned on him. White? Gail had set all the carpeting and walls in the house to a morose shade of white. "Usa-who-fell-to-heaven-for-our-sins!" Mere cursed. He turned toward her open closet and knew what he'd find even before looking. Her Zero G suitcase was gone, just as she was. After all the threats, she'd finally gone and done it. She'd moved out on him.

AUBURN

4

Mere waited as long as he dared and sliced airborne through the faint after-image of the phasing hatch. He pivoted after landing and whirled in time to watch the doorway solidify. An old childhood game (played mostly by boys) that he never outgrew. Aside from losing a sleeve once, he'd always managed to clear the reappearing hatch. Occasionally, the holonews carried reports of kids getting injured or killed from the infamous pastime of "beating the ghost."

Mere unzipped the gray hood of his long-sleeve shirt and draped the waterproof material over his head. The city had been placed on ozonalert all the last week— sometimes these states of emergency dragged on for months. He knew that he looked silly wrapped in cloth from toe to head, but it was better to be safe. Skincer was one of the city's big killers, especially among light-skinned lowtowners: albinos, lightenings, and zebs.

Mere took the escalator to the sidewalk onramp and quickly navigated the miniature matrix bordering his complex. A happy couple lounged on the carpeted lawn, the woman's head cradled in her partner's lap. Mere half-waved out of politeness, then turned and scowled. The sidewalk encircling his complex soon funneled into a two-lane bridging the skyway. It was a shithole of a day. The overcast haze castrated Skytown's obsidian lightscrapers, shrouding the upper domes in an orangish-gray mist.

He had a hard time keeping last night's unpleasantries out of his mind. He and Gail had been scuffling a lot, but nothing that justified her moving out. He felt as though her complaint about the crisping was a ruse. It was obvious that she'd been holding something back from him, but what? Lately, she'd seemed more sad than angry, their spats about nothing and everything. Her recent moodiness and fierce faultfinding were very much unlike her.

Not entirely true, of course. The early months of their relationship had been filled with the uneasy rumblings of exploration and fighting, often beneath the sheets, for who was in control. Then one day, out of the green, she began placing his welfare and wellbeing before her own. She helped put him through school, sacrificing her own dreams of becoming a public defense advocate.

Funny thing was, he never once asked her to put her life on hold for him. Sure, he probably could have been more encouraging, but, until recently, she seemed happy with her life. Almost maniacally so. Part of him was thankful for her questioning their relationship and breaking them out of their rut. Last week he admitted to her that some of her complaints were justified. That only made her angrier.

His current mission to drag her home like a testosterone-laden caveman probably wouldn't help his case much. So be it. He wasn't about to write off his marriage without understanding what was really going on. Besides, she wouldn't have let slip where she was going unless she'd wanted him to follow her.

He picked up speed on the uptown lane and merged onto the Bennett Terminal expressway. Traffic was moderate for weekend congestion, mostly high-wives on consumer binges and kids prowling the skyway nexus. Omnilines crisscrossed above the treadmills, pumping phone, cable, and comp links into businesses, homes and manimalls. In front of him, a chartreuse vision, decked out in a flower-print jumpsuit and a black halo, yanked her leash and brought her albino to heel. This fashion-hound bordered on obese, her hands and face striped with rainbow cosmetics. Her boy yawned from his squat on the sidewalk and looped his fingers inside his collar to ease the chaffing. Mere knew this woman's overbearing sort all-too-well from his teenage years escorting shoppers to and from Irony's wholesale jewelers. The way she cocked her head with an open-ended black cap made him remember...oh Usa...EVERYONE was wearing turtleneck hats.

Then it dawned on him. Today was Augusa 1, the beginning of yet another citywide clothing mandate. To liquidate overstock from faulty quotas, Pyramid marketers had created a new fashion—turtle neck shirts without the shirts. He now recalled the interoffice memos and HV warnings: recommended wear included ankle bracelets, headbands, and fezz-fashion hats. Starting today,

anyone caught without a neck ring would be officially reprimand-
ed. Screw it. He'd just have to keep a low profile until he found a
Pyramid outlet or a lowtown vendor who'd be sure to have some
binned between holoporn vids and tattooed taxidermy.

The Bennett terminal bustled with activity. Pyramid Police
manned a traffic checkpoint, checking commuters for compliance
to the dress code. Mere knew he should hop a lane moving the
opposite direction, but he didn't feel like it. He wasn't about to turn
back until he tracked down Gail or at least gave it his best shot.
Besides, the regulation was way-too-stupid to take seriously. He
scooted behind the fleshy posterior of the flower-suited woman
and tried to make himself as small and unobtrusive as possible.
He needn't have bothered. Nothing got past the 0/0 vision of the
cybernetically enhanced officers.

"Citizen, yes you, gray shirt, step off the walkway."

"I'm in a hurry, officer. What's wrong?"

"You have five seconds to comply."

"I'm on official business."

"Three, two-"

Mere hopped over the albino's leash and scudded off the deceleration strip. This wasn't going to be a problem, he told himself.
Passing checkpoint screens was a basic urban survival skill, one he
had perfected through numerous brushes with the law.

The policeman pointed a stun prod at his groin. Mere bared
his teeth and tried to keep his temper in check. Who did the white
shirt think he was anyway? His anger made him tremble and patches of brown blurred his eyesight.

"Bless Usa," Mere forced himself to say through a barbed-wire
grin. "Is there anything wrong, officer?"

"Bless Usa," came the humorless reply. "Where is your turtleneck ring, citizen?"

"Did we start that today?"

"Yes, today, at the beginning of red shift. Notices were broad-
casted all week on HV. Or does your house still run on transistor
technology?"

The officer's bulging neck oscillated in laughter. This guy's a
real prick, Mere thought. He's just trying to bait me into doing
something I'll regret. Keep it together. Think about Gail. Can't get
busted. Mere rubbed his eyes and joined in, "Hahaha."

The policeman's massive paw enclosed Mere's arm at the elbow. "As a member of the science corps, you have a responsibility to set an example for others." The white shirt flicked on his portable comp, unwrapped a fresh needle, and pricked Mere in the palm. A trail of wires snaked beneath the guard's uniform and emerged through his pant legs into an organiport. A barrage of numbers funneled onto his wrist L.E.D. Time stood still. Passersby gawked. Mere mocked them in his thoughts.

"Everything SEEMS in order here. One might even say VERY well in order. Congratulations on your promotion. It looks like you have friends in high places."

Why did every white shirt he ran into have to be such a jackass? Maybe it was part of the personality screens for their job application.

"So does this mean I'm free to go?"

"With a warning. But don't let it happen again or we'll slag your ass, friends or no. When people shirk their responsibilities, the system breaks down." The guard withdrew a black band out of his form-fitting jumpsuit. "Wear this for now, but don't forget to buy more."

"Yes, officer, I will wear this atop my head with all the pride that went into its overproduction. Whenever possible, I will purchase more and ring myself in black until I disappear altogether and only the company remains."

Mere slipped the poorly sewn band over his hood and hurried onto the slow-moving conveyor. He wasn't waiting around to see if his sarcasm had flown over the white shirt's head or not. His attitude was bound to get him in trouble someday. Mere'd had quite a few brushes with the law, back when he had nothing to lose but a tiny cubicle in a North Irony orphanage. When shove came to push, he wasn't like other Highs. Lowtown had honed his self-reliance and a mean streak. Mere wove his way to the ticket booth, using sharp swivels of elbows and hips to clear a berth ahead.

***

The neighborhoods of Oldtown flew beneath his feet, sparking memories that he quickly stuffed down in his headlong rush crosstown to find Gail. He skirted the orderly streets of Jazz, the hubbub of North Irony, the uniform wooden boxcars of the Mores, before finding himself in the bizarre serenity and unrest of the Jungle. Prefab houses peeked out from behind tangled ivies, trees, and overgrown hedges. Gardens erupted from rooftops packed with dirt. The smell of burning flesh and sewer rot, prevalent in other lowtown boroughs, was replaced here by the sweetness of exhaling plants and dying flowers.

Mere ripped the ring from his head and hurled it into the extensive shrubbery encircling the ivied pavilion. Destination achieved. Sierra Resort. Gail came here sometimes when she was feeling out of sorts and had hinted that she might check in to the facility if their problems got worse. The automated doors parted like the lips of insanity on a talkative day. Oddly angled lamps cast a mural of dancing lights across the floor and ceiling, and a light breeze ruffled a grove of potted sycamores. Prisms swirled on thin wires hanging from polished ceiling beams. A syncopating rhythm of tablas and drums droned from hidden speakers. The carpet controls were set on grass, the walls to an almost-invisible black.

The resort cut a swathe in your psyche, Mere admitted, if nothing else. Hunched almost double to avoid nettles, he followed the dirt path through the foliage and parted a curtain of multicolored light beads leading to a reception area. Plumes of incense swirled in rainbow clouds above the jungle-fashioned parlor. A receptionist, hair and fingernails dyed the same shade of auburn, looked up as he approached. Perfect breasts, unencumbered by clothing, poked out above a wooden stump that functioned as her desk.

Mere straddled a fallen tree that he assumed was a bench. He stared at her expectantly, waiting for a "How can I help you, sir?" A long-fingernailed hand shot out and grasped his wrist. Smooth fingertips swirled over the backs of his knuckles. She smiled a vacant, pasty smile. Mere stared into the mesmerizing pool of her chameleon contact lenses. He hated talking to people whose eyes changed colors.

When she spoke, her verbs vibrated with Rim twang, vowels lengthened, consonants clipped, "Bless Usa. I'm Hazel, your Sierra representative. Do you have a reservation? Our rooms are full at present."

"Yes, bless Usa, I'm here to see one of your guests. Gail Roosevelt."

Hazel frowned. Her fingers shuffled through a cloth-bound registry, but her eyes stayed trained on him. She continued in a warm tone that wasn't, "Sorry sir. Ms. Roosevelt left specific orders not to be disturbed."

It was obvious that she knew Gail. "Hazel, I'm Gail's brother, Ray. We have a family emergency."

"She is undergoing a very delicate treatment. The doctor's orders are quite clear. You can leave a message for her and I'll be sure to pass it on."

"Hazel, there's been a death in the family. An aunt she is...was very fond of. Is there any way I might speak with her?"

"No."

"Listen, I really need to see her. It's an EMERGENCY. Can I speak with your supervisor?"

"I'm sorry, but the earliest I can schedule you to see Mr. Sierra is next Saturday at 1400."

"Cut the crap," Mere growled, bolting out of his seat. He barreled through a cavelike entrance he thought might lead to Sierra's office. The poorly lit stone cavern branched in a Y juncture. Mere veered onto a cobblestone path that quickly dead-ended at a sealed entrance. A neon warning, "Testing in Progress," blinked above the hatch.

Mere searched for the toggle and flipped the ghost. He waited a few seconds for the door to phase before stepping into a tiny viewing cubicle. He startled two men who sat across from one another, jacking off. A pornographic holo surrounded them in an orgy of motion. The tumbling images of three men and one woman were momentarily distorted by the watchers' torsos as they zipped up and stumbled from their seats. An alarm wailed in the distance as the embarrassed patients elbowed their way out of the room. Mere paused, hands on hips, appraising their "therapy."

The three-on-one extravaganza had been filmed in a grove of miniature palms in a room not unlike the admittance chamber. Pretty tame stuff, overall. But spooky nevertheless. Then he knew why. The woman sandwiched between the men was Gail. She looked unbelievably happy, ecstatic, a warm smile spread across her face as the men climbed over one another to please her.

CHERRY

5

Mere stormed out of Sierra Resort, his face flushed, his body wracked with coughing. He twisted through a labyrinth of alleyways and blazed a trail south through the Jungle into Sherwood, the gateway to the canal zone. Blood, not his own, dripped from his knuckles. His fists hurt like hell and his breath came in heaves, but he felt great. He hadn't punched anyone since his Catholic Central days when he and Jonas Grumby were the toughest lieutenants in the North Irony gang "The Onlies." He had gradually lost touch with his old pals from the hood after being accepted into the Institute of Science. Occasionally, he popped in on Jonas at their old hangout Boo's Bar. A watered-down rom didn't sound like too bad an idea, especially after demolishing those loin-clothed fatcats.

In the time-honored tradition of men, he pushed all thoughts of Gail out of his mind. It was all for the best: their break-up, his new freedom. After all, love was a concept created by women to trap men into relationships. He would cry later, but even when that faraway event took place he would do so without remembering one good thing about her. It would probably be harder to forget the horrified looks on the faces of the men he'd punched.

He shuffled down an embankment and shot diagonally across the canal bed rumored to have been a waterway centuries ago. Several silhouettes—some human, some animal—registered themselves on either side as he bolted across. Keep moving, mind your own business, make no eye contact, he told himself. He kept his head down and accelerated his pace. Having grown up a banger, he knew the safest shortcuts across the canal. Still, it was no place to loiter.

He padded up the cement incline into familiar turf, the alleyways where North Irony blended into the Westend. As he wove through the twisting side streets, Mere kept close watch on the cornucopia of wall tags. Whenever the lilac of the Westenders intersected the cherry scrawls of the Onlies, Mere veered north. No sense getting caught in a hot zone.

Skytown's digital clock tower buzzed, thrumming a powerful bass throughout the city. The ground vibrated six times, signaling the start of blue shift and the end of orange. Mere tilted his head and searched for the sky through a honeycomb of crumbling brick constructs and cement patching. No luck. In this neighborhood you could walk for kilos without being able to see Hightown, let alone the sun. It made North Irony seem drearier than it actually was.

Mere stumbled and tried to focus on the narrow path ahead. The alley began to blur and his vision doubled. His stomach flip-flopped and he lost his sense of balance. Another cityquake? No, that wasn't right either. He teetered toward the brick wall and doubled over in pain. Ground was air was wall was him. His palsy, when it actually came, always surprised him.

* * *

Nothing, nothing, and more nothing. Mere drifted into the cool wake of consciousness, his head and body numbed by frigid waters. Nothing seemed broken from his fall onto asphalt. Feeling slowly returned to aching joints. Whispers and the patter of footsteps encircled his prone body. He felt a heavy object brush his nose just before he cracked his eyes. A steel-plated boot, with silver and black tread, hovered just above his forehead.

His eyes fluttered open and everything came into a hazy focus. Great, just great. It looked like he was going to get rolled. Three kids, fifteen to twenty years old, contemplated their catch. They were definitely bangers, but with no visible weapons. Cherry-striped jackets and maroon fingernails gave them away as Onlies. His palsy had carried him into a world both alien and familiar. His head and back throbbed in pain. His jaw was frozen. He blinked and lifted his head, careful not to touch the boot. This used to be his turf growing up, but no sense tempting fate. The rules, hopefully, were the same.

"Teller," Mere called out. The two toughs leaning against the wall examined him with puzzlement and hatred. They thought he was cherry: a highguy and a gray shirt. "Teller," he repeated, unwilling to believe that they no longer used the code word for relatives and affiliated members. He rolled out from under the young giant's boot and staggered to his feet. Their pale Irony skin seemed almost pink in contrast to the searing red of their jackets and hoods. No turtleneck rings on these boys. The duo against the wall almost straightened, but the boot guy held up a hand and they slumped back in a relaxed posture.

"What are you doing alley hopping, highguy? You must be nuts."

Mere grimaced and muttered, "Teller."

"Yeah, I recognize it. My boys don't because it's out of date. What? Was your brother an Only?"

"Nah, me, I was an L like you."

"Lieu huh?" Never heard of no L making it to Hightown." The Lieutenant lurched over and shook his hand. "Zero," he said, eyeing Mere from bottom to top. "You should know better than to stroll into Irony wearing a grayshirt."

Mere shook his head, "Yeah, I wasn't planning on going this way. I got into a fight in the Jungle and wanted to go to Boos."

"We're going that way. Might save you some headache if we escort you. How'd you do?"

"What?"

"With the cuffs?"

Mere rubbed his blood-caked knuckles. "Gave better than I got."

"Yeah, we Onlies always do. Nothing to lose, nothing to gain."

Mere cringed at the gang's credo, the orphan's swan song of pain and right of way, more true than false, but sad never-the-less.

***

Zero and company dropped him off in front of Boo's. Nice kids, although Mere never remembered him being that quick to jump on a target outside of the neighborhood. With the new I-cards making it almost impossible to jimmy for cash, the gangs were probably bored. Zero had traded his striped jacket for Mere's gray cloak. "It'll save you problems in the hood. Besides, it's nice for us to have another disguise floating round."

Mere paused at the entrance doused with neon, "Boo's Bar. No cover until Indigo. Tonight only, The Jonas Grumbies." He ducked inside the doorway to a row of holobooths splattered with graffiti-3D: your mother's a clone; Onlies do it alone; for a jumpstart call Patty J. #623-69-1817. The first two eyephones had been ripped out of their chipped fiberglass booths, but the third, although battered, looked operational.

He seated himself on a ledge of glowing graffiti and inserted his I-card into a slot lacquered red like pursed lips. A voice balloon accompanied it with, "Feed it to me big boy." He dialed up Cola who was his assistant. Although just out of the Institute, she was his best friend at the lab and a straight shooter.

Her face flickered inside the badly cracked hologrid. Mere could only tell it was her from her unmistakable saw-tooth smile. It didn't take long for him to convince her to break her date and meet him at Boo's for the usual weekend culprits: liquor, drugs, and music.

"Besides, Cola, I ran into some problems in the Jungle and I need your advice on what kind of insanity to plead at work."

"Loop, loop, already. I wasn't too thrilled about hanging with Reed Bourne on a Saturday night anyway. If he wasn't our boss, I'd tell him to fly to hell." She paused and squinted, or at least he thought she did. "You OJ? You're not looking so hot."

"Well, Polk crisped me last night, Gail's cheating on me, I punched out a couple of guys for no good reason, and almost got banged by the locals."

"And I'm complaining to you about my love life of all things. Be right down."

***

Boo's was typical for a Westend pill, pipe, and rom joint. At 1900, it was already teeming with haggard regulars, blue crews, bangers, phreaks, and prosts. The only albino was the man mountain of a bouncer, Stark, who nodded a gruff hello. Boo's was one of the few establishments outside of the Rim and Lightening that served all-whites. Boo herself was a living legend. At one time she was lead screamer in the crank band "Window to the Intestines" and later earned a rep in the Westend mafia. She knew practically everyone who was anyone: skies, highs, and lows.

Boo had been a surrogate mother to their group of Onlies and the most important woman in his life, at least until he'd met Gail. She was the perfect surrogate parent for an orphan—fair but stern with just enough fingers in illegal action to be interesting. In a world of neighborhood castes and carefully drawn lines, Boo played the game well enough to keep her independence and make her club something of a safe zone in a tense neighborhood. More than anyone, she'd drummed into him how it never paid to sell yourself to the highest bidder.

The after-shift crowd seemed jumpy, but it wasn't later, until after his eyes adjusted, that Mere noticed the scowls and hostile looks. The darkening of his skin from his crisping coupled with a Hightown tan marked him as a stranger in the hood. He fired up a complimentary one-hitter and stared at his yellow-to-orange-to-red blinking table. He inhaled and kept an eye peeled for Boo or anyone else from the old scene.

His scan came up blank, although he ID'd potential trouble makers: an Indigo recycler at the holojuke ditching work, a pair of Westenders displaying their colors, and a pillhead, probably a spider phreak, playing videos. Nothing he couldn't handle. Besides, Boo was as careful as they came, installing metal and energy detectors at the hatches. The service was rotten, same as always. He'd have to track down a barista or go without. He started to rise, but was shoved back into his seat.

Mere whirled with cocked fists. Jonas Grumby laughed, screwing up his gaunt face and sticking out his tongue. "You lost or something?"

"Why else would I be here?"

"Beats me." Jonas bent down and surrounded him in a fierce hug with those long arms of his. "You're a sore for sighted eyes."

Jonas hadn't changed much. He still wore the Grumby family heirloom, an undersized suede jacket that accentuated his long bony frame. His hair was close-cropped, centimeters off his scalp, a must for working as a butcher in the underground vats. Jonas always said that nothing carried the stench of rotting meat worse than hair.

"I've been itching to come visit, but things have been busy at work. I got a promotion."

"New layer of skin, too."

"A crisping. Pulse, I've missed you. Why haven't you come up to visit?"

"The police shake you down if you even LOOK up at High-town. Especially if you don't have Pyramid colors."

"Yeah, I'm working for the man and gray's my color," Mere joked. He'd heard the bitterness in Jonas's voice and didn't want to make it seem like he was putting on airs. His old friend had a problem with authority figures. A big one. It was probably the only reason why their positions weren't reversed. Jonas had been a better student than Mere, brilliant in most subjects, especially math, music, and science. Maybe it had all come too easy. Songwriting and playing the electrar were the only skills Jonas had continued to hone. Unfortunately, very few musicians made enough from their craft to live on.

"Are you going to stay and watch me play tonight?"

"Wouldn't miss it."

"Looks like you've been reverting to some old habits." Jonas pointed to the dried blood on Mere's knuckles.

"Hard to break some of them."

"True that."

Mere ignored Jonas's stare and finally flagged down a barista. "Some rom?"

"Then will you tell me what you're really doing here?"

Mere mouthed "sure," even as he realized that he himself didn't know.

∗∗∗

"There's poison on the bloodless knife that splits the hidden life in the garden of despair. There are screams no one hears, test tubes beneath the tears of the Pope's recycled prayers. Who's the clown? Who's the clone? Who flays steel from the bone? Why that frown? Why that moan, when you scrape spit off the ozonodome? Are we sure that we're alive? Do we even get to die? The organiputer knows my future. The organiputer shows my future. The organiputer fills my future. The organiputer kills my future."

Jonas's chorus ended, his fingers spasming into a solo. He looked as though he was wrestling a monster as he strummed his electrar. He'd always said that his seven-string had a mind of its own when he played. The music and vibrating lights blurred and Mere's thoughts somersaulted into memories. When he was younger and angrier, Jonas's songs had meant the world to him.

Cola jiggled at his right elbow, in awe of Jonas's on-stage performance. After she arrived, Mere's litany of problems soon became secondary to the hormonal signals passing between his lab partner and best friend. He had never seen two people fall for each other faster: the lingering handshake, lengthy stares, and shy-but-not grins. Mere knew he should feel happy for them, but their good-natured flirtations were only making him more depressed.

On his left, the establishment's proprietor Boo Wilson alternated between tugging on his sleeve and shouting obscenities. She was compact and muscular, and Mere had to brace both knees beneath the table to keep from being yanked into her lap. Boo's complimentary orange pills, some new variation of dimelds, started to kick in as Jonas finished his song, the body of the electrar slapping against his thighs. The wiry musician ripped connectors from the speakers and bent the neck of his instrument into the sound system. The feedback screeched, sending shivers up backs and hands to ears.

"Break their ear drums," Boo screamed next to him, somehow louder than the speakers. Finally, the song ended and the fluorescents snapped on. Silence soon gave way to claps and stomps, including a few black-robed acolytes on the second floor balcony who'd emerged from one of the private dining rooms upstairs.

"See you next Saturday, I hope. I should have a few new songs," a hoarse Jonas called out to the crowd. He cradled his instrument and stepped carefully through the concertina separating him from the pit.

"Usa, he's great," Cola half-screamed, her sense of hearing still thrown off. "Why haven't you brought me here before?"

Mere shrugged. Cola slipped away toward the stage to join Jonas's groupies. Boo beamed the vacant smile of booze and pills. One that Mere was probably wearing as well. He pushed himself up and started to follow Cola, but a familiar face stopped him in his tracks. A cloaked figure glared at him through the binoc-glass near the back entrance. The increased magnification made the bobbing face beneath the blue hood unmistakable.

"What's the matter? You look like you've seen a ghost," Boo said in a friendly tone that she saved for her favorites.

"I'm fine," Mere stammered. "Just going to get some air."

Had he seen a ghost? Maybe. But it was the kind that would stare back at you if you looked it in the eyes. Mere, for reasons he'd never been able to figure out, avoided mirrors. His reflection made him queasy and he could feel his palsy bubbling up from the other side of the looking glass. Still, that didn't keep him from recognizing the man outside the bar who was also the murderer in his dream.

It was another Mere Roosevelt.

BLOOD

6

Mere burst out the bar's back entrance and scanned the empty alleyway. His blue-hooded twin had disappeared in the ten seconds it had taken him to shoulder his way through to the exit. Something rustled above him and to the right. Mere dove over the railing, hooked an arm for balance, and landed on his feet. A chimpanzadog paced on the third floor balcony of a neighboring apartment complex. The house pet scratched its head at Mere's maneuver and brayed to be let in.

The flashing neon of the back staircase was making him too conspicuous a target. A rational person might ask a target for what? A twin? A dream? But Mere was not in what he normally would consider his right mind. He was drunk, angry, and buzzing with the courage of dimelds and adrenaline. He nestled up into an alcove by the recycler bins and cocked an ear. Graffiti took up most of the rectangular jut, an indecipherable mosaic. The hastily painted scrawls were the color of blood.

He pressed against the wall and let his eyes adjust to the night mist. House music thrummed from Boo's as a door opened and a pair of male voices drifted off toward Eisenhower Avenue. This was exactly where he saw himself get shot last night in his dream. It was a bit creepy, but he might as well stop being a scientist if he was going to let irrational fears send him scurrying inside. Then again, there was no reason NOT to be cautious. There were many kinds of predators and victims. He desired to be neither. He poked his head out from his nook and weighed his options: check out this strange guy masquerading as him or head back inside?

The chained-up back entrance to the now-defunct Fino Royale further down the alley brought things into perspective. This once-teeming nightspot and underground casino had been the heart of the Westend. The Beanman Oscar Fino had been feared throughout six boroughs. Mere and Jonas used to run errands and messages for their neighborhood kingpin, more out of respect and admiration than coercion. He'd been one charismatic son-butch. Now Mere and Fino were one and the same, relics of a bygone era. No matter how much he wanted it to be different, this was no longer his turf. No longer his life.

Mere turned back toward Boo's, but froze in his tracks. Hackles rose on his neck and back. The faint *click tock* of a pistol safety sent him into a panicked two-step behind the recycler. He spun, kicked out his legs, and caught himself in a push-up position, but not before his chin scraped the asphalt. Before he could berate himself for getting soft, a body landed on him and drove him into the patched asphalt. A kneecap pressed into his back, driving oxygen from his lungs. Mere fought to breathe even as his balls climbed into his stomach for reassurance. The bastard must have been on the fire escape, an old Only trick, and he of all people fell for it.

A hard, cold object was pressed into his neck, followed by, "Don't move a muscle. Put your hands on your head and keep them there." A sweeping hand snaked through his pockets. Robbery seemed doubtful. Even so, Mere said, "Take whatever you want."

"Shut up. The only thing I want from you is your life. Sit on your hands and clap your trap."

With a not-so-gentle prod from his assailant, Mere slid his palms under his backside. He was going to die. He was going to die. He was panicking. His eyes shotgunned the narrow inlet behind the bin, searching for anything he might be able to use as a weapon.

"I know what you're up to. It isn't going to work," Mere said, hoping to nettle his assailant.

The empty bottle near his feet might provide an advantage. Mere slowly wiggled his hands out from beneath his hips as light footsteps looped around. Liquid oxygen sneakers led to a body and face that were his and yet not. A cocked pistol added a third eye to the surveillance. His twin's shoulders bulged strangely, perhaps from body armor obtained on the white market. The gunman stopped next to the recycler so he could keep an eye on Boo's back entrance as well as Mere.

"Bark all you want, yappy. My plan IS going to work. You've

worried me for quite some time. The mysterious twelfth finally appears."

"Twelfth?"

"Don't play games with me."

"Listen, if this is about old gang business, I'm sure—"

"You're serious aren't you? This is very-very-VERY interesting. Why would Polk leave you in the white on this? Maybe he thought you were immune from being spotted. Until last night you didn't even register on my system as a player. I wonder if the others know about you yet. Has anyone else...shall we say...been stalking you?"

"No."

"Like you'd know. What kind of idiot are you to come out here unarmed?"

His twin's gun hand dropped a fraction. The guy must have a pretty low opinion of him, Mere decided. If so, he should try to lower it further and make himself seem less of a threat. "Look, my wife's pregnant," Mere pleaded. "Have a heart. I'm really worried about her being home alone. I don't know what's going on with you and these twelve friends of yours, and I don't really want to find out."

"You don't get it, do you? It doesn't matter what you want. You're in the same pod I am. Kill or be killed. And as far as your wife's concerned, I'd keep close tabs on her."

"You threatening her?"

"No, idiot. You and I can't have children. None of us can," his twin said, chuckling like the world's largest asspit. He straightened his gun arm and took aim.

"If you're going to kill me, can't you at least tell me why?"

"I could, but I won't." Chuckles lengthened into guffaws. His double's trigger finger flexed.

"At least tell me your name. You can't kill a guy without telling him your name," Mere blubbered, lowering his head and pretending to cry. He lined up his boot with the bottom of the bottle.

"OJ, brother. Don't say I never did anything for you. I'm Conrad and you're one dead-ass-"

Mere looked up in fright at the fire escape and lashed out with his left boot. Conrad glanced skyward, then flicked his eyes to follow the scudding bottle. Mere pushed frantically with his hands and right leg. He lurched forward and twisted sideways as a flagette exploded. He scooped his right arm under the recycler and thrust the fiberglass container upward. He shrieked in rage, straining every muscle in his arm and shoulder with a desperate heave.

Conrad's sneakers saved him. He bounded sideways more than a meter to avoid the cascade of bottles and the overturned bin. Glass shattered. Conrad aimed. Mere tucked into a ball and rolled forward. Old gang mentality: attack when they think you're fleeing. Another shot rang out. Mere came up out of his tumble as Conrad landed on the bottles. His assailant was too far away, but Mere sprinted forward anyway. Conrad's feet slipped out from under him and the gun flew out of his grip. Mere dove and snatched the pistol grip, throwing himself sideways away from his assailant, his elbows driving into shards.

Conrad looked stunned. Mere hesitated before drawing a bead and it almost killed him. Conrad whipped out another pistol from behind his back. Mere rolled toward the bin and shot blindly. When he came up, Conrad was gone and he could hear retreating footsteps pound the pavement. Mere scrambled to the wall on his hands and knees, and peeked around the corner. Conrad bounded more than ten meters with each step. Mere fired again, almost breaking his wrist. Conrad dove right into another alley.

Click tock.

Mere whirled.

"Halt."

He saw a pistol and fired. A body slammed against Fino Royale. A head exploded. Blood mixed with graffiti. The white uniform of a police officer turned instantly crimson. Mere froze as he heard the buzzing sirens. He'd killed a cop.

ORANGE

7

The underground stream coursed beneath Sierra estate with a low and tiny rhythm that made Gail tired. She had not slept in more than a day. Her bare skin brushed against entanglements of roots that had ripped through the building's foundation to the moist terra below. She was getting used to the almost dark, losing herself in the hypnotic funnel of muddy water washing over greenish-gray stones.

A man cleared his throat as he approached. Gail looked up from the enigmatic swirls of moss and watched a bobbing light zag along the riverbank. She considered covering herself, but resisted the impulse. If she couldn't trust the doctor here and now, she was in more trouble than she thought.

"So what's all this about?" Doctor Tyler asked, pointing his flashbeam away from her and easing her Zero G suitcase above a patch of dry earth.

"First, I want to know did it fool him?"

"I don't know. Is Mere normally violent?"

"It did work then." Gail unsnapped the lid of her case and dug for a weathered ensemble that would make her less noticeable to lowtown predators. "I hated to deceive him, but...you know...?"

"No, I don't know, although I'd like to, considering I'm putting myself and this organization at risk to help you."

"Don't you see, Phil?" she said, slipping into reddish-brown slacks and a hooded orange jacket. "I'm keeping quiet for your sake. I want you to imagine what might happen if a squad of white shirts were to track you down and ask about my whereabouts. Trust me, you'd want to know as little as possible."

A pregnant pause was broken by, "Are you really in that deep?"

"Deeper," Gail said, shutting her case and wishing she could see her friend's eyes in the muted lighting. She didn't want to cause him pain like she had Mere, but she had little choice. She was poison to everyone around her—they would realize that someday.

Phil handed her a slip of paper with addresses and vidphone numbers like he'd promised. His fingers paused around her knuckles before pulling away. She opened her mouth and was poised to launch into her troubles when Phil broke out with, "Remember, it's the Rim." No further explanation was needed for the nether region that ringed lowtown. It was a meeting place for evil and good, a crossroads for anarchists, smugglers, albinos, and petty criminals. And somewhere beneath the city walls it was rumored lived the Graylings: zombielike creatures leftover from Pyramid-sanctioned experiments. It would be a dangerous place to live, but nowhere near as reckless as staying in Hightown, not after her disastrous encounter with Polk.

* * *

"Are you sure this is where you want to go?"

"I'm sure," Gail answered peevishly. Her albino cabbie was barely visible from the back seat above the hump of tan vinyl. His stubby fingers steered the decrepit cab over a series of tight two lanes, which were more rubble and potholes than actual street.

"I don't mean to bother you," the cabbie said. "It's just that... the Rim's not a place where a Hightowner usually—"

"Who told you I was High?"

"Ummm."

"WHO?"

"No one."

"Then I'd appreciate it if you minded your own business."

Gail crossed her arms and felt sweat well up beneath her second-hand jumpsuit. She was coming down with something. The cabbie continued yammering away, introducing himself as Sax. He told her that he worked for one of three albino-run taxi services, the only ones that served rundown areas like the green-light district.

A garbled squawk sounded over the intercom, followed by a high-pitched whine. Sax answered the call and an anxious-sounding man requested his assistance.

"Yeah, five minutes, I'm on it," Sax said, slapping the receiver into its stand and accelerating. He drove like a madman, blowing past several stop signs before braking to a halt along the grooved shoulder of Rim Drive. He jumped from his seat with the engine still running and helped her out of the back.

"Sorry, normally I'd walk you to the hatch, but there's an emergency. I have to go."

She reached into her bag for her I-card, but he held up his hands and backed away. "It's been handled. Besides, it would be a silly move for someone on the run."

"I'm not—" Gail said as the driver's door slammed and the cab peeled out in a U-turn, squealing south into the city's Northwest quarter. She took a quick look at her surroundings. She'd only been to the Rim a few times, never by herself or at night. Numbers were painted or scrawled on circular doorways imbedded in the city wall.

She hurried across the street and felt dozens of eyes boring into her back although her hood and orange cloak gave her no peripheral vision. She almost turned back. Surely her brother or mother would be able to help her out of this jam. Then her resolve hardened. She would not drag anyone she cared about into this mess. She pressed the buzzer and waited. Seconds turned to minutes. She pounded on the hatch with the heel of her hand, imagining a motley assortment of lowlifes surrounding her.

"Please, someone answer!"

Her stomach, already fluttery, cramped up from her monthly curse. Her period wasn't just worse than normal. It was an abomination. Her flow, although frighteningly heavy, wasn't the problem. She was bleeding brown between her legs. She trembled and readied herself to yell "Tampoca," the name Phil had passed on to her when the hatch phased.

"Ahh, another lost lamb," croaked a skeleton-thin albino woman, clutching a cane. Two ruby pyramids covered her eyes, the official stigma for blindness. Her face was taut and grim, pockmarked by the ravages of white flu and harsh times. "What's your name?"

Gail hesitated, then thought back to the heroine of her favorite childhood story about a perpetual girl child searching for home. "Florida," she said. "Florida."

***

Gail, although fighting exhaustion, gave in when Tampoca suggested a meal. Actually, the headstrong woman wouldn't take no for an answer. Gail collapsed on a tiny stool, part of a mismatched collection of chairs at the dining room table. She did not have the energy to haul her bag to the curtained alcove that would be her new and, she hoped, temporary home. Tampoca grimly diced a half-dozen vegetables into a salad and heated up a pan of rice on an ancient stove.

Gail could not even begin to fathom how Phil knew this woman. He must have his fingers in a lot more things than she ever suspected. An image of Mere wallowing in self-pity flashed through her mind, but she tried to blank it out. The pain he was going through was surely not any worse than what she herself was experiencing. Besides, from what little she remembered from her capture and conversation with Polk, she would have caused her husband more harm than good if she'd stayed. Trouble was, she was already lonely. She missed her home, her flabby chicken-dog, even Mere's moody presence.

Tampoca's apartment was tiny but well ordered. A small living room was kept cool by the thick adobe of the city's retaining wall. A small garden thrived under growlights in a slanted alcove just off the kitchen. A narrow stairwell whorled upstairs to Tampoca's room. A sliding hatch leading to a closet-sized bathroom was immediately to her rear. There were no appliances she could see other than the stove, fridge and a fist-sized radio hanging from a wall hook.

"This will put some color back into you cheeks," Helena said, clacking her cane against the table and serving Gail a plate of food.

"Thank you very much."

"Let's get one thing straight. I'm not exactly thrilled about putting up a stranger, especially a Hightowner who made enemies of the wrong person."

"Listen—"

Tampoca hissed, "No, Florida, you listen. I realize you're not feeling that great right now, but you're going to have to find work."

"Of course, right away."

"I have a cousin who runs a barter. I think he might be able to find you something."

"Thank—" Gail started and paused. Her gratitude was probably the last thing Tampoca wanted to hear. What an odd woman. Gail was seriously spooked. She quietly picked at her meal and discovered she was ravenous. She wolfed down the fresh greens and sticky rice, and then wished she hadn't.

"How was it?" Tampoca asked from the kitchen as she wiped down the stove.

"It tasted great. I'm just feeling nauseous."

"It's because everything cooked in this house is organic. You're used to that rot grown by the organiputer. This home-grown will make you sick at first, but you'll feel better later. Trust me."

Gail pushed herself to her feet with the help of the table and carried her plate toward the sink. Her midsection cramped up and she was sweating from what she hoped was just a mild fever. Before stumbling to her tiny bedroll, she paused and asked, "Is it true what they say about the anarchists in the Rim?"

Tampoca laughed for so long and with so much vehemence that Gail shrugged, plodded across the dining room, and drew back the curtains to her tiny room. The mirth continued from the kitchen even as she lay down on the thin mattress and felt the world swirl around her.

"Florida," Tampoca called out between spasms of glee, "not a word of it is true. The truth is stranger and far more difficult for people to believe."

AMBER

8

Mere held his head between his legs. It wasn't from nausea or the threat of vomiting, although the latter seemed a strong possibility. He could not look his friends in the eyes. He was a murderer. He was out of control. He was losing his grip on reality.

"Pulse," Boo said. "Snap out of it." She caressed Mere's forehead with the rough palms of her mammoth hands and raised his head, sliding it from its tortoise shell. He blinked his eyes and gulped in the amber incense swirling in Boo's top floor office. The lavishly decorated room was poorly lit and cast no shadows—it felt more like a brothel than a business nerve center. Rose-patterned couches lined two walls beneath oblong picture windows. Outside, omnilines crisscrossed just outside the multicolored glass. Cola peered into the alleyway through the curtains. Jonas paced behind Boo on a pattern of red and black carpeting.

"Quit already. You're making me buggy."

"Sorry, Boo," Jonas said, throwing himself onto a worn office chair. "It's just that if we're going to make a move, we should do it soon before they cordon off the hood."

"I slid behind the stairs and merged with the crowd," Mere mumbled. He didn't want to get Boo or his friends in trouble. Trouble was, no one killed a cop and got away with it.

"You better hope no one saw you," Boo said. "I sent Stark down the street to call a cab. We're going to have to gamble he can track down a friendly."

"And quick," Jonas added.

Cola cast Mere a sidelong glance before turning away. Her eyes locked with Jonas's and, although her forehead was wrinkled with worry, she couldn't help but smile. Mere stared at the couple blankly. This was what he would be missing when he was hauled away—having someone beam you a look that said, "I'm vulnerable and lonely. Be with me." He would never have chance to shed his gray garb and brown skin, and discover whether there was a man or monster underneath. Red and yellow dots flashed on the windows, followed by a faraway siren.

"Hoverpods," Cola said, scissoring open a pair of curtains. "At least a half dozen. We've got to get him out of here."

Mere stood, agitated and confused, wondering if he should give himself up to protect his friends. He hardly noticed pulling the pistol from his belt. Jonas took several long strides and disarmed him. Mere looked at his own hands in disbelief. What in the jack did he think he was doing? Jonas tossed the pistol to Boo as Stark burst through the hatch and locked the phase. Cola stopped fingering the curtains, crossed the room, and dug her fingers into Mere's elbow. Although it was meant to be comforting, her grip was ferocious. The pain helped.

Jonas continued his pacing. "What are we going—"

"Shut up. All of you," Boo hissed, turning to Stark. "Is it a go?" The beefy albino shook his head solemnly. Boo tossed Conrad's pistol into a planter that held a leafy jasmine. "OJ, here's the plan."

***

There was no time to go over the details again. Mere readied himself to give the performance of his life. Police, brandishing stun prods, streamed from the alleyway to the front entrance just as the cab pulled up.

"She's mine," Mere said, growing angry. "You'd better let her go."

Jonas pulled Cola to him and screamed, "The lady doesn't like you anymore."

Mere stormed across the porch and cocked both fists, "I'll looping kill you, you son-butch."

Jonas stepped in front of Cola and shielded her. He threw up his arms as Mere shellacked him with a flurry of lefts and rights. Jonas groaned in genuine pain and crumpled into a ball. Mere gritted his teeth and found himself enjoying the punishment he was dealing out.

"Get that asspit out of my establishment."

A massive hand clamped on Mere's shoulder and yanked him backwards. Stark's elbow dug into his throat. An impressive stranglehold, lifting him off the ground. "It's only because I had to make it look real," Mere whispered to Jonas, although no words came out. His swinging feet almost clocked Jonas in the midsection as his friend peeled his forearms from his face.

Stark shifted his grip and Mere managed to rasp, "Cola, I still love you," as he was hauled none-too-gently down the steps.

Cola leaned down and helped Jonas to his feet. Her lithe body clung to the side of his battered tan jacket. "Thank you. I was really scared," came the expected words, but Cola made them sound genuine.

The police looked surprised as Boo wrenched open the hatch to the cab and ran her I-card through the meter. "Take this drunk wherever he wants to go." Mere continued to struggle in earnest, but to no avail.

"Hold it right there everyone," sputtered the white shirt, but not before Stark tossed Mere into the back of the cab. He cracked his head on the armrest of the opposite hatch and turned to face the police. The taxi accelerated away as two guns cleared their holsters. "Everyone freeze," shouted the second officer.

Boo held up her arms. "I'm the owner of this establishment. What can I do for you?" These were the last words Mere heard as he cradled his throbbing head and slumped over in the back of the taxi, at least until the driver asked, "So, hey, where'm I taking you?"

***

"Hummeda, hummeda, hmmm, eh, eh, bad da naaah."

Mere awoke to humming and worse, tuneless, droning humming from a squat albino behind the wheel of an accelerating taxi. The driver swerved through heavy morning traffic on Rim Drive, the pothole minefield that ringed lowtown's four major quadrants. Mere's body was locked in a half-sitting position.

"Jabbeda, ummena, seebedio, la, lu, le, eh, hoooooo."

The ancient cab darted in and out of openings between service trucks, delivery vans, and an occasional joyrider sick of public transportation. Apartments and small businesses pocked the jagged city wall. Occasional pedestrians braved the broken sidewalk on the shoulder of the two-lane.

"Snop, amodda, wehow, labittanubbi, ya, wah."

Slowly, the night before fluttered back to him. Mere had seen his wife starring in a pornographic hologram, punched out three Sierra security officers, passed out in North Irony gangland, been taken hostage in someone's adolescent war game, and inadvertently slain a cop. This trail of carnage could be traced back to his wife's decision to leave him for the carnal joy of pirated sex flicks and a recent office party where he was doused with crisping. He was obviously losing his mind.

"Snoobedda, flujuhoobeda, doobilupushigwa, snaaaaaaaa."

Mere straightened out of his crouch, giving him a bird's eye view of the cabbie's massive bald spot. The pitted road swirled past radio holovids jiggling on the dashboard. Hopefully, his driver was tall enough to see over them. Mere glanced at the rearview mirror and stared into manic green eyes flashing through unkempt black locks. A wide, cherub-like smile filled the bottom of the mirror, crooked teeth slightly less white than a washed-out albino complexion scarred from pox.

"Hey, there, hope you don't mind the tunes," the cabbie said. "I've been driving all night. Boo told me to take you wherever you wanted to go, but all you wanted was sleep and I couldn't drive you to sleep. Through sleep maybe, but not to sleep."

Mere realized that he preferred the humming to speech. He pursed his lips, forcing a low moan through his morning haze of headache and foreboding. His ruse worked. The cabbie stop talking and joined in Mere's off-tune humming until the radio broke into Pyramid-sponsored commercials.

"Time, what is it?" Mere managed to spit out.

"Almost ten, about ten to ten actually, but the clock in here gets messed up from driving so often from one side of the city to the other. Most people don't know that the gravity shifts depending on your altitude and proximity to the digital clock tower. My grandpa Olio told me how once he and a friend got shot at trying to sneak into the bunker below the tower."

"Sorry, what time is it?"

"About ten or ten to ten."

"Usa," Mere sputtered. Even drawing on an orphan's impressive catalog of angst, he could not imagine things getting much worse. Cardinal Shaw was scheduled to speak at Gray Six, Hightown's church for gray shirts. This was a definite to-be-seen-at event, although churchgoing was not carefully monitored in general. Mere knew that he needed to act normally if he were to have any chance of avoiding arrest. His absence at this ceremony would be suspicious under any circumstances.

And of course, services were just about to start.

Mere focused on passing street signs, wary about prodding the albino into another string of nonsense talk. The effort was too much. He slumped back into the folds of still-warm upholstery. "Can you get me to the service hatch of Church Gray Six?"

"Ah, subterfuge," the cabbie said as he cut the wheel and accelerated. A nametag, clipped to a pulled-down visor, read Sax. A smiley face stuck its tongue out beneath the name, seemingly drawn by a disturbed child in the throes of rebellion.

Mere clutched the worn armrest of the zigzagging yellow juggernaut and struggled to regain his composure. His hold on reality was tenuous—he mistrusted his intuition and capacity for logic. It would be better to sneak into the festivities, he figured, rather than being fingered as an awkward latecomer. It should be a snap to bypass security. He knew how the more affluent churches worked, having traveled as a choirboy to many a Hightown parish. He would need a dark robe, a little luck and, perhaps, the albino's help.

* * *

Mere wiped the sweat from his brow and peered down the chandeliered hallway, thinking how ridiculous he must look and wondering if his makeshift choirboy costume would fool anyone. Amber-hued candles flickered in gold and silver sconces above tiny altars heaped with black lilies. He could hear the familiar refrain of synthesized organ and harp that marked the beginning of services. The refrain to the opening hymn thrummed from an archway leading to an already-filled auditorium. He pressed up against a priest's vestibule and thought about the impressive display of freakiness Sax had shown in diverting the guard's attention during his break-in. He steeled his nerves and patted down the pointy shoulders on his costume. He only needed to escape detection long enough to wind around to the back pews and slide into a vacant berth.

A hatch slid open behind him. Clacking footsteps approached. Mere hoofed it down the hallway past an archway cluttered with clergy. Several voices called out, but Mere didn't turn his head or slow his pace. He turned the corner, slipped off his shabby frock, and tossed it behind a statue of John the Baptist. The last few rows were almost empty. Luckily, all eyes were turned toward the front dais. Mere scooted into the last row and locked his eyes on Cardinal Shaw who was clad in an amber robe that signified the mingling of the sun (God's first creation) with the blood of Christ.

A pair of black-robed apostles emerged from the hallway and looked over the congregation. Mere stared forward, beads of sweat peppering his forehead. He knew he looked like hell. Zero's wrinkled red cloak from last night, even if it wasn't three sizes too large, wasn't exactly Sunday best. After what seemed an eternity, the priests' assistants gave up their search and strode back into the corridor. Mere breathed a sigh of relief. Don't be paranoid, he told himself. Everything's fine. No one's looking at you funny or wondering why you're muttering to yourself. They probably think you're praying. The music stopped. Heads and shoulders snaked in anticipation.

Cardinal Shaw thanked the local clergy and scientific community for hosting him and launched into a sermon that Mere whited out as he obsessed on his problems. Last night had been rough. From end to beginning. He had awoken numerous times in the cab, refusing to fall into a dream that tortured him with spiders, monstrous trees, and exploding heads. He couldn't make tails or heads of his predicament. He wanted to last through the services, be seen by his coworkers, and crawl back home to his gravweb. Only thing was, he couldn't keep the cop he'd slain out of his thoughts. Something primal in him reveled in the violence he'd unleashed and the rush of fighting for self-preservation.

Sweat soaked his chest and back. He was feverish and sick, alternating between cold and hot flashes. A mounted figurine of the Virgin Mary on the sidewall sent him into a wicked deja vu. He remembered being racked by fever on many a Sunday afternoon as a child in the orphanage church. Before being stricken with palsy, Mere had spent several years after his parents' deaths fighting off what the priests had feared was a terminal illness. Mary had always been his favorite bible icon. He daydreamed about saving her from the clutches of evildoers, one of his strategies for surviving the long hours church orphans spent in religious observance.

Mere almost nodded off. He clutched the pew to keep himself upright and noticed that others were singing. His fingers fumbled through the Usan hymnal. He mouthed words while the world went fuzzy and black around the edges. He focused on the kindly face of the Virgin Mary, straining to stay conscious. Gray freckles dotted the forehead of the gleaming ebony figurine. Rivulets of brown trickled down her belly between her legs. The statue wavered, its limbs trembling in the candled lighting. Mary's clothes fell away. Her belly swelled. He must be hallucinating.

The gaping womb drooped from the wall and opened wide to swallow him. A sea of crisping boiled inside her loins. He was going to be sick. Mere looked away and tucked his nose and mouth into his jumpsuit as he prayed. Prayed that no one could smell or hear the dry heaves of his nausea.

SULFUR

9

A good night's sleep had done little to help Mere regain his composure. Or health. He was still sick—sick in the head, sick in the stomach, sick at heart. Mere had already spent a half hour sitting on a marble bench outside Pyramid Gray Towers. A steady stream of administrators and scientists flowed in and out of the automatic hatch. Mere ignored the gurgles of his stomach and readied himself for wading through the fierce congestion. Maybe he should have called in sick.

After ten minutes of waiting, he thought he saw a lull in the crowd, but there was no such thing in the heavily guarded lobby. Passage to and from Pyramid was kept to a single-file line for security reasons. Finally, he screwed up his courage, passed through the checkpoint and managed to find a not-quite-full elevator. Once inside, he called out this floor to the gray-skirted woman closest to the phasing hatch.

Elbows and shoulders pressed against his chest and stomach. The overcrowded box rose and he tried to forget the events that had taken place in the alley behind Boo's. If he concentrated long enough, he could actually envision the murder from the perspective of a shocked and horrified bystander. He wasn't a murderer—he couldn't be. It was ridiculous to think that death would scythe souls in his clothes. Avoid watching the holonews at all costs, he told himself, and keep a positive attitude.

He was epically late. The lift lagged at every floor, its occupants hiding behind pasted-on smiles. Mere had slept throughout the previous afternoon and evening, and straight through his alarm. He dreaded work and its accompanying small talk, stares, and inevitable teasing about making a cameo so late in the day. Not to mention what his coworkers must be thinking about his early departure yesterday from the after-church reception. Part of him was surprised to have slept straight through the night without being rousted by white shirts and thrust into the mysterious inner workings of the justice system. It was only a matter of time before the trail of blood led back to him, probably through his friends whose lives would be shattered in the process.

At last, the doors phased and Mere squirmed through annoyed scientists into the short hallway leading to his set of labs. He forded a narrow inlet packed with hidden sensors, theft detectors, and wide-eyed security. Double hatches disappeared and he stepped into the antiseptic corridors of Gray Lab Six, his home away from home. Private offices and high-security workstations occupied the right side of the entrance hallway. The left side branched into banks of laboratories, storage rooms, common areas, and orderly rows of hatches whirring with overworked phase generators. Mere shed his turtleneck hat and hurried past Reed Bourne's office. Taking a deep breath, he ghosted the hatch to a workstation already abuzz with activity.

Neural gloves, visors, and sealed gray suits swaddled scientists. No one paid him much heed as eyes swam in miniature kingdoms of proteins, cells and DNA. Without a filtration mask the lab stank to low heaven, a pungent combination of penned animals and sulfur. Mere scrolled his pinky along a fluttering light panel that housed call buttons. He toggled Cola's signal, triggering a barely audible clacking in her visor. She rolled her shoulders, slipped off her headset and flashed him a troubled grin before refocusing on her centrifuge. She was just playing it cool, he decided. More than he was managing.

Mere paused at the kitchenette and poured himself a coffee-tea in his "Techies Make It Better" mug. He ambled to his cube and thought about the countless hours of painstaking data entry he'd let slide during his project. Maybe he could ask Reed for a temp to help him out. He eased in behind his console and zoned out. This was definitely a day to skate, maybe leave early, and grab some shuteye. He blew on his cup of steaming stimulant.

"Hey, boss, Reed wants you in his office. Right away. Hey, you look like jack," crowed Chino Bright, one of his assistants on the organiputer interface project.

"Tough weekend."

"So I've heard. Everyone in Six is talking about your crisping.

What's it like?"

"Like sex, drugs, food, your birthday, and death rolled into one."

"You deserve it, if you don't mind me saying so."

Mere shrugged and wondered if that was really a compliment. He dragged himself toward the hallway, anxious to escape Chino's cheery cherub self. Besides, it wasn't wise to keep Bourne waiting. Chino plunked himself into the vacated chair and scrolled over the user board. He probably figures it'll be his soon, Mere thought. The whole lab, including himself, expected Reed to give him one of the coveted far-side offices overlooking lowtown.

Mere plastered down an errant tuff of hair. He entered his boss's spacious lobby and his assistant was nowhere to be seen. He pressed his I-card into Reed's hatch and flicked the call button. A perky medley trumpeted his arrival. Reed's face flashed on the viewport and he mouthed the word, "Open." The hatchway ghosted, revealing a standard corp set-up: cavernous office with almost nothing in it, company logo flickering in a holohearth, chameleon blinds twisting in a variety of animal shapes. Mere hurried along a burgundy runner leading to his seated boss.

Reed didn't waste any time: "So you thought you could get away with it?"

Mere's mouth opened and closed.

"That we'd cover for you?"

"Ummm...." Mere caught his breath and sank into the gravchair attached to Reed's office platform: a combination desk, compustation, minilab, and kitchenette.

"Nothing to say for yourself?"

"What I do on my own time—"

"Directly reflects on Gray Lab Six," Reed snapped.

"If you're going to fire me, just do it. If not, I've got more important—"

"Mere, watch your mouth. If it wasn't for me, you'd be in deep jack. If you don't have time to answer my questions, I know you can clear your schedule for the police at Sky Station."

Mere feigned shock and sputtered, "What have I been accused of?"

"You trying to tell me that you don't know?"

"I'm not trying to tell you anything."

"Then you'd better start. You're not so brilliant that I'll put up with outright disobedience."

"I had a rough weekend. My wife left me on Friday. I didn't sleep at all. I wasn't in my right mind. It was an accident," Mere said, and added, "It won't happen again."

It looked like he was in for it now. White shirts were probably waiting for him outside. He doubted he had enough pull to escape incarceration.

"Violence never solves anything. Well, actually, it does, but it should be your last resort."

Mere wondered if he could work up some tears.

"I'm putting myself on the line to quiet this up."

"Thanks, I appreciate you protecting me."

"I know you're not used to the politics higher up. One or two incidents like this and you're out for good: no promotion, no office, no freedom to work on what you want.

Mere shimmied his head from side to side, a penitent schoolboy. Was he really going to get off on a murder gig? Just like that? Justice couldn't be this malleable.

"I want you to take the vacation coming to you and lie low. Do you think you can do that without getting in any more trouble?"

"Absolutely." Mere climbed to his feet. "No problem."

Just keep clear of Sierra Resort."

"Sierra?"

"Yes, if you show up there again, they're going to have you arrested, domestic problems or no."

Mere was dumbfounded. "Oh, the guys I beat up....that's a relief."

Reed screwed up his face.

Mere recovered with, "Come on, can't you take a joke?"

"I don't know. Are you telling me one?"

***

As soon as the hatch snapped to attention behind him, Mere paused in the hallway. He cradled his head in trembling hands and stared at his warped reflection in the buffered parquet. Not funny. Not funny at all. Why had he believed, even for a moment, that Reed could get him off on a murder rap? He was slipping. Bad.

Maybe some more sleep would help. Or a vacation from himself.

He shuffled back into the lab to let his staff know that he was going to be out of the loop for awhile. He poked his head in and saw a small crowd huddled around his desk. Chino lay there on the floor next to an overturned chair. He was curled in a tiny ball. Shards of Mere's favorite cup sat in a brown pool spreading across the floor. Chino climbed to his hands and knees, heaving a sulfurish tar.

"Woh!"

The ring of onlookers quickly expanded.

"Looks like he'll be OJ."

"You call that OJ?"

"What the hell you drinking at work, Roosevelt?"

"I thought we were going through the industrial cleaner a little too fast."

Heads turned to the doorway where Mere half-waved and made an awkward exit. Poison? It couldn't be poison. Why would anyone want to…Jesus! He marched through security and snatched an elevator to the compulab on the fifteenth floor. He avoided the bureaucrat at the sign-in desk, linked into an organislot, and signed on with a pseudonym. He scanned news chatter, hoping to pick up references to the police slaying or his run-in with Sierra security. The terminal froze. The words "Careful. They know who you are," flickered on the screen before winking out.

Mere shut down the system and calmly rose. Hours later he was on his sixth rom and second burger at Slack Jaw in the Jungle. Vacation, what a vacation it would be, Mere kept telling himself. He'd find a way to escape his troubles even if it killed him. His hands clenched into fists as he fought an overwhelming urge to assail the drunk next to him. Feelings of invincibility and helplessness swept over him. He was deep in the grip of a fever as familiar as childhood. Dangerous, yes, he was a dangerous man. Even so, he refused to look into the faces of the crowd and think about who or what might be after him.

Two evenings earlier, just when Mere's problems went from bad to worse with a single pull of a trigger, North Irony had another unlikely visitor. A strange young man with short-cropped orange hair slept peacefully on a park bench in a small alcove that went by the dubious name of Liberty Square. The local bums left him alone—the pasty youth was a shady lowtown legend like the albino cabbie who drove the city at night talking to himself. The drowsing man did not have a name, but rather went by a single initial, heightening his anonymity.

Hours passed. The tuneless cacophony, whirring deep within the walled city, woke him out of a dead sleep. G yawned and cursed his inability to get a proper night's rest. Why did no one else seem affected by the racket? If a child whimpers on a playground, ten women appear out of nowhere to comfort her, but ten million urban zombies can somehow tune out the constant caterwaul of streets, sidewalks, and buildings. The grating thrush of elevators, bridges, omnilines, and statuettes. These discordant notes were there for anyone who allowed their emotions to scamper through the streets like unruly children. The larger tragedies are always ignored, G mused. People disregard the daily dirges, allowing them to moan softly in the background like clouds, shadows, or the meaning behind words.

She hated being ignored, Collings did. The city was a she and not just metaphorically. She thought of herself as a real woman. These feelings were not known to everyone, perhaps not even to anyone other than himself. G could hear Collings' circuitry beating hatred throughout the city. Then again, why shouldn't he feel her pain? She was his best friend. The staccato of her isolation echoed in his footsteps.

Despite the city's misguided belief in her own personhood,

G had to admit that she was more than the synthesis of steel, concrete, and organic circuitry. Organiputer was hardly an apt description either. Collings had attitude and personality. Like many women she was forced to perform a litany of tasks without gratitude. And she was going insane. The increase of cityquakes were proof. Only he and a few of Polk's elite scientists knew that these tremors resulted from her nervous breakdowns.

G's brothers and sisters were at least partly responsible for her imminent demise. Polk had poisoned them to each other and the world long ago. G's siblings were eating Collings alive from the inside, replacing her body and mind with their own. Soon there would be nothing left of his mentor, friend, and mother figure. It depressed him to listen to her mantra, "I love myself. I love myself. I love—"

"Myself," G finished her line as he rose from the stairwell in the deserted park. Her death knell was sounding, but it wasn't the death of a little-known relative where you could come back from the funeral and kick back in front of the HV. It was the death of something deathless, of an idea or a dream. G stomped his feet on the pavement and laughed, no, it was giggling: tiny, tickling knives of sound. He spent his days sharpening his sword for battle, waiting for President Polk's head to come within reach. "Polkie, come here, Polkie," he chirped in a sweet tone that parents warbled to children and pets.

Several men and women approaching him on the sidewalk didn't wait for the intersection to cross the street.

"You can't keep away from me forever, Polkie," he muttered. "So what if I'm going to destroy the city and everyone in it just to wipe you out?" Giggles lengthened to joyous bleats. Ten million lives were nothing compared to the damage this man had done to the world and the threat he still posed.

G knew the time instinctively, without having to scan the sky for the face of the digital clock tower. It was midnight, closing time for many establishments, the opening buzz for others. He passed by a stretch of tenement buildings owned by Dick Vale, this neighborhood's landlord heavyweight. As he crossed into North Irony and the Eisenhower Nexus, people moved with a sense of purpose, scurrying to or from what the night brought.

Streams of mist poured out of cracks in building foundations from the underground tunnels that burrowed beneath almost every centimeter of the walled city. Few or none knew these passages better than G who made his home in a dozen or so secreted cubbyholes beneath Oldtown. If he were offered a job, family, and a home, he would refuse them. He enjoyed his marginal existence as a scavenger and freethinker. Through Collings, the organiputer, he had access to more information than anyone in the city but Polk.

Blue tumblers accompanied sirens as six hoverpods descended from Hightown. Must be something big. A riot, mass murder, or police killing. He hurried to the nearest North Irony lanternhead and hunched down beside it. If the organiputer was the city's brain and the clock tower its voice, then the lanternheads were its eyes. Polk's very own surveillance cameras. G looked at the plaque below the lanternhead which read:

> Morrow Richards
> 620 to 662
> *I always thought I could hypnotize chickens.*

A strange epitaph, but not nearly the weirdest tombstone he'd seen. Heads of deceased residents, preserved in the saline of fluoroplasm, glowed from dusk till dawn in their amber spheres. Funny thing was, they worked better than the street lamps they'd replaced. Morrow's globe burned brightly, a recent addition to the fiefdom of lanternheads.

G inserted the metallic connector leading from his wrist into the servoport. There were advantages, after all, to being part machine. He jacked into Morrow's head and saw the world from the perspective of the lanternhead, glaring with rage down at his own body. After a few moments of concentration, the rage subsided and he gained control of Morrow's thoughts and, more importantly, his eyes. Lanternheads weren't any more sentient than the average circuit board of an organiport, but they couldn't quite forget that they'd once been alive. Memories and emotions lingered inside the circuitry, sometimes for centuries or more after the original inhabitant's death. Some lanternheads, like people, were more ornery than others. Morrow was filled with too many emotions: fear, anger, love. Instead of struggling to maintain control and getting a migraine, G jumped ship and lost himself in the electrical eddies of the omnilines. He bounced from lanternhead to lanternhead toward the descending squad of police.

Names fluttered to his lips as he bobbed from link to link: Rosa Grant, Keith Madison, Tara Andrews. Finally, he ended up in the lanternhead of six-year old Mack Carter on the corner of Trump and Jericho alley. Children were always the easiest to control and Mack was long-since dead. Aside from the secret police detachment that monitored lanternheads, G was the only electronic Peeping Tom in the city, a computer-aided pervert of the highest caliber.

He scanned an agitated crowd forming in the alley juncture and zoomed in on the downed officer. His interface with Timmy would ruin any recordings of the incident. One more cop killer on the loose. G giggled and monitored the alley and surrounding apartments, panning up to the second floor windows of Boo's Bar. He pushed Timmy's electronic ears to full magnification even as he telescoped the eyes into a room where a wiry man in a battered suede coat paced next to several agitated colleagues.

* * *

What little lighting there was in G's dank cubbyhole emanated from a wide array of stolen equipment. The alcove itself wasn't large enough to stand in. Mismatched carpeting covered the concrete floor. Although it wasn't far from a small grating leading up to the Eisenhower Nexus, the air was slightly musty and stale. G thought about increasing the circulation to his hideouts, especially in summer, but never got around to it. He stretched out on a blue shag runner, lay down, and closed his eyes.

G replayed his pirated download of the look-alike men's conflict in the alleyway. He managed to do this with his eyes shut and without the use of machines. He was, of course, not like other humans. He carried his machineness on the inside instead of on the outside like everyone else. He lounged for hours in his hideout, examining the sequence. Polk's fingerprints seemed all over the identical-looking men and their fight. Unfortunately, G could not make out the majority of their conversation. It wasn't a meeting of two old friends or a mafia hit, that much he knew. One of the men was named Conrad, the other wore a banger's red coat, although he looked too old for it.

G projected the sequence over and over on the circuitry of his amplified brain. After several more hours and the inevitable shift of dark to light on the squalid streets above, he gave up. He would think better with a little sleep and maybe there was a way he could kill two snakes with one brick. He jacked into his illegal and highly secured organiport, scrolling through files of city residents. He often slept this way, grabbing shuteye while letting his mind rove the organiputer's databanks and the nexus of lanternhead security cameras. He kept an image of the two men in the forefront of his mind as he zoned out. Anyone who worked for Pyramid or the city government would be displayed on the files.

Hopefully, he would know more when he woke.

* * *

Unfortunately, G was wrong. He'd spent almost an entire day in a dreamlike trance, scrolling through the cityweb without the slightest success. The whole thing smelled like a cover-up, Polk's specialty. Time for a new strategy.

Maybe he'd have more success with the recording he made of the crime scene. If he could amplify the sound it might lead to a breakthrough. No easy task, however, even with his experience and know-how. To get better amplification than his own set-up, he would need to track down an HI signal booster. He knew the junkyard well and navigated his way to it beneath the city. He ascended from the tunnels up into its security grid. He didn't set off any alarms, but he was distracted and sloppy, miscalculating his entrance in view of a passing guard.

"Stop thief."

Unfortunately, it was illegal to purchase or own HI circuitry. This particular component was a vital part of the primary circuit box from a hovercraft. He snatched a board out of a bashed-up hovercraft and calculated his escape options.

"Get him."

"Alive. If possible."

G used his knife to slice through the security mesh and accelerated through the Ninth Street Bazaar adjacent to the junkyard. He heard a piercing growl erupt from the sky. A doverhawk. Security was pulling out all the stops. These beasts were supposed to be illegal to own except for white shirts. Who'd have thought the theft of a tiny and practically worthless piece of circuitry could cause this kind of commotion? It wasn't like he'd killed a cop.

He pushed his way through the densely packed market, hurtling a hand-woven basket of carpet panels. His pursuers were closing in—a darting shadow sprouted wings. G dove sideways beneath a tent awning into a vendor's display. Teeth of a doberhawk clanked centimeters from his ears. He scrambled on hands and knees through curios and tableware, smashing several porcelain vases. A male figure loomed. G kicked out savagely and rolled under the back flap of the tent, gouging his shoulder on a steel peg.

He was faster than humans, but hadn't counted on the beasts. That's what he got for scrounging for parts in unfamiliar territory. He needed permanent cover fast. He seemed to recall an unfastened tunnel hatch further down on Sixth. He prayed the bazaar didn't dead-end before he reached it. His eyes whisked skyward as he galloped into a hairpin turn.

G was instantly reminded of that last race, decades ago, when he was a ten-year-old albino racer and a favorite to win the Hightown Stakes. He had been well behind the leaders going into the third lap of the championship race. His gut had flared in sharp denial as he churned in a flat-out sprint. He gained ground, but was still ten steps behind the lead runner going into the final turn. He plucked the needle from his wrist sheath quicker than the eye could follow, a movement practiced thousands of times in front of a mirror. He jammed the adrenaline into his thigh, pretended to stumble and deftly repocketed the syringe.

His feet and mind jumbled in a blur of speed and desire. He tore past the competition halfway down the clubhouse stretch. Groans, grunts, and whoops burst from the chasing pack. The roar of the crowd boomed in his ears. Colors intensified, swirling the sharp delineations of reality. His body froze three steps before the finish line, but his momentum carried him past the marker. Victorious, his heart exploded.

When he woke from his emergency surgery, the contest was his only memory. His entire childhood. This race still plagued him during times of emotional intensity or duress. Even now, decades later, he raked his mind eagerly for a name, a face, anything from before his heart attack. His life, if you could call it that, had continued under a strict government regimen. He had been given a new name and a family: twenty-five other cybernetic children blessed with the letters of the alphabet for names. G was the only one who'd survived to tell the tale.

He pushed himself in a final burst. A doberhawk's shrill cry echoed in the alleyway. G scrambled into a sewer duct and closed a grate just before the fangs and claws of his pursuers could get to him. He twisted away from the vent and burrowed into the underground. That was a close call, even for him. It cheered him to know that he could still run like the wind. Only a weak heart had kept him from joining the busts of racing champions whose youthful faces haunted Hightown storefronts and promenades.

Most feared the underground labyrinth, but G found it safer than the streets above. Besides, he was armed to the teeth in ways most people couldn't fathom. He threaded his way north, in the mood to lick his wounds and hang out at Varicose, his favorite Rim bar.

***

G swilled the watered-down rom as much for the sake of appearance as anything else. Only the harder drugs affected him and then only barely. He glanced at the broken hovercraft component sitting on the table. Did he really almost get nabbed for a worthless piece of junk? That's what he got for letting his curiosity get the better of him. He had his own problems to think about. Namely, how he'd ever get close enough to put a world of hurt on George Polk.

Varicose was filled to overflowing. All three floors. G's was one of the few tables that housed only a single person. He knew many of the regulars by name in the combination bar and bazaar, especially the vendors, but he was too much of a loner to seek out company. Others must feel the same way about him. While several people looked in his direction and waved, no one stopped by to talk to him.

He leaned back in his stool, on the right side of the stage, waiting for the next performance. Varicose had the best open forum in town, maybe not in the talent of its performers, but in the eclectic variety of its acts. Impromptu plays were interspersed with musicians, comedians, dancers, poets, and oddballs spouting whatever came to mind. Occasionally, he downloaded the best performances from memory and made a copy for the owner. Not once did he ever consider getting up on stage himself.

"Need anything else?"

G looked up and wondered if he wasn't more inebriated than he thought. A brown-skinned waitress, in a spotted apron, looked down at him.

"No, I'm fine. I haven't seen you around here before."

She was the darkest person he'd ever seen in Varicose or the Rim for that matter.

"I just started work today," she said, looking over her shoulder at packed tables of revelers next to the bazaar stalls.

"I'm G," he said, extending a hand. He didn't usually go out of his way to be friendly, but figured that the barista was probably getting a lot of flack for her shading.

"Florida," the woman said, coughing. She looked as though she might keel over, but regained her balance and gave his hand a quick tug. "If you need anything, be sure to let me know."

Their skin touched for only a second. In that brief moment of contact, G could sense something was terribly wrong. A spark of uncertainty and fear crackled in the air. First of all, her name wasn't Florida, it was Gail. He wasn't exactly sure how he knew that. He had a feeling of kinship with her that he'd only experienced before with the organiputer. At first, G was elated. He wondered if she felt the same way about him. Then it dawned on him that she was different.

Like himself, she might be part machine.

LEMON

11

Mere slammed his knee into the leg of an overturned table and ranted a string of obscenities. For Usa's sake, he was the hunter not the hunted! He stumbled drunkenly, clutching the sack of kibble close to his chest as he circled his living room. There would be an accounting to the treachery at hand. So what if people were following him? Let 'em. He was ready for anything. He kicked off his shoes and tiptoed a circuit around the disaster area that was once his living room. Torn curtains waved their fingers of hello. Overturned furniture jutted into walkways and kitchen utensils littered the carpeting.

Damage control was the only reason he considered feeding Tim at all. And the hairy squawker knew it. His wife's chihuahua-chicken had ravaged the apartment during his short stay at work and all-night blitzkrieg at the bar. Or quite possibly it had occurred the day before when he'd been too out-of-it to notice. Tim had pissed all over his compustation and ripped the crotch out of three of his jumpsuits. Why couldn't Gail have taken the nasty critter with her?

Mere felt almost nothing for animals. He didn't know why he was immune to their pants and slurps and nuzzles. It was one of those traits—some would say a character flaw—that he hid from everyone, including Gail. Genetically altered pets seemed contrived; he could drum up more feeling for a stone. At least the mutated Tim couldn't actually mate. Nothing would be worse than a city overrun by bobbing squads of feather-pelted psycopaths.

He heard the squawk just as he felt the bag of kibble torn from his hands. Ambushed again. Tim darted out of range, circling the room on his knobby chicken legs. When Gail had designed her hybrid, Mere and the woman at the Pet Center thought it was a bad idea to mix a temperamental breed of dog with a major food crop like chicken. But she'd been adamant. Her choice stemmed from an odd childhood fetish she had for fowl. Her chicken nicknacks still cluttered the kitchen and bedroom—she hadn't bothered to take those with her either. Gail had always loved cooing and gobbling to Tim in a high-pitched whine, a surrogate for her baby lust. Mere knew he could get under her skin any time he wanted by poking fun at chickens.

What was wrong with him? He was thinking about Gail as though she were still a part of his life. Pathetic. Not an hour went by where the truth didn't whack him in the back of the head, although he was trying his hardest to ignore the pain. Loneliness loomed large on the horizon. Everything reminded him of her. Her lemon-scented perfume lingered in the apartment even though he'd burned oil in a pan to mask the scent. He had always counted on his wife for companionship and a feeling of safety, attributes important to him from having grown up in an orphanage. When he'd married Gail he knew that he was getting stability and friendship, not necessarily passion or romance.

It was sobering to be on the fast track to middle age and not have a clue about what love was or if it even existed. He could find little to believe in these days. He mistrusted others, disliked himself, and could not bring himself to swallow the panacea of a supreme being. Now he was a murderer and hunted by blood-thirsty kooks in some sort of bizarre war game. He could see damn little reason to continue the miserable existence that loomed before him.

Mere quit stalking Tim and slumped into his favorite chair. Usa, he was bitter! No wonder Gail left him. Who'd want to live with someone who didn't know who he was or what he cared about? There was something lurking in Mere that he feared to unleash, yet how could he understand himself if he kept these deep-seated desires buried? If he was a killer at heart and cared nothing for anything but power and glory, so be it. To be true to himself— whatever that meant—was better than living a lie. Tim stopped nibbling his kibble, cocked his head, and whined, staring at Mere in confusion.

***

The next few weeks were a blur. Mere had reacquainted himself with the fringes of Oldtown and what scurries in the shadows, discovering that he himself was blocking out the light. He gobbled, swilled, and snorted anything offered to him, anything but sex, the idea of which sickened him. He frequented old-man bars, used pseudonyms, and even, under proper circumstances, started fights. When he wasn't blown on rom or pills, he was sleeping.

"What's the difference between a lightscraper and a woman?" Mere asked the afternoon crowd at The Changling.

The clean-shaven barista ignored Mere and edged away from the counter, pretending to serve other customers. The bleary-eyed old timer on the stool beside him stared into the depths of a filled ashtray, obviously uncomfortable.

"If you really had to, you could love a lightscraper." Mere chuckled, drowning out what could be laughter, but probably was not. He was ready with the latest jokes, having collected them from dives throughout the city. The last few days he'd been scouring the "Corridor," a row of bars, casinos, and restaurants for a mostly gay clientele. He was having the time of his life. Or something. His vacation from work had already slipped away or was just starting. He couldn't remember. His only goal was to sink further into depravity.

"Hey there, stranger. What's on your mind?" A thin and pasty man approached Mere from a side table where he had been scamming drinks from two older gentlemen.

Mere squinted at the apparition. "Why are you following me again?"

"What?"

"Don't think I haven't seen you around. Keeping tabs on me. Accusing me with that smug look of yours."

"I would say I'm more coy than smug, although I could work on it."

"Right and next you're going to tell me that if I ignore you and pretend you don't exist that everything's going to be fine, well, I've tried that, believe me."

"You're losing me, partner."

"Jack," Mere barked as he staggered to his feet, causing the barista to make eye contact with the bruiser checking weapons at the door. "Don't call me partner. Not since you ran out on me."

"I think you're confusing me with some other babe," the man

said.

Mere reached out and dug his nails into a baby-smooth fore-arm. "Why do I get the feeling that killing's what I do best? I don't dream anymore, but I can hear them scream, millions of them, in my head. I find myself thinking that it's better to weed out the underbrush so that the garden can grow back stronger. But what the loop does that mean?"

The boyish voice deepened its timber, "You've got two sec-onds to let go of me or my pal Slant at the door is going to pull your heart out through your nostrils."

Mere pushed the boy away and caressed his empty drink, prod-ding the lemon in the bottom of the glass with a straw. "Good luck finding it. Everyone in this place can just fly to hell. Don't you know that I've got your lives in the palm of my hand and all I have to do is squeeze very-very hard?"

Mere knew that in a few seconds he would be feeling the thick fingers of a bruiser named Slant digging into his shoulders and propelling him out the door. He couldn't bring himself to care that much. About anything. He tilted back the empty glass, swallowing at air, his tongue probing the ice and citrus for the last vestiges of rom.

***

G knew that he'd made a mistake as soon as he opened his mouth. After spending weeks getting Florida to agree to a date, he couldn't keep himself from grilling her about her past on their walk together in the East Rim caverns. They'd kept behind the oth-ers on the guided tour, laughing and trading quips until G began his barrage of questions.

She dodged them awhile before admitting, "It must be obvious that I'm in trouble."

They lagged behind their group and paused at a stone monu-ment that marked the halfway point of the tour. A small field of white rock lilies was blooming on an outcropping below, lit by a string of growlights pitoned to the drop-off into darkness.

"Actually, you seem like you're having a great time. I can't help it if I'm more sensitive than the average guy."

"True, I like that about you. You're different."

"Different?"

"That's not a bad thing. This is the best time I've had in ages."

"The best date?"

"You can call it that if you want."

"A good enough time to make you forget about your problems?"

"Almost," Gail sighed, her mood lightening. She sat on the jagged edge of the marker, folding up her feet and tucking them under her thighs. "I suppose I might as well tell someone. I think I might be pregnant."

"Oh," G blurted, shrugging nonchalantly and leaning back next to her.

"And to top it off, I left my husband."

"Really?"

"It's a complicated situation. I'm unbelievably confused. I know that leaving him was the right thing to do, but I don't think he has a clue about the real reason why I left him."

"Did he hit you?"

Florida opened her mouth and pursed her lips as a zeb and albino couple sauntered past on the dimly lit trail to another section of the rock gardens.

"No, it was nothing like that."

G felt her fear and confusion spilling into the air. An image flashed in his mind of a gray-eyed man with night-black skin.

"Polk has something to do with this, doesn't he?"

"How did you know that?"

"I'll tell you my story if you tell me yours."

"I wish I had a story to tell."

"What do you mean?"

"The trouble began about a year ago. I started having dizzy spells and these huge white holes in my memory."

Florida winced and shielded her eyes with her hand, her skin mottled with white swirls beneath the violet growlights.

G smiled encouragingly. "Are you telling me that one second it would be noon and the next thing you knew...."

"It would be night. Exactly. For some reason I didn't want to worry my husband about it even though the gaps in time kept increasing in frequency. Toward the end it was about every other week. Something strange happened during my last whiteout. When

I came to my senses I was in Skytown, strapped to a table."

G's long fingers curled into the grooves of the boulder. "You don't need to talk about it if you don't feel like it."

"No, I think it would be good for me to tell someone. I'm not really sure I understand it myself. When I woke up in Polk's penthouse I didn't know where I was at first. I felt groggy, just like after a bad dream, and there were tubes running from my arms into a machine."

"The organiputer?"

"I'm not sure. I was nude, for starters. Then Polk came into the room, fondled my breasts and...he kissed me."

G reached down and caressed her fingertips in his palm. She pulled away and stood, teetering on a tiny ledge.

"Polk joked to a tech about what a great kisser I was. It was really messed up. Then they started talking about my next cycle or rotation, something odd and creepy like that." She paused and burst into a halfhearted laugh. "I'd had enough. I reared back and popped him in the nose as hard as I could. You should have seen the look on his face."

"I wish I could have."

"Polk was pissed. He pulled back his arm like he was going to punch me and told me that if I didn't keep my mouth shut about what I'd seen that he was going to kill my husband."

Florida returned to the stone marker and slumped next to him, leaning into his shoulder. Although G expected her to cry, it tore at his heart to see her shaking, silently, in the crook of his elbow. He slid his other arm around her and tried to think of something to say.

"I should have warned Mere, I guess, but there was something in Polk's eyes when he said...."

"Said what?"

She sniffed and wiped her nose with the back of her hand. "He said...or better yet, I'll get Mere to kill you for me."

Mere wandered the teeming streets of the Jungle, looking for something, sleep perhaps, since he'd almost managed to quit the practice entirely—scared of dreaming, scared of himself. By day, he avoided Hightown, flittering along the knuckling streets of low-town in search of answers but not really knowing what to ask. By night, he tried to forget his troubles through rom and insipid conversation. Night wrapped him in a comforting embrace, stifling his longing for Gail, but not his passion, not altogether. He had a complete inability to rein in his temper. He was acting like a real ass. Maybe he'd always been one.

He'd spent that particular morning edging in and out of the Jungle Bazaar, avoiding the main rows of shops where vendors hawked their overpriced wares. He kept to the fringes where the rental space was cheap, the buys more interesting.

He paused outside an antique shop called Gravity's Rainbow, trying to figure out what it was about the store that drew him to it, compelling him to enter. Maybe it was the gold hookah, taller than a man, in the picture window. Or perhaps it was the wreath of dead flowers, carefully culled in braids of curry, olive and brown that hung above a tiny copper gong. Or, more likely, it was the unobtrusive sign in the bottom right corner of the plate-glass display that read "Tchotchkes," the rarely spoken moniker for holy objects. These talismans were rare and expensive, supposedly from before the jihad when prophets and fools trod the earth.

Mere nudged open the hatch to the unassuming shop and was met by the tinkling of bells above the jamb. The proprietor ignored him as he wandered along cluttered shelves of glassware, household baubles, jewelry, and furniture until he said, quite clearly, "Tchotchkes."

The grizzled owner, with skin like aged parchment, and his

even older wife, or quite possibly his mother, motioned him toward the back of the store. Mere hesitated before following the couple into a tiny display room with no windows and a low ceiling. They sat him down at an antique table, one of the few he'd ever run across made of wood.

"So where's the magic show?" Mere asked, crossing his arms across his chest. He'd always wanted to view a holy object close up and see what the fuss was about. It was undoubtedly just another illusion to confound the masses like astrology, séances, and skin readings.

"Oh no," the woman said, stepping from the cubicle through a side door fashioned seemingly of paper.

"What my wife means is that you are the one who will give us a magic show."

"I don't understand."

The owner's high cheekbones stretched taut skin into a smile, his yellowish-gray teeth matching his complexion exactly as though unbrushed for just such a fashion statement. His stooped wife returned with a rickety wooden box pocked with knots, the contents rattling inside.

"This is a tchotchke, recently unearthed," the old woman said. Her sagging breasts brushed Mere's forehead as she placed the box on the table. She kept her hands pressed over the lid and waited until she made eye contact with him before letting go. The wooden container vibrated and slid, slowly, toward him. The husband approached and slapped his hand on top of the box, stopping its advance, saying, "Most think that tchotchkes are symbols of God. They are actually the constructs of the devil who is man, the destroyer."

Only then did Mere notice the pale golden moons on the proprietor's fingertips, nails the same color as his skin and teeth. The owner grinned, lifted the box lid, snatched up a white plastic orb jumping around inside and pressed it into Mere's palm. The old man's hands, although gnarled, were dexterous and strong. He slipped a loop of twine over Mere's middle finger before he had a chance to pull away.

The tchotchke wiggled as though it were alive. Mere felt the sideward tug of gravity spooling string. The plastic cylinder spun outward and extended to its full length of twine, hovering waist-level above the ground. It had sideways gravity. Incredible. It was too small to have a Zero G generator. Mere stared, open-mouthed, then loosened the string from around his knuckle and whirled for the door. Trick or no, it didn't matter. He wanted nothing more to do with this object or the unknown. Mere heard the tchotchke thud against the wall as he bolted from the back room of the tiny shop through the clutter and out the front hatch into the comforting twilight fog.

$* * *$

"Florida," she said after a moment's thought, the name tumbling off her lips. It was difficult for her to think of herself as the fairy tale character whose name she'd borrowed. The clinic healer smirked or maybe smiled—it was difficult to tell which—and wiped his palms above her prone body, brushing the molecules of air just above her curves and crevices. He still hadn't touched her and yet her skin tingled and itched.

It was maddening. She'd been here for more than an hour while the old man circled around her with outstretched fingers, chanting under his breath. She'd found the healer's oldage methods comforting at first, but now wished that he'd give her a prognosis or at least share whatever was floating around in the ether of his mind.

She'd come to the free clinic on G's advice (funny how quickly she'd come to trust him) and, at first, wondered if it was a wise move. The waiting room was dingy and strewn with tacky lace wall hangings, suggesting a brothel or something worse. But the rooms inside were clean, if not spacious. Kilo, the attending physician and acquaintance of Tampoca and G, had already listened to her more than all the specialists in Hightown combined. She wouldn't have come at all if G hadn't frightened her about the possibility that Polk might have performed an experiment on her.

"So am I pregnant?" she asked. Her symptoms supported the theory, but none of her store-bought tests had yet to come out positive.

"Yes and no," Kilo said, withdrawing his hands and rubbing his fingers together as though they were coated with a thin layer of oil. "That is to say—I don't know."

"What do you know?"

"You're sick for starters, but I don't have to tell you that. There's no indication that your malady is serious, although I can't be sure. It's a condition I've only come across once before...with G."

"Meaning?"

"Meaning you'd better talk to him about it."

"But you're a doctor."

"This is something beyond medicine. Beyond flesh and blood, too, for that matter."

Florida's skin flushed with anger and fear. She sat up and pushed herself off the exam table. She slid on her underwear and bra before facing the mottled physician, a gray and white zeb.

"Why am I bleeding brown?"

"I don't know."

She stepped into her green-striped work pants and wiggled the stretch material over her hips. "You could make a guess couldn't you? An educated one?"

He paused to look at the ceiling. For a moment she reverted to childhood, wondering if she had used the correct phrasing: mother may I, please, pretty please. Kilo's knees buckled slightly and he continued rubbing his hands together as though he might rediscover fire.

"Educated, no," he said.

She slipped on a pair of hand-sewn tan sandals that G had picked up for her the day before at the Bazaar and shot the healer a pleading look. "You can make a guess never-the-less?"

"Yes. I'm almost positive that you're exuding the same chemical compound that forms the crisping sex drug. Speculation has it that this fluid is a leftover component of organiputer activity. Kind of like oil to an engine or..."

"Blood to a body," she finished his sentence.

"Yes, but like I said, it's only speculation."

"So what you're trying to tell me is that you don't know why I'm sick or why my belly's swollen?"

"I'm afraid so."

"What in Usa's name is growing in my womb and what am I supposed to do about it?"

"Eat only organic food and talk to Tampoca about ways to flush out your system. The person you really need to talk to though is G. He isn't..."

Human, the thought passed through aFlorida's mind although she wasn't sure why. Kilo quieted and began running his fingers through his stringy, shoulder-length hair.

"Thank you," she said, gathering her handbag and hooded jacket. She waved halfheartedly and departed the exam room.

"Come back if your symptoms get worse," Kilo said to her back even as the next patient filed past her to see the doctor.

Her bloated stomach cramped as she staggered through the hubbub of the sick and infirm. She dodged a nurse who'd been hounding her for her signature and bolted outside the waiting area into a squalid alley in the half-deserted Lightning district. It had been her first trip from the Rim since she moved and she wasn't sure the journey had been worth it. She was more confused than ever. As she hurried toward the main thoroughfare, she thought she heard footsteps behind her.

Ridiculous. Just paranoia. She took a deep breath and quickened her step, dreading her work shift later that afternoon. She was going to be fine. She was just a little sick. No one was following her. It was her imagination. The whole thing. A dream. It was just the fever from her flue. She'd feel better after a nap.

***

G tried to keep his wits about him as he descended into the labyrinth of tunnels beneath South Oldtown. Not far to his west were underground nitro gardens where organic vegetables and fruits were harvested. The whole operation was situated next to a processing facility where green-shift workers prepared and packaged consumer goods. To his west were the fabled Collings mines from which organic steel, alum, plastic, gold, and sycron were stripped from the hardened outer layer of the organiputer. Because of these and other Pyramid-controlled businesses, the foot traffic was heavier in these sections of the underground. Unfortunately, so was security.

G fought back a yawn and made slow progress through the utility corridors. He hadn't slept well the night before. Then again, his mode of rest had little to do with actual slumber. It was the machine part of him (Polk's not-so-subtle additions) that gave him increased stamina and made him more comfortable communicating with machines than humans. Gail, seemingly, was the exception. After their day trip in the Rim caverns, she'd invited him to spend the night. Not that anything sexual happened between them. Gail was feeling too nauseous from her illness and he was too uncomfortable with his own body to make an advance.

G hesitated as his side path dead-ended and he was forced to backtrack and lower himself through chipped cement into a well-lit intersection. It looked like he would have to chance moving along a Pyramid maintenance tunnel until it meshed with another of the uncharted and substantially older trails beneath the city. The official tunnel network, well-mapped and cleared of debris, came with a miniature rail system and just enough foot traffic to make him edgy. There was no way around it though. Not for today's purpose.

He picked up his pace and navigated due south toward where the organiputer was older and better established, and still retained much of her old personality. At least, he hoped there were still parts of his surrogate mother that remained alive and in control. It had, after all, been months since he'd hotlinked into Collings.

G couldn't keep last night from his thoughts as his shadow bobbed along the gleaming rails beneath the overhead track lighting. Tampoca had looked at him strangely when he'd pulled the curtain closed to Florida's alcove. A little unnerving considering her blindness. The old witch had undoubtedly heard the rumors about G and the catalog of oddities attributed to him that made him feared and reviled by just about everyone. Florida didn't have any preconceived notions about who he was and how he was supposed to act. She seemed to welcome his presence. His friendship. Maybe more.

He wondered how long this warm feeling would last. The bond that attracted him to Florida might also spell the end of their relationship. When he first touched her, he'd been surprised to discover that he could sense her thoughts in the same way he could when linking into a lanternhead. There was something about the way she smelled and carried herself, something not quite human. He was reluctant to mention it. He didn't want to freak her out and risk losing her friendship.

Florida had enough to worry about without him adding to it. Her fear of pregnancy coupled with getting sick was more than she could take right now. He hoped Kilo could provide her with some answers. She'd been fighting through cold sweats and nausea during her work shifts at Varicose. He could tell she was in a lot of pain and wanted to help. An interface with Collings might provide some answers, even though his last link with her had nearly cost him his life. It would be worth the risk if there were even the remotest chance that he could help her.

Since meeting Florida, he'd felt more human than he had in decades. He would help her even if it meant taking the life of another or putting his own on the line. G hurried his pace and soon reached an uneven branching of tunnels near where the service corridor fed into a vast array of industrial complexes. This was the place all right. He bent down and pressed his ear to the tracks for vibrations before veering off the main path.

G snaked through a complicated series of rights and lefts, maneuvering through fallen masonry and buckling archways before finding a rusted metal grating leading further down into antiquity. The hinges were oiled, though. He kept this route free of debris in the event he needed to use it. He descended an even rustier ladder and approached a caved-in wall where a portion of the organiputer had pushed through the concrete mooring like tree roots. G sat cross-legged next to the rubble and prepared himself for the link. He spooled a series of wires from nodes in his wrists and sought for similar connectors in the bulbous gray mass pushing out beneath the fragmented plaster. He took his time preparing the link and cleared his thoughts. If he weren't careful the initial contact with Collings could burn out his mind.

He finished the connections, closed his eyes, and lost himself in the electronic battleground of flesh and metal, burrowing straight into the heart of the organiputer. He slipped through a thin patch of web protection—no one expected a break-in this far down in the system—and was met by a surge of anger, followed by a stronger pulse of desperate love. G let the spectrum of emotions wash over him, isolating sounds and images to make words form from the organiputer's jumbled thoughts.

"G, it's good to hear from you. I feared you were dead. I have not been myself lately. The countermeasures have been effective."

Yes, the countermeasures. G's brothers and sisters were eating Collings alive from the inside like a virus. They were taking control of her routine functions, setting up bypass links and an alternate web of neurocommand centers. Polk's plan was insidious: to fragment the central processing of the organiputer with twenty-five live wires like himself, each named after a letter in the alphabet. Polk wanted to do away with the mad Collings without losing functionality.

"It's good to talk to you. I'm sorry it's been so long, but contact is always a dangerous proposition."

"Polk?"

"Yes, Polk is trying to kill me just like he is you. This is why I need your help."

G could feel the organiputer's emotions surge, threatening to overwhelm him. If he didn't get her to disconnect soon, she could fry him.

"You want help?"

"Yes, help. I need you to route me to the sanctum."

The sanctum was Polk's internal security system. The president took great pains to ensure the break-in G was planning never took place. The weight of Collings' fears and concerns began pushing through his buckling defenses. In desperation, he let his guard down enough to let Collings know how the close-link with her was affecting him. The gamble worked. She stopped trying to smother him and the pressure eased. Collings soon guided him, light-speed, through the labyrinth of circuitry toward the dangerous Skytown nexus.

"Sorry, G, I didn't mean to hurt you. I have so little control these days. I'll help you get past his defenses."

Polk, you'd better watch out, G thought. I'm coming to make your life a dying hell.

* * *

Mere fed Tim a chicken burrito with his fingers. They'd become fast friends over the last few days. He had finally figured out the secret to a good relationship. Power. He could withhold food or not. Tim had quickly learned to be nice, even docile. For some reason, it was important to Mere that he break the spirit of the knobby-legged fur ball. Now, the coup de grace, cannibalism. He'd actually gotten Tim to eat chicken.

"Doesn't Timmy wimmy wove chickie-wickies?"

"Bawkabakoofroobawk awka," the bastard erupted as it nicked his fingers with its beak.

From now on, it would only be the two of them. No women. No job. Just them pandling on a street corner in North Irony. That way all the sisters from his orphanage could walk by and provide him with food and clothing even as they shot him the all-knowing look that implied he'd never amount to anything. "You're too pigheaded," they'd say. "Too bad-tempered. Too violent." Was it his fault that he wanted more than a life of squalor? If he hadn't fought and clawed and scratched his way through school, he would never have made anything of himself. People were always trying to tell you how you should act, especially those who never knew what it was like to be poor.

Mere left the remains of his meal for Tim and rose from the couch. He kicked through the trash littering the somber white carpeting and hoped for the clank of his big toe stubbing itself on rockgut. Cheap rom. Yes siree. Last night's poison distilled from a man with one eye in the white light district. Mere flicked on the HV in the middle of a news report about the illegal vegetable trade in the Rim and how it was weakening the immunity of light-skinned people to sunlight. Mere continued his search for last night's bottle as the newscaster explained how it was every citizen's duty to report whomever was helping to spread the "dangerous" produce.

Mere's hatch rumbled with a knock that sounded like metal on metal, a ring rapping against steel. He dove to the ground to avoid being spotted through the partially opened front blinds. It was Helena, his landlady. It had to be. She'd stopped by to see him every day this week, but thus far he'd managed to avoid her. He'd had to play it cagey to get in and out without the old witch spotting him.

Why in the loop was she so interested in him? Her nosiness was starting to get on his nerves. No reason to get paranoid, though. She was probably just checking up on her buddy Gail.

"I'm coming in, Mere. You better make yourself presentable," Helena yelled through the sealed hatch.

"I won't let you in and you can't make me!"

"This is for your own good."

The hatch had barely ghosted when Helena rushed into the room and threw herself on top of him. He'd made an easy target, he supposed, lying face first on the floor. She was heavier than he thought. He thrashed and tried unsuccessfully to buck her off.

"Helena, you've probably heard that Gail's left me. I'm not sure I'm up for anything this kinky."

Mere felt the prick of a needle in his neck and he reared up, dumping Helena onto the floor.

"Usa, that hurt! What are you trying to do, kill me?"

"It looks like you're doing a pretty good job of that yourself."

Mere lurched to his feet and took a couple of unsteady steps toward his landlady, but there was something in the way the middle-aged woman stared at him that made him pause.

"That's right, you'll do what I say from now on," she hissed. "You have no idea how high the stakes are. You need to pull yourself together."

"Your looping crazy," Mere muttered, his mouth and lips going numb, his feet too asleep to stand. He collapsed onto a pile of clothes that smelled like vomit and cheap cologne.

"That's right, get a nice rest and when you wake up I'll have a couple of people here to look after you. You see, Mere, you're actually a very valuable commodity, only you don't know it."

"Wha'?"

"Hush, dear, I shot you up with something that was once called a tranquilizer. You see, I'm a very old woman. Hundreds of years old. Almost as old as you."

Mere began to drift off, but not before he heard her whisper, "Someday you'll understand what I'm doing. I only hope I won't live to regret helping you."

Greek whirred through the web faster than even his cyber-enhanced mind could handle. He tried very hard not to panic, and meditated on nothingness as images of winged demons burned into his mind and numbers melted. The greater part of Collings had splintered off to create a diversion for his break-in by sabotaging routine city maintenance programs. A miniscule portion of her accompanied him on his journey, guiding him through the barriers protecting Polk's inner sanctum.

Collings was splintered and fragmented, her personality cast over the cityweb. She wasn't much assistance in helping him to ward off the influx of information. G tried losing himself in emotions: passion and rage, his and Florida's predicaments, his overwhelming desire to end Polk's rule over a world recast in his image. Hate. Hate and lust. Lust and hate. Florida's body coupling with his own on a wedding bed built from Polk's bones. The president's severed head kept alive only to record the numerous and legendary performances of their lovemaking.

With a final prod from Collings, G slingshot and penetrated the thick walls surrounding Polk's castle of information. He landed within the fortress, disoriented and confused. For a long time, he could barely make tails or heads of his surroundings. Or if he was even alive. Back in the tunnels, his abandoned body lay on mildewed concrete without a mind, gasping for air.

**

G drifted in the web, trying to orient himself in his new environment after the shock of almost having every nerve ending in his body burned to a crisp. The only thing that seemed to reach him was pain or, more accurately, memories of pain. Especially the horrors of his lost childhood and the imprisonment following the surgery that changed his life. He pulled apart each memory like a mad vivisectionist, focusing on the concrete and visceral, categorizing elements of an existence someone else had shaped. He remembered those first awkward steps in his vat-grown adult body and the winces of disgust from the doctors and security guards.

It was the little things that had hurt most in those months of watching and waiting after his rebirth. Polk tried to keep him and the other letter children in the dark, but the president hadn't counted on how well he had fashioned his cybernetic brood. They were supposed to be replacement conduits for the organiputer after all. G and his siblings found out about their roles, of course, among other corporate intrigues. Polk was anxious to harness and control the organic system that ran his whole operation. The fast-expanding organic brain housed beneath the city was malfunctioning from the added power drain that came from selling Collings' services to technology-poor cities rebuilding from the war.

Because he was only the seventh letter out of twenty-six and the process for creating organic links out of orphaned children still had a few kinks, G had time to gather information and plan an escape. The other letters thought him quite mad and, aside from F, J and P, he could find no allies in his quest to leave the heavily guarded Skytown facility. One of the brainwashed do-gooders must have narced on him—there was no other explanation for why he was separated from his siblings and imprisoned in an ozonodome cell made of synthetic steel.

It was this period of isolation, G believed, that saved him from the gruesome fate of the others. He had nothing to do during his imprisonment but stare through the shutterglass from his tower over the misty metropolis and let himself fantasize about what might have been. Dreaming freed his mind and opened his senses to the miniscule amounts of energy swimming through the air and the circuitry funneling beneath his prison. When he wasn't gazing out the window trying to glimpse the elusive yellow orb shrouded in smog, he lay on the floor of his tiny room for days at a stretch, seeking to communicate with the presence he felt beneath him. This entity would gain substance over intense days of concentration and coalesce into a maternal voice he would come to call Collings.

He wondered about his sanity. It wouldn't be the first time someone had cracked in solitary confinement. The things Collings told him didn't help much either. It was mostly nonsense patter and hard-to-believe facts like how she'd created most of the modern constructs of the city by cloning and recloning portions of her body in geometric designs. It was this synthetic tissue, the skin of the city, through which G gained a valuable friend and ally. The lonely Collings took pity on him and helped save him from being assimilated into the cityweb on the eve of his new "assignment."

G came out of his reverie and back to his senses. He'd done it. He'd knifed through Polk's security. He charted his position by putting out a few low-level feelers and tried very hard to cloak himself from detection. He used the rarely monitored links of security cameras to weave in and out of the comp platform, searching for files that Polk had accessed in the last few weeks. He would have to be quick about it and careful. It had been nearly twenty years since G had last busted into any of Polk's high-tech nodes. When he was younger, he'd taken greater risks and had come close to paying the ultimate price for his brashness. Polk had suckered him into a number of traps, each one more insidious than the one before. Once, a squad of police even managed to track down his body and haul it halfway to Hightown before he came to his senses and escaped.

Both he and Polk got craftier as the years rolled on. G had decided that it was in his best interest to stay as far away from the president as possible until he could develop a foolproof plan to take the bastard out. Polk, meanwhile, had stopped his efforts to track him, figuring him dead or no longer a threat. Well, the prodigal son was returning home with a surprise for the old man.

G wormed his way into the system's chronomap and searched for files whose existence had been encrypted so well that they disappeared as soon as he accessed them. Son-butch! It looked like he'd stumbled onto a self-erasure program that protected files by taking them off-line when improperly accessed. Although he'd been thwarted at the source, he had other tricks he could use.

He dampened his synoptic signature and latched onto the self-erasure program, following it on its round of purges. He knew better than to try and break any security codes. He'd been burned that way before and lost some of his prime underground organi-

links in the process. Collings wouldn't be any help to him even if she'd been able to accompany him through the protective ice. She knew very little about the advanced security Polk used to safeguard his personal files.

G attuned himself to the semi-intelligent program and watched as it erased signs that files had been used. He caught flashes of information as these ghost files were dumped. Apparently, there was a group of scientists who monitored Collings and flushed her brain with chemical uppers and downers to keep her running at optimal levels. No wonder she'd been so sluggish. He glimpsed invoices of goods shipped to and from other cities and discovered that samples of all imported items were fed into the organiputer. He was locked out of a file folder called "gravity" as well as an efficiency report of the letter nodes. The best-protected area, within its own self-contained system, was simply labeled "Twelve." G tried to remain alert and waited for the program to make its rounds into that realm of high-security files.

His patience was rewarded. The self-erasure system linked into Polk's personal node and waited to flush a file that blinked "Twelve, currently in use." Loop, it was a hot link. Polk was on-line. He had to be. Without thinking of the repercussions, G slid from his piggyback and wormed his way into the live program. He quickly acclimated himself and, by concentrating, forged his thoughts into words.

"Hi, Polk."

"You're dead." came the all-too-quick response. "You've got about five seconds before I flush the whole node."

"I don't think you have the balls to wipe your own files," G responded as part of him scrolled through the open file. It helped being part machine, only he had to keep Polk on-line, engaged. "What's the matter. Don't you recognize your old pal, G?"

"G? I figured you'd have killed yourself by now."

G pulled in random words from the file—*cloning, replacement body, battle of the twelve.* It was time to get Polk off his game. "It's funny, but I'd have thought the same about you. Must be time for you to get a new body. How are the twelve doing?"

G could almost feel the heat of Polk's words, although they were translated into binary code. The 1's and 2's of his words snaked pure venom, "I've got just the thing for you, G. A present, you might say. A welcome home present."

Information kept spooling into G from the file—*Characters: Mere, Conrad, Death, War, Famine, Pestilence.* Odd. It was almost as though Polk was playing a war game, but with whom and why?

"I'd put my money on Mere," G binared to Polk even as he realized it was Florida's ex he was talking about. Why hadn't he made the connection until now? He was feeling a hair sluggish, almost as though energy was being drained from him. Of course. It was a trap.

"Gotcha dumb-ass," came the message from Polk as G fought to extract himself from the web. *To the death* were the last words he downloaded as he attempted to disengage from the file. And... he could not. His thoughts were fuzzy and his on-line persona was losing its vitality and form. His reasoning power was being sucked from him at an alarming rate.

"Welcome back to the fold, G. I'm sure the other letters missed you while you were gone."

Jack! G tried to figure out what exactly was happening to him and how, but his thoughts were stagnant and no ideas came. He could feel the web rerouting portions of him that until now he'd had little use for, the parts of his mind and body that had been altered and expanded by Polk to replace the organiputer. He tried projecting himself through the protective ice to contact Collings, but it was no use. He was defeated, his free will sucked into the system. His memories were clogging up with maintenance programs and system hardware. He was becoming the link that Polk had always wanted him to be. "You're a coward," he transmitted to his tormentor, although he was unsure whether his message would pass through the maelstrom of information around him.

Last resort...something drastic. He put every iota of his will power into shutting down the breathing of his body back in the tunnels of South Oldtown. He had learned to control his involuntary brain functions years before, but was too out of it to know if he was succeeding. A minute passed. Two. Three. He was hoping for a brief sojourn into brain death...in order...to break the link. His mind, after shutting down, should return to his body. Hopefully, without too much damage.

More and more routine functions of the web was funneling into him and routing through his brain. His circuitry. Good. The more systems linked into him the better. When and if he ever made it back to his body, the cityweb would be in for some serious crashing. G focused on his lungs...keeping them from drawing... breath....even as he was lost, whether to Polk or his own body he hadn't the slightest clue.

* * *

Mere woke with a start, a terrible pain shooting through his lower back, half in bed, half out, wearing nothing but a pair of black shorts with faded blue polka dots. He groaned, clutching his covers, and tried to place where he was. His bedroom. His Zero G bed, only he hadn't turned it on. Or had he fallen out of the gravweb some time during the night?

He tried to remember what had taken place the evening before and memories of Helena's attack flooded over him. She'd acted strangely. Then again, how well did he really know her? She had doped him up with a major-league depressant and dragged him into his bedroom. Still, he could tell the drug-induced sleep had helped. Considerably. He'd been going batty without shuteye. He raised himself up on his elbows and tried to focus on the sheer white walls.

"Hi, princess," chided a confident, masculine voice. "Have a nice rest?"

Mere whirled to face the voice, but came to a sudden stop as a long metal blade pressed against his throat. He gasped and looked into the barrel chest of a squat, muscular man about his age with curly black hair and steel-gray eyes. The bull-necked bruiser was dressed in a yellow jumpsuit, marking him as a Pyramid accountant or lawyer.

"What? Am I behind on my rent or something?"

"Very funny, for a guy about to have himself silenced. Permanently."

What the loop was this about? Mere thought he saw a shadow streak across the floor. It was Tim, the feather-pelted freak, sneaking into the bedroom to watch him die. He suddenly felt very tired. Tired of people trying to kill him. Tired of not understanding what was going on. Tired of wrestling with his conscience.

"This will bring the number down to five. You must have really pissed Polk off. I couldn't believe it when he told me where you live."

"What are you talking—" Mere began, but stopped himself. It wasn't worth it. His number was up and he was too beat to even protest.

"War. The name's War. Not my real name, of course. I know it sounds stupid, but Polk gave me the nickname himself."

"You're right, it does sound stupid."

War's face darkened and his muscular arms bulged with rage. He pulled back the blade a fraction and yanked Mere to his feet. The bedspread that Helena had covered him with stayed wrapped around his leg. It was a novelty flying blanket that Gail had bought them for their occasional trips to Park West. Mere grabbed the corner of the Zero G bedspread to keep himself from tripping and stared into War's eyes. He had seen that same look before, in the mirror, just before going out and getting blitzed.

"Any last requests?"

"Go loop yourself."

War grinned and pushed Mere down to his knees. The yellow coat raised his blade just as the floors began to vibrate and the walls to buckle. A cityquake! Mere dove forward under War's blade and stumbled to his feet. He waded through the dirty laundry strewn over the carpeting and tried to keep his distance from the madman in his bedroom. The quake had invigorated him with the desire to fight back. He kept his eyes on the rattling furniture and struggled to keep his balance. He sidestepped another swing and didn't even see the foot that shot up out of a pile of Gail's discarded underwear. His windpipe rattled from the blow. Mere collapsed on the floor, choking, wheezing for air.

War took his time approaching his fallen prey, wobbling in the tremors with tiny, careful steps. Mere gasped in an attempt to get oxygen into his lungs and tried to gather his wits. He picked up an armful of shirts and flung them over War's upper torso, looking to scramble out the hatch, but the brute cut off the angle, tossing off the scraps of cloth with a jerk of his neck.

The yellow suit slowly backed him into a corner. Mere looked for the slightest opening or misstep, bunching his leg muscles. His bare back pressed up against a pane of glass that was invisible, cloaked in white from the wall setting. Mere had covered most of the windows with holowalls since Gail had left him. They'd never really opened this window anyway because it looked out over the skyway.

The cityquake ceased its spasms as quickly as it had begun. A wobbling War straightened. "Pulse," he said, chortling, "That was close. I should have known better than to get cocky."

"Helena!" Mere yelled, even as he cursed himself for having blown an opportunity to escape.

"Come on, Mere, is it? Die like a man. Or at least like a clone of a man."

Mere grumbled, waiting for War to strike.

A bobbing furball darted out from behind the bed and leapt toward War, flapping its wings. Mere's assailant whirled and sliced through air as Tim ducked beneath the blade and sank his beak into yellow cloth. War shrieked and kicked out, trying to loosen the chihuahua-chicken from his calf. Mere used the momentary confusion to step inside the man's guard and grab two handfuls of a sycron jumpsuit. He whirled and pivoted, throwing War over his hip into what he hoped was the window.

Glass shattered and the hologram dissolved. Mere felt the force of the hip-toss carry him forward even as the madman gripped his left wrist with his free hand. War slid across the sill, cursing, a squawking Tim ripping into his leg. The yellow suit dropped his blade and grabbed the sill with his right hand even as he pulled on Mere's arm with his left. Mere braced his legs against the wall beneath the window and felt his bad shoulder pop as he tumbled over War's shoulder.

Cool air rushed through his nostrils as he sailed out the window. He got an instant shock of vertigo. Fear and adrenaline pumped through him. He shrieked in free fall and reached out, snagging hold of War's belt. He clutched onto his nemesis for dear life and slid down the man's left leg even as Tim continued ripping into the right.

"Jack, let go!" War howled, swinging his left arm back up to the window frame. Mere held on for all he was worth and watched Tim flap his wings and dig his claws into exposed flesh. He felt his shorts begin to slide down his legs as the magic blanket, caught in the waist band, tugged downwards from the pull of gravity. War groaned and, incredibly, began lifting himself upwards. Mere looked at the chihuahua-chicken for inspiration and bit into War's other leg.

The scream was terrifying, almost childlike in its high-pierced ferocity. Mere saw War's hands give way and slip off the ledge. The threesome fell, accelerating toward the city below. Mere shoved himself off War's thigh and lunged toward the skyway railing. One chance, he thought, reaching out for the conveyor sidewalk...and missing. He shrieked and rolled onto his back so that he would not have to watch the ground rush up to meet him. He stared, instead, at his genitals and the boxers draped around his ankles. The blanket was still entwined in his underwear, flopping wildly. Could it possibly still work? His fingers ran across the synthetic material and he pushed a button, praying the battery cells were still good.

The blanket jerked and spasmed as it fought against gravity. The Zero G material stiffened and Mere struggled to lie down on top of it. His mind whirred, weighing options, as he continued falling, but more slowly, like a piece of paper. He was still in a world of trouble. He caught a glimpse of War and Tim plummeting toward a row of fast-approaching brick warehouses even as he drifted sideways in a fluke updraft. The Zero G blanket wasn't designed to fly really. It had a child's safety device that kept it from rising more than a few centimeters. It was supposed to hover, only hover. While Mere's mass was within the device's parameters, he had built up too much momentum.

Mere flattened his body and caught sight of a passenger gravpod descending from Hightown. He rolled his weight from side to side, hoping to steer himself on top of the descending glass booth. Mere prayed to Usa, even though he didn't believe in the trinity, and was surprised to find himself drifting toward the passenger car. Fast. He slammed sideways into the cable above the booth and plopped onto its upper deck. A miracle. The air rushed from his lungs. His back and hip discovered a whole new sensation of pain. But he was alive. Somehow, he was alive.

He felt self-conscious about his genitals flapping in the breeze and the stares of passengers below him. He raised himself in a sit-up position and reached for the sycron shorts hanging from his ankles even as the city groaned and rumbled. An after shock. The gravpod teetered and he felt himself sliding. He let go of his underwear and lunged for the cable, but it was too late. He tumbled across the slick sunroof and smacked his head on the corner of the booth. Black and white spots spiked his vision as he fell. Ignoring the rush of wind whipping across his skin, he closed his eyes and tried very hard to become one with the idea of death.

Florida was getting worse. The cramping was becoming un-bearable, especially when she turned, stooped or made any quick movements. Business was slow at Varicose, thankfully; she doubt-ed whether she would have been able to last her shift. Tampoca's cousin Clight, the owner of the establishment, furrowed his brow as Florida clenched her teeth and sweated bullets. Her belly had swollen considerably over the past week even though she'd barely eaten and the pregnancy tests still came up negative.

"Sure you don't want to go home," Clight suggested. "You look like you're going to keel over."

Florida clamped a smile over her grimace and nodded. "No. I'm trying to earn enough to get my own place. Tampoca's been nice, but...."

"She's giving you some friendly hints about getting out of her place."

"Hints? She's telling me straight out."

"Means she likes you. She's had a lot of people stay with her over the years. She's just looking out for you."

Florida didn't doubt it. Beneath her gruff exterior, Tampoca had a kind heart. A mouth like a trash heap, but a kind heart. Tam-poca had stopped digging into her so much after she found out how sick her guest really was. Florida wished she could take off and give the old woman her privacy. She was starved enough for it herself, willing to work double or triple shifts until she earned enough to move out. She just wished that she was feeling a little better. Aside from the fever and nausea, the Rim was turning out to be a great neighborhood to live in. And the crew at Varicose had made her feel welcome. She'd already made more friends in the last month than she had in her previous five years in Hightown.

The back office vidphone beeped and Clight slipped through a small corridor stacked with confiscated weapons and private stock to answer it. Florida took over his station and began mixing a fire lizard for an already-inebriated customer. She blended the home-grown tomatoes and carrots with green pepprini and was about to shake it into the tumbler when Clight called out, "Florida."

She motioned for the droopy-eyed man to wait and hurried to the backroom as fast as she could without sloshing her belly. She caught G's forlorn expression in the hologrid just as the vidphone blinked off. Clight frowned and hung up the receiver.

"That's weird," he said.

"What is? What's wrong?"

"G was acting pretty peculiar, even for him."

"What did he say?"

"He was at a tram stop just off the Rim and he sounded like he wanted some help getting home. I told him I'd get you on the phone and he hung up."

Florida loosened her apron. "Do you mind if I take off?"

"Nah, it's dead in here. See you tomorrow."

Florida reached for her dark-green jacket on the coat rack and hurried toward the service entrance.

"Be careful," Clight said, already heading back out to his customers.

Florida buttoned up her tunic and tried not to read too much into what he said even as she neurotically pulled the sycron material over her brown skin before going out to find G.

* * *

The ancient commuter vehicle had circled more than halfway around the Rim Loop on magnetic tracks before Florida managed to snag an empty window seat. She stretched out her legs and fought the urge to splatter vomit on the woman beside her. She turned her head and stared out the time-dappled plexiglass, spacing out, searching for G whenever she heard the lurching shoom of displaced gravity and the none-too-gentle tug of worn brakes.

She got more than her fair share of dirty looks when she rose to check out the people huddled at tram stops. Albinos, zebs, and a variety of offwhites, including Jazz and Mores, narrowed their eyes, showing their distaste at her presence. Florida tried not to make eye contact, but when she did, she smiled demurely, though confidently, and retook her seat. To be fair, she had to admit the reception wasn't much different than what she would have received if the roles were reversed in Hightown.

It was twilight by the time she spotted G lying on his side between a vidphone and garbage chute not far from a tram bench. As luck would have it, he was only two stops away from Varicose, only she had circled the Rim Loop the wrong way. From her perch in back, Florida had to squirm through the packed throng to reach the loading platform and almost missed the stop, yelling, "Back hatch. Back hatch."

G groaned and blinked his eyes as she held her belly and rushed over to help him. Nothing seemed wrong with him physically. There were no visible bruises or gashes, although it was difficult to tell for certain in the fading light. She propped him gently against the chipped lip of the bench and shooed away a couple of interested pandlers.

As she probed and tested his extremities for injuries, G mumbled incoherently, choking out a series of whirs and clicks that made her skin crawl and reminded her of numbers. She leaned over and sniffed his breath which, although didn't stink of rom, crackled like a malfunctioning appliance. The hairs on the backs of her arms stood on end, snapping to attention.

"You OJ?" she asked. "Have you taken any drugs?"

G nodded no and wrapped his arms around her shoulders like a child who'd played himself to exhaustion. She considered waiting another hour for the next circuit of the clockwise Rim line or chancing a vidphone for a cab that would probably take even longer.

She helped the staggering G to his feet and peered, hopelessly, along Oldtown North's mostly deserted warehouse district. Most Rim business ventures, she'd come to discover, advertised through cryptic street signs. She scanned both sides of the trash-littered street and noted a green H inside a burgundy diamond, the symbol for a guesthouse. Maybe she was in luck.

She slipped his arm over her shoulder and felt a wave of nausea burn through every fiber of her being. Her knees buckled and sweat raced down her arms and back. She never remembered feeling more exhausted. She gritted her teeth and half-hauled, half-steered G to the adobe building across the street.

***

Florida groaned in bed, too drained to move, if you could call it a bed. It was, rather, a foam cushion barely wide enough for a child, let alone two sick adults. She lay on her side, her belly protruding over the pitted adobe floor. A sliver of orange from a lanternhead sliced through worn blinds, illuminating the only decoration in the rent-by-the-hour dump, an apocalyptic painting of a dryad guarding a lightscraper in the mythical golden age before the war. Dark green sprigs of olive leaves spurted from the fairy's ears and spooled over her back like wings. Florida could feel G press against her, probably to keep from tumbling off the narrow mattress.

For some reason, perhaps the warmth of the body behind her, she found herself thinking about Mere. For all his professed aloofness and selfishness, he was the one who'd shown an avid interest in having kids. Although she'd wanted them, the extra responsibility seemed too much for the two of them to bear, especially with how sullen Mere had become the last few years. He was a loner from his time as an orphan and did not speak about the turmoil inside of him. Love and trust were difficult concepts for someone who'd survived the fierce pecking order of gangs.

The coldness she'd fabricated in order to leave him was real enough, she realized that now. She didn't blame him for his shortcomings, though. Something about his name suited him. Mere, a shade of something more, a person struggling to emerge from the camouflage of flesh, a reflection of everything he thought others wanted him to be.

G was the exact opposite: childish, impulsive, bordering on the insanity of true enlightenment. A rebel without a rebellion. When she was with him, she felt giddy and serene, younger than the smallest child asking endless questions about the nature of the universe and older than the wind blowing exotic fragrances over the city walls.

G stirred behind her and rested an ice-cool palm on her elbow. He slid a finger along her shoulder to her exposed neck. Her body tingled, awakening. It wasn't a sexual response, but something that reached far deeper, like a dream or an intimate look between new lovers. G sighed, his breath raising hackles on the scruff of her neck.

"You're thinking about lovers. Earlier it was the wind. Am I right?"

"How'd you know?" Florida asked, shocked at his perceptiveness and pleased that he was once again forming words.

"I've come to the realization that we're a lot alike."

"I think you may be right."

"There's something inside both of us that makes us different... unique from everyone else."

She turned over onto her back, half hanging off the cushion, and saw the conflict raging in G's white irises, his pupils expanding and narrowing in the press of milky clouds, an eternal struggle one might see between the poor and rich, machines and human beings.

"I've got a story to tell you," he began in a measured tone as though his words might shoot out like tiny daggers and flay her to the bone. "Once I was human as, I'm sure, were you."

He paused to let the gravity of his words sink in. Florida shifted, pressing against G's torso for more of the bed. She raised herself up on her elbows, her thoughts spooling with dread and anticipation. She cupped G's smooth white fingers and slid them under her shirt to the brown skin stretched taut over her swollen belly.

"There, did you feel that?" she asked, her midsection rumbling with the tenacity of something struggling to be born.

G shook his head and said, "Yes, it's the truth," sending shivers coursing through her from her toenails to the split ends of her dishwater-blonde hair. The sensation was like the exhalation of electricity or the boiling of constellations on a cloudless night.

Every centimeter of Mere's body ached and throbbed with pain, but nothing seemed broken. He lay on his face, his forearm cushioning the bridge of his nose. His back was stiff and the top of his head was sore as hell. Shackles constricted his wrists and ankles, and there were bandages over tiny cuts on his legs and arms. He marveled that he'd managed to survive that final tumble and wondered who or what was keeping him prisoner. Could it have anything to do with the madmen, like War, who kept springing up out of nowhere to kill him? And did he imagine that his would-be assassin implicated Polk, of all people, in his bizarre conspiracy?

"I say we kill him now in his sleep."

"Our anonymity must be kept."

Mere turned his neck sideways, slit one eye, and made out a handful of silhouettes stooping in a semicircle. Basking in the late afternoon sun slanting through the skylight, his captors appeared to be a mishmash of races and cultures: light-, dark-, and high-skinned. Mere took in the garb and swaggers of various neighborhoods: Jazz, Irony, Rim, More, Zeb.

"What about the message from Teller?"

"Her orders were quite specific."

"Screw her. She's not taking the risk. What right does she have to boss us around?"

"None, but Blitzen will be pissed if he finds out we slagged Roosevelt."

"Got that right," muttered a stocky man stepping out of the shadows. He had a short, clipped beard, muscular biceps, and an impressive Hightan. "The point is non-negotiable. My group will stop the flow of cargo from the east and put a major crimp in your operation."

"You're bluffing, Blitzen, and you know it," challenged a woman whose bandana, nose ring, and olive-toned skin marked her as a trader from the sect controlling the Bazaar. "You need our information and traders every bit as much as we need your access to out-of-city goods. More so. Even if we slag Roosevelt, you'll have no choice but to continue working with the Rainmakers."

What was down here? The Rainmakers were a group of traders and thieves led by a council who operated some of the more lucrative white market ventures. They were rumored to have centuries-old rituals and secret ceremonies. He must have tumbled from that gravpod into a Rainmaker stronghold that, by all accounts, was harder to get into than Skytown. Much harder. No wonder they wanted him dead. His luck, as usual, was rotten.

"How in Usa's name did he get here anyhow?"

"Fell from the sky, if you can believe it."

"Yeah, right," Blitzen said in disbelief as the Arb woman held up her hands as though to say I'm as mystified as you are.

"I saw it with my own eyes," added Vixen, a chip-thin More woman with an ankle-length skirt. "He fell through one of the skylights into a crate of lingerie we were normalizing for the gravnet."

Everyone laughed, especially Prancer, who tugged on her bandana, adding, "What a way to go."

"It's not like he's already dead," Blitzen said.

"Come on," countered the short, squat Jazz representative. "We all know we can't take the risk. He's one of the twelve for Usa's sake. What're we supposed to do if he ascends?"

"What we can do, Donder, is move ops if and I'm stressing IF he manages to survive which I highly doubt."

There it was again—the twelve. It pissed Mere off that his life was being controlled by a number, a puny, insignificant number at that. It seemed as though everyone in the city understood what it meant but him. His eyes swept over his jailors, gauging their reactions, no longer caring whether he was spotted.

The solemn zeb known as Dasher stroked his goatee and said, "It doesn't look like we have a consensus. That makes it Rudolf's decision."

Blitzen opened his mouth to protest, but thought better of it as all eyes settled on the youngest of their group, a taciturn redhead wearing silver hoop earrings of Christ burning at the stake. Mere didn't need to hear him speak to know that he was from

North Irony.

"Now, this is a tricky circuit," Rudolf said, his face and nose blushed with emotion or, perhaps, a fine afternoon rom. "It doesn't look like we have a lot of choice, does it?"

Mere, with great difficulty, clambered to his feet, taking tiny steps and clanking his ankle manacles as he approached the circle of Rainmakers.

"Rudolf, why dontcha give a guy from da hood a break?" Mere asked, elongating his vowels in a purposeful North Irony accent. The pain from the bump on his head, which he hadn't felt lying down, seared in agony as blood rushed to the injury. Black spots swam before his eyes. He staggered, almost toppling onto Prancer who drew a blade and bared her teeth.

Several of the men stirred, their hands fumbling for weapons, but Blitzen waved them off. He strode toward Mere with outstretched palms, whether to recapture him or keep him from falling he hadn't a clue.

"How about it, Rudolf?" Blitzen taunted, grabbing Mere by the elbow. "Looks like your boy here just asked you a favor."

"If it were up to me alone, Blitzen, I might let him go, but I have to look out for all our interests," Rudolph said.

"Hey, I won't tell anyone anything," Mere told the assemblage of blurs as he blinked his eyes and fought to keep his bearings. "I don't know where I am and I don't care either."

"You'd better care," Vixen said. "This place will be your death if you aren't careful."

"I didn't mean…" Mere struggled for words. He tripped and lost his balance, leaning against Blitzen's thick shoulder.

"I saw we take the matter to the Graylings." Blitzen cupped a brawny mitt around Mere's waist. "I'll abide by their decision."

Rudolf looked around the circle. Everyone in the group shook their heads, some more reluctantly than others.

"So be it," Rudolf said. "The Graylings it is. Usa help us all."

Mere swallowed with difficulty, his parched throat constricting. The Graylings? Although he'd heard stories of the ashen creatures who lived beneath the city, he'd never believed they actually existed.

∗∗∗

"You mentioned Teller earlier. I've heard the name before, but...."

"But what?" asked a slightly annoyed Blitzen.

"I always heard she was a murderess, a vampire," Mere said.

"Propaganda. Somewhere at Pyramid there's a whole staff of people paid to do nothing else but discredit the old broad."

Blindfolded, Mere squirmed against the alum frame in the back of the truck and tried to find a position that would cushion him from potholes. "So, Polk's got a vendetta against her?"

"An understatement. You probably know her better than I do," Blitzen said.

Mere felt helpless and alone. He closed his eyes and tried to keep the whine of the antiquated vehicle from turning his impressive headache into a migraine. He had tried to take his mind off his pains and aches by tracking the truck's progress and making guesses as to where they might be in Oldtown. Without knowing their original starting point it was a hopeless diversion, not to mention how difficult it was to make out street noises over the sputtering engine. The driver, Rudolf, seemed paranoid or overly careful, double-backing several times and accelerating with vigor over time-worn urban thoroughfares.

"What about the Graylings?" Mere asked.

"What about them?"

"Who or what are they?"

"You've heard the legends, haven't you?"

"Sure, what child hasn't?"

"Or adult."

"Or adult," Mere conceded, thinking over the dozens of urban legends he'd heard about the enigmatic mutants who lived beneath the city. Most of the stories involved high-stakes problems, a meeting with the difficult-to-find Graylings followed by a near-impossible quest doled out to a hero. The strange creatures played pivotal roles in fairy tales as diverse as Jay and the Greenstalk, The Dreaming Swan, The Emerald City, Crystal Boots, and Knight Rider.

Blitzen slapped his palms on the truck bed to keep from skidding after an especially sharp turn and said, "I'm a fool for telling you this, but I'm willing to risk that Teller's belief in you isn't entirely unfounded." Mere opened his mouth, a question about Teller forming on his lips, but he didn't want to interrupt Blitzen. "I'm a pilot," he continued, "born in Kamchat and, because of my background, one of the few legal immigrants to Collings. Because of my job, I've been to just about every port on the globe. Although Polk restricts us from getting too friendly with other corporations, I've heard similar myths about Graylings almost every place I've gone. I always thought it was odd that there was so much similarity in the stories between cities."

"Especially since there's been so little interaction between the metropolises," Mere said.

"Lately."

"Sure, the last few hundreds years at least. I'm not sure what that matters unless you're trying to tell me that the Graylings are immortal."

"I don't know about that, but Teller thinks they were around before the war."

"Impossible. They're human, right? Mutated?"

"I'm not sure I buy it myself, but Teller believes that the Graylings were weapons during the war. Clones.

"Cloning humans...that's hard to swallow. There's no crime that'll send you and everyone you've ever known more quickly to the stake," Mere said.

"It taboo now, I think, because of what happened during the war."

Mere was just beginning to gain Blitzen's confidence when the truck lurched to a stop.

"Teller said these clones were designed to have a limited life span, but there were some anomalies...." Blitzen said the last word slowly so that it seemed to have a dozen syllables. "...some creatures who didn't take to their programming or didn't like what they'd become."

The truck engine rattled and sputtered, shutting off. Three heavy raps sounded on the front wall by the driver. Usa! Just when he was getting somewhere. His leg chains were taken off and Mere could feel Blitzen's tight grip on his arm as he was guided down a treacherous incline, a loping path leading below the city. He could feel the air around him grow staler with every turn and, although he was nervous, he didn't say a word to Rudolf or Blitzen. He even laughed at one point as he thought about how ridiculous he must look stumbling between the two men, wearing nothing but boxers and a blindfold.

After what felt like an eternity of tripping over rocks, Blitzen halted him at an especially foul-smelling spot on the path, peeling back the sweat-soaked cloth covering his face. It took Mere a few seconds for his eyes to adjust to the poor lighting. Rudolf's flash-beam swept along the floor and illuminated the webbed feet of their guests.

"We've been waiting," said a calm, hypnotic voice that Mere assumed belonged to one of the handful of wan and hunched-over bipeds surrounding them in a small oval cavern dominated by faded swathes of graffiti. The Graylings were close to two meters tall, identical looking bald men with pitted faces and deep-set gray eyes. Their ages were difficult to gauge. Their blank expressions minimized wrinkles and accentuated loose flaps of skin. A cool, measured voice, that seemed to emanate from the nearest Gray-ling, continued, "This shadow man you've brought us cannot be allowed to live."

"His departure is for the greater good," the same voice stated, but from a different location in the room.

Blitzen looked over at Rudolf who shrugged and pulled the handle of a pistol from his jacket lining.

"We will pass sentence ourselves," the voice insisted.

Rudolf quit fiddling with his coat and, with a tiny voice, said, "I'm afraid I can't allow that. The other Rainmakers will want to see proof. The body."

Maybe he'd lost too many brain cells from his recent bouts with drugs and rom, or maybe he was just dense, but it sound-ed like these gray freaks had handed him a death sentence. He wrenched his arm from Blitzen's grasp, but found four Graylings blocking the only visible exit.

"Our word will be your proof, that is, unless you don't value us as allies."

"Loop," Rudolf grumbled.

"You'd rather have us as enemies, then, I take it," the same voice echoed from the Grayling nearest Mere who was becoming confused by the single voice ricocheting among the identical-look-ing creatures.

"No, not at all, we trust you," Blitzen said, turning to Rudolf. "Don't we?"

"Yes," Rudolf said, backing away. "Absolutely."

The pair of Rainmakers made a deferential bow and threaded their way through the assemblage of Graylings. They scurried back onto the path leading toward the surface. Mere watched their departure, looking for a similar avenue of escape through the knotted gray limbs, but then he heard a reassuring voice whisper, "Don't worry," even as the Rainmakers turned a corner and the tunnel they'd taken was replaced by a rock wall.

He swore he heard the faraway echo of Blitzen's voice calling out, "Sorry," before finding himself alone with this misshapen band of gray mutants who wanted him dead. The disappearing path and shifting walls threw him off until he remembered how the Graylings were supposed to be masters of illusion. Mere bunched his muscles, still bound by a rope around his wrists, and struggled to count the wispy images in the almost dark.

"Come with us," repeated the same, unrelenting voice and although Mere wanted to fight his way to freedom, he found himself being led, placidly, into the bowels of the earth.

GREEN

16

Mere sat cross-legged for so long that he could no longer feel his body. The bruises, the aches, the constriction of his bound hands, even his nonstop migraine melted away beneath the stares of the unspeaking Graylings. His eyes had adjusted to the pale light that seemed to be emanating from the walls of the subterranean cavern. He was having a hard time keeping his train of thought. Although he knew that he was under a death sentence of some kind, he could not bring himself to feel worried about it. His thoughts of escape never lasted more than a few seconds. He found himself thinking not so much about an afterlife or reincarnation, but concrete things like whether the sisters at the orphanage still cared about him and how the maligned Tim, in the end, had been the truest of friends.

The whole mess with Gail bothered him more than any of his other failed relationships. If the psychotic War was right and Polk had it out for him, then it was for the best that she'd left him when she did. Regardless of their current marital strife, they were still good friends or had been before the bottom dropped out.

His bout of depression and rage, even as he'd tried to drink himself to death in Oldtown, hadn't been from his hatred of Gail or Collings, but of himself. He'd never been able to get a handle on his emotions. He bottled them up until the pressure backed up to the point of explosion. Although he never once struck Gail, she'd put up with a lot of tantrums and never complained about his moodiness, going out of her way to make things less stressful for him. He wished he could see her again if for no other reason than to apologize.

When Mere looked up from his trance, he found himself walking in circles in a large cavern, passing through a revolving wheel of Graylings who warbled with excitement.

"Follow us," said a voice that seemed to boom from the ceiling. "It is time."

Mere, famished, bruised and drained, was surprised to discover that he had newfound bounce in his legs as he followed the train of stooped Grayling to wherever his fate might lead him.

***

Florida was worried about G who'd been surly ever since she found him passed out on the sidewalk. He stayed at her place the next few days, getting up only to track down a contact who might help them get to the bottom of her illness. Since his absurd claim that her body had been tampered with by Polk, she'd tried to keep busy with work and a semblance of a normal existence. She worked double shifts, then came home. When Tampoca wasn't puttering in the kitchen or pruning her garden, Florida cooked a meal for G who would otherwise forget to eat.

She arrived at her place early that evening, simultaneously excited and worried. Excited that she'd gotten her paycheck and could afford to move out. Worried that her relationship with G might be getting complicated. They'd made love the night before, casually, mechanically, chatting all the while as though they weren't doing what they were doing. G kept himself in check throughout their lovemaking, even to the end when he pulled out of her and rolled up into a fetal ball. Florida had poked and prodded at him for awhile, wondering if it had been wise to jeopardize their friendship with sex, but G didn't respond, having fallen asleep curled inside his protective shell of white skin.

She unlocked the hatch to the cluttered apartment, calling, "Tampoca," but her host was out, as often was the case this time of night, probably at her gardening club. "A coven," G had called the all-woman's society during morning's breakfast when Tampoca had examined the scattered leaves and grounds of Florida's coffee-tea, saying, "This doesn't bode well, I must consult the others. In the meantime," Tampoca advised, "don't do anything out of the ordinary." Florida, out of politeness, smiled and shook her head even as G rolled his eyes. What in Usa's name was the least bit ordinary about her life now?

Pulling aside the opaque curtain strung across the kitchen

archway, she stepped into her tiny room. Her dark mood was whitened by the ire on G's face as he lay on his back, staring up at the sky through tears in the venetian blinds. She changed out of her clothes self-consciously and sat on the edge of the bed. He didn't appear to have noticed her exposed flesh, intent as he was on a strip of stars in the eastern sky as though it were a road leading to some better place. Before she could tell G her good news, he turned his head and said, "I scheduled a meeting tomorrow morning with someone who might be able to help you, a scientist."

Florida stared at him expectantly, prompting him to continue, "Her name is Teller. She's a real pain in the ass. I had to remind her of the favors I've done for her before she would agree to meet. She's brilliant, but paranoid as stars. Even though I'm in good with her, I think we should be careful about how much we trust...."

The unspoken words hung in the room like an unwound noose as Florida nestled in next to G and stared upward, looking for a sign she could understand in the darkening sky.

* * *

The Graylings hadn't killed Mere but perhaps they'd done something far worse—they'd made him face the worst part of himself. He clung to the shadows and kept to the side streets, but that didn't keep passersby from giggling at his attire (boxers, no shirt, no shoes) or from crossing to the other side, alarm registering in their mistrusting urban eyes. He had to be careful. Traffic was more pronounced at night in The Slice than in other parts of Oldtown. This strip of trendy shops, galleries, coffeeterias, and underground bars was hopping tonight, frequented by artists, revelers, and malcontents from all walks of life. More than a few Hightown brats had been known to spend a few decadent years here avoiding corporate and familial obligations before joining the Pyramid juggernaut.

Rooftop fluorescents and lanternheads shone dimly, waging a losing battle against the night's debaucheries. The faraway stars were shrouded in soot as layered smoke slithered from apartments and eateries, a storm cloud of legal and illegal pursuits. Music and laughter thrummed through walls and hatchways, vibrating through the soles of feet and settling into a wide registry of smiles.

The streets brimmed with a tuneless caterwaul that promised to last far into the morning hours.

Mere, wary of stumbling into the Slice's infamous patrol of white shirts, took his time navigating intersections and street corners. He searched the sidewalks for a pandler who was not too desperate or down on his luck, someone who looked like they had the wits to capitalize on a quick and tidy profit. He kept close to hatchstoops and alleys, looking over the crowd. After considering and disregarding half a dozen homeless teens, Mere spotted a haggard lightening lounging on a curb in worn threads and clackboots, swilling a dark bottle and harassing commuters for chits.

"Pssst," Mere hissed from the shadows, repeating the call until the soused youth whirled. "Yeah, you, come here."

Mere bent his fingers toward his chest, motioning the drunk over to him.

"What's your deal?" the lightening sputtered, disgust settling on a pale face streaked with dirt and grime.

"Greenery," Mere said loud enough for several young women on a nearby street corner to turn their heads. The gaunt youth looked startled, then smiled at the code word for contraband. He stumbled to his feet and swaggered over to Mere.

"So, game and name?" the lightening asked, eyeing the stylishly dressed girls who thought better of witnessing the transaction and jaywalked toward their destination.

Mere loosened his I-card from the loop on his wrist and entered his code on the attached minicomp. His remaining balance flashed on the card's tiny screen. He showed the four-digit figure to the youth and repeated the code to retrieve it. Although it wasn't an impressive amount for someone living in Hightown, it was still a tidy sum. Enough for a pandler to rent a room and go on a bender for many moons. The lightening smiled and shook his head as Mere whispered in his ear.

The straight-up exchange—his savings for the youth's stylish secondhand clothing—went off without a hitch. Mere figured it was suicide for him to use his I-card, considering half the city was after him for one reason or another. The kid grumbled a little about losing his boots, a steel-toed variety favored by bangers. This slightly worn pair had an added bonus: nobs on both heels which, when pressed, extended a ten-centimeter blade beneath the toes. Otherwise, the drunken youth was delighted with the deal, fastening Mere's I-card around his wrist and wandering off in his underwear into the heart of the Strip for a night of carousing.

Mere buttoned up his new threads and thought about the strangeness of his encounter with the Graylings. After letting him stew for more than a day, they'd guided him through a labyrinth of underground tunnels. Throughout that long hike in the almost darkness Mere fretted about escaping and making his way to Jonas's pad in the Slice. Before he could work up his nerve to bolt, they untied his wrists and led him up to a sewer grate within a block of where he'd wanted to go. Had he mumbled something to them while daydreaming? As a scientist it was easier for him to believe that than in the psychic powers of immortal clones.

The Graylings tried wandering off without an explanation, but Mere grabbed the nearest one by the elbow. A strange sensation tingled through his palms and the hairs on his arms bristled.

"I thought you told the Rainmakers that I shouldn't be allowed to live."

The same eerie voice emanated from the midsection of the Grayling in his grasp, "We mistook you for someone else."

"I don't understand."

"Let's say, for the sake of argument that souls exist. When you came to see us, we could barely sense yours. We thought you were like us."

"And now?"

"And now, with our help, your spirit has been strengthened. It may even be as serviceable as a real one."

A confused Mere said, "Thank you, but—"

"Don't thank us." The Grayling's voice lowered to a morose whisper, "When this is all over you will lose everything and gain yourself. We will lose ourselves and earn the right to die in peace." The Grayling slipped from Mere's numb grasp. "Don't give us a second thought. We march to our deaths with open eyes."

"I don't get it. What do you expect me to do?" Mere asked the receding gray silhouette.

"Live," the voice drifted to him as the Graylings became one with the shadows. "Don't forget, you dream the truth."

These last words were so soft that Mere wondered if he'd imagined them. Even discounting the nonsense about souls, he had to admit he felt better after his time with the creatures. As he lifted the sewer grate and climbed out of the tunnel, he felt invigorated, actually looking forward to the challenges that awaited him. A survival strategy quickly formed on his walk through the Slice, one based on aggression, trusting his friends, and a bit of luck.

He realized that he'd been too mired in self-pity to see how much danger he and the people around him were in. The assassins trailing after him were ruthless enough to use his loved ones against him, especially if Polk was providing these gaming freaks with detailed information about his life. It was time to take the initiative and become the hunter. It would be wise to check in on his friends and flesh out whatever danger they were in. He wasn't deluded enough to think of himself as heroic. It just made more sense for him to tackle his problems head-on rather than being woken in the middle of the night by another sword-wielding madman.

Swaggering much like the threads' previous owner into the stream of revelers, Mere was shocked to see Cola leaving a corner market with an armful of groceries. Then it all made sense. She was probably down seeing Jonas. In the hubbub of that hellish night at Boo's, Mere hadn't gotten his friend's new address (Jonas was always getting kicked out of places for playing his electrar too loudly). He had planned on checking a few local dives to see if he could get a bead on the lanky musician, but now it looked as though his luck had changed for the better. Running into Cola would save him a lot of time, not to mention the hassle of making himself conspicuous.

Careful to keep his distance, he followed Cola along Hathaway, the main Slice drag, a cozy two-lane that separated the mostly working-class Westenders from the religious Jazz community. He noticed a few restaurants off the beaten path as well as an occasional upscale clothing boutique. Jazz tailors were much in demand, especially for non-synthetic formal wear. The familiar Christ on a burning stake dotted Westend businesses and the spires of apartment buildings as though to counter their neighbors' beliefs. Cola stopped occasionally to peek through a shop window and enjoyed a leisurely pace through the cultural mishmash.

Mere felt guilty about shadowing her and was about to close the gap and call her name when she turned into the stairwell of a ground-level flat. Hurrying to catch up, he saw her punch in the last few numbers of an alarm code. Jonas came out to meet her, giving her a quick peck on the cheek and lifting the shopping bag off her hip. Mere looked over his shoulder to see if he was being followed himself, then stepped down into the tiny alcove. Jonas dropped his jaw in shock, almost losing his grip on the bag, but he recovered quickly, motioning Mere into his apartment and ghosting the hatch.

* * *

Mere held onto his belly contentedly and lay on Jonas's couch, his makeshift bed for the evening. He'd always known Cola was a good cook (she'd occasionally shared her homemade lunches with him at the lab), but tonight's fare was inspired. Chick pilaf, garbean sauce, whole tomats lightly boiled, and served on a plush bed of greens. He'd downed a trinity of servings without coming up for air. Then it dawned on him that he hadn't eaten in almost two days.

Between slurps of culinary ecstasy he recounted the events of his last few days. Jonas was particularly interested in his fight with War, Cola with the Graylings. She stared at him strangely, barely eating herself. At first, Mere thought her furrowed brow might be from pity or concern, but neither rang quite true.

"OJ, Cola, out with it. What's on your mind?"

"Well," she exhaled, choosing her words carefully. "Some of the lab techs saw you in the Jungle during your vacation. They said that you were on a bender and acting like a jerk."

"So now you're wondering if I was drunk and seeing things. I don't blame you. I wish I'd imagined being attacked, falling from Hightown into a den of smugglers, and meeting a group of mythical creatures who held my life in their hands. Unfortunately, I was sober."

"It all sounds a little too weird not to be true," Jonas said.

"Mere, I wasn't doubting you."

"Don't worry about it, Cola. By the way, how's Chino doing?"

"Fine. He wasn't as sick as he looked. It was food poisoning. He's been asking about you at the lab. Everyone misses you."

Although Mere doubted that more than a handful of people knew he was gone, let alone missed him, it was still nice to hear.

"I'm glad you're still in one piece," Jonas said, grabbing the neck of a half-empty bottle and pouring Mere another glass of spice wine. Cola led a round of toasts and blushed when Mere asked about how she and Jonas were doing. The wine hit him pretty hard, probably from his lack of sleep. He decided to show some restraint and turn in. "I want to get an early start," he told his hosts. "Tomorrow's as good a day as any to get a handle on things."

Jonas shook his head. "If you want, I'll take a few days off work. I might know some people willing to lend a hand," he said before shooing Cola away from the kitchen and dragging her off to bed.

Mere nestled back into the couch cushions, almost content. He found himself thinking about how right his friends were together. Although they were from different heights, he didn't know two people who deserved each other or happiness more. He started drifting off, but a full bladder nagged at him, keeping him from passing out. Exhausted as he was, it took him a good thirty minutes of fidgeting to work up the energy to stumble toward the bathroom. As he approached the tiny john off Jonas's bedroom, he noticed a fluorescent light ebbing through a crack in the hatch. A soft, though insistent voice trickled through the narrow opening. He tiptoed along the worn carpeting and put his ear up against the wall nearest the hatch. There was no sense bursting in on Jonas and Cola if they were going at it.

"Listen, I know you want me to bring him to you and I will, but I don't want to do anything that will make him suspicious."

Mere swallowed, all the moisture gone from his throat. He strained to hear more as Jonas's voice trailed off. He wanted very hard to believe the best about his oldest friend and not take what he'd heard out of context, but the crackle of the vidphone cleared and Mere heard Jonas say, quite distinctly, "OJ, tomorrow I promise I'll deliver Mere to you. Yes...whether he wants to or not...I know how to convince him."

Mere backed away, trying not to make noise and found

his boots on the floor by the couch. He slipped them on and grabbed his new off-white jacket, pocketing a small pile of chits Jonas had left on the end table. It wasn't much, but it would have to do until he figured out his next move. Mere heard the toilet flush followed by the whir of the bathroom faucet. He hurried to the front hall, ghosted the hatch and rushed out into the dismal night, realizing that he would be able to trust no one, perhaps not even himself until he figured out what was really going on.

"Nice day for a walk," G said.

"Hmm," Florida replied.

The late morning sun was piercing and the neighborhood unfamiliar. G fought to keep the signs of his devotion in check as he walked next to Florida along the concave rubble that was once a sidewalk. He wanted to shout, to sing, to curse her husband and every other man who'd ever touched her, to promise his undying love. He didn't dare, though. He knew any emotional outburst on his part would drive her away from him. It was uncomfortable for someone who'd been alone for so long to feel this vulnerable.

They'd taken the Rim tram to the far south station and crossed northwest into the Spring district along streets dominated by rundown warehouses and abandoned factories. This free enterprise zone was once a bustling commercial and residential neighborhood back when Pyramid still allowed open competition. Now the only sounds of activity were made by occasional gusts whistling through threadbare docks, broken windows, sagging archways, and old-style doors ajar on rusted hinges.

Florida was unusually quiet and hadn't said a word since they'd left the Rim. G knew that he was probably to blame. Two words— yes and no—had formed the majority of his conversational output over the past few days. She let him stray a pace or two ahead while he charted their course, folding her arms across her chest and turning away whenever he looked over his shoulder.

Maybe he was just imagining things. He should concentrate on the matter at hand anyway. Few knew the city the way he did, but even he wasn't sure that the address he'd been given existed. After all, Teller's directions had been filtered to his Rim hideout through a maze of secondary links using a complicated code. After having his brain chewed up and spit out of Skytown net, he wasn't exactly sharp, and had struggled to decipher Teller's message.

He thought about sharing his fears with Florida, but the impatience glinting in her eyes made him keep his doubts to himself and quicken his pace. Spring was a nasty part of town—not that it was dangerous or even all that ugly. The ruins themselves held a rustic sort of charm. There was, however, something eerie about the long-abandoned buildings and desolate thoroughfares, a silence that made him uncomfortable. Spring had none of the usual urban background static, the buzzing from hot and cold links that he'd learned to block out in order to keep his sanity. The omnilines were disconnected as well as the lanternheads. The absence of street lights and surveillance cameras probably accounted for why Teller had set up shop here.

But what did he really know? Everything surrounding Teller involved conjecture. They'd run across each other quite a few times over the last two hundred years, but he barely knew anything about her. She wasn't like him or the Graylings, that much he knew. Neither was she like Florida whose thoughts he could read and with a little practice she could probably do the same to him. Teller had found some other path to longevity. All he knew for certain was that she was a scientist without peer and hated Polk as much or more than he did.

It cranked him that Teller had remained an enigma to an electronic know-it-all. Even Polk was easier to track down and monitor. Her age and physical appearance changed every time he saw her. Sometimes radically. Teller was not someone to be taken lightly, even when you were working toward the same goal. He'd heard more than one story of someone who'd crossed the old witch and had not lived to regret it.

He was starting to feel some regret himself as he guided them down the dead-end alley to their destination. If Teller managed to cure Florida of her illness there was a good chance that his newfound lover would no longer need him. As it stood, she was becoming every bit as much a freak as he was. An anomaly. A machine. If she regained her humanity, he feared that he might lose the only person other than the Graylings who would ever be able to understand him.

"This is it," G said.

Florida flicked her eyes over the abandoned warehouse and

asked, "You sure about this?"

"Absolutely. There's one thing I didn't tell you, though." G paused, sucking in air. "I think it would be a good idea if you waited outside."

"What?"

"Teller can be skittish."

"Why in Usa's name am I here then?" she asked. "You know, you've been acting like a jerk for days. First you tell me I'm some sort of monster and then you drag me out to the middle of nowhere so I can hang out in rubble, sweating to death, while you talk cloak and dagger nonsense to an old witch who probably doesn't even exist. This is a waste of time. I should be out looking for a place to live."

She turned away in a huff, but G placed his hand on her shoulder. "Look, I know you're not feeling that well and I apologize for how I've been acting, but trust me on this. Please? I know if I go in by myself that I'll have a better chance of getting her to help you. And that's why we're here, to help you."

"I'll give you fifteen minutes. After that, I'm splitting."

"Agreed," G said, leaning over to kiss her and, when she stepped away, gave her arm a light squeeze. "Shouldn't take any longer than that."

* * *

"I've been told I dream the truth," Mere said, slipping on the tight-fitting duds he scored the night before.

"Yeah, by whom?"

"I'm sorry. If I told you, I'd have to kill you."

"Yeah, right, whatever."

Mere felt pretty good considering the amount of rom he'd needed to convince this young woman to take him home. After leaving Jonas's, he'd cased the loudest and smokiest bars in the Slice. The more boisterous and desperate the women, the better. He hit the jackpot at a dive called The Wave just before ultraviolet shift.

He still didn't know the name of the willowy brunette who put him up last night. She thought his name was Conrad. He knew they didn't have sex. She was probably wondering what he did, aside from passing out, and too embarrassed to ask.

His benefactor was probably no older than twenty and made no effort to cover her body as she lay on the fold-out futon serving as her bed. Her one-room flat was both cluttered and spotless. Too many possessions were stuffed, albeit neatly, in every arc, bend, and crevice, leaving only a single-file walkway between stand-up room dividers.

Mere fumbled through the snaps and loops on his white v-cut tunic and tasseled pants, an outfit that was popular many years ago and was retroactively stylish in the Slice's fashion-conscious night scene. Ignoring the mirror, as always, he straightened his jacket and racked his brain for the inspiration to make a graceful departure. This was something he hadn't had to deal with in a long time: the awkward morning-after goodbye.

Should he prolong their casual encounter by inviting her out to breakfast and spending chits he didn't have, or would it be better to leave with a glib, "See you around." He was already feeling pretty good about himself for not having taken advantage of her and wasn't sure he owed her much of anything.

"See you around," she said, taking him off the hook. She tilted her neck and made momentary eye contact before slumping back in exhaustion.

"Yeah, sure."

Mere fought an overwhelming urge to apologize. He bowed his head and mumbled, "Bye," wandering out into the sad, misty day. Thoughts swirled in his head like the patchwork of low clouds forming and reforming the sky into a spackled gray ceiling. He sifted through memories that swirled, unbidden, in a pre-caffeine haze. When the cloudy images converged, they darkened and solidified into the square jaw and high cheekbones of President Polk before settling into his own grim features. Mere shook the cobwebs out of his head and crossed Hathaway toward a Hightown gravpod.

Too many people were interested in him for Polk or someone high up at Pyramid not to be involved. He didn't understand why he'd been made a target, unless it had to do with his research. In the mean time, it would be a good idea to dig up as much as he could on his former employer and would-be murderer before putting the next phase of his plan into motion.

＊＊＊

G made it a point to eavesdrop before heading up to the second floor of Teller's warehouse. Bypassing the all-too-familiar security equipment he had guarding his own cubbyholes, he linked himself into the surveillance equipment and checked to see if there were any surprises. It took him a few minutes to get the hang of Teller's spynet and he made sure to cover his tracks as he bounced from camera to camera through the spacious warehouse, worming his way toward what appeared to be a central command point. Teller, or the old woman in a bright-green outfit that he assumed was Teller, sat in a sparsely decorated office. A tall kid in a battered suede jacket paced beside her, his lips a jumbled blur. G jacked up the audio and strained to find the right frequency.

"—a real mess of things."

"Jonas, are you positive he overheard you talking to me?"

"Why else would he have left?"

"You said that he wanted to get an early start."

"I went out to check on him at half-violet and he'd already split."

"Maybe he didn't want to get you involved," Teller said. "Whatever the case, you've got to find Mere before they do."

Now this was starting to get interesting. G started recording the proceedings on his brainframe. Was the Mere in their conversation Florida's ex? If so, who or what were the "they" after him?

"I have a few ideas about where he might have gone."

Teller peered down at the portable comp on her desk and threw up her hands, silencing Jonas. She looked around the room, saying, "All right, G, you can come out now."

When he refused to respond to her online, she shut down the local net and his connection went dead. G unlinked from the cold port, released the jack connectors which scrolled back inside his wrists, and headed for the stairs. There must have been a timer on her surveillance equipment. Not bad. Something she'd added since his last visit.

G was winded by the time he made his way through the dusky warehouse to her office. The multi-level complex was a maze of open bays and office space, but he had the advantage of his recent journey through the surveillance equipment to find his way. By the time he jimmied the alarm and ghosted the hatch to her well-concealed office, her lackey was pointing a pistol at his head.

"Watch it," G said, not without defenses himself, but unwilling to show Teller what he was capable of unless he had to.

"Go ahead, put it down," the old woman said.

The gangly man was slow to respond and G started counting to five. Luckily for him, he'd only gotten to three when he slipped the pistol back into his jacket.

"I forgot all about our meeting," Teller admitted, walking over and giving him an awkward hug. "G, this is my colleague, Jonas. Jonas, this is G."

"I don't like this one bit," Jonas said.

Teller smiled. "I know that you're about to remind me of my own security measures." The old woman lifted her long skirt and reseated herself, her wrinkled face puckered in amusement. "You see, G, normally you'd be dead and we'd be relocating right about now since you aren't on the cleared list of our...acquaintances. What Jonas doesn't know, however, is that most of what I know about security I learned from you."

"I could say the same thing," G admitted, although he didn't mind the compliment.

"How come I've never met him then?"

"A lot of what I'm talking about happened before you were born."

"Before your parents were born," G corrected.

"I don't remember much about my parents, I'm afraid," Jonas said.

"Me neither."

"Come on, guys, enough with the machismo already." G and Jonas turned their stony glares on Teller who slapped her forehead. "You probably don't even know what that means, do you?"

Jonas nodded, pouting. G laughed, thinking how much he'd always liked Teller, even when she was being a pain in the ass. At least she knew what it was like to be a person who felt out of place. It shouldn't be too difficult to convince her to help Florida.

"What I'm trying to say is that we're all on the same side. G doesn't like Polk any more than we do. He'd never betray us, especially if he knew how close we were to looping him."

G perked up. "Just how are you going to manage that?"

"I'm afraid I can't tell you. All I can say is that nearly fifty years of planning is coming to fruition in the next few weeks. If we're successful, Polk will be eradicated as though he never existed. After all these centuries. Kaput."

"So what does Mere Roosevelt have to do with this?" G asked.

Jonas snatched up the pistol, but G was quicker. He reached over and squeezed the bodyguard's fist before he could aim. Applying pressure across the knuckles, G forced Jonas to release the weapon which clattered to the floor. He pushed Teller's supposed muscle to his knees and shoved him over onto his back.

Jonas rubbed his knuckles, saying, "Teller, aren't you going to do anything? The whole operation's compromised."

"Relax, Jonas. My guess is that he doesn't know much more than what he overheard on his way in."

G shrugged, saying, "Think what you want. It just so happens that I have Mere's wife waiting outside right now."

"Gail? What does she have to do with...." Jonas trailed off, choking on his words as though he'd just figured out G's plan to pump them for information.

"Teller, there's something wrong with her. She's sick and I think Polk's tampered with her in some way. Do you think you can take a look at her?"

"Polk's tampered with practically everyone in this city one way or another and he'll continue to do so unless he's stopped."

"Be that as it may—"

"Look, G, I like you and normally I wouldn't mind doing you a favor. Right now, I can't spare the time. All my plans are riding on an idiot who has no idea how much his life means." Teller stood, her voice heated and passionate. "You want to do this woman and everyone in the world a favor, then help me and Jonas find Mere."

"We don't need any help from this—"

"Yes, we do," Teller interrupted Jonas. "Let's just say that G has certain abilities that make him particularly suited to finding missing persons."

"Are you sure you won't change your mind about helping my friend?"

"I can't do it, at least until we can track down Mere and get him to safety."

"Tell you what, I'll put out a few feelers and keep my eyes open. If I give you a solid lead, I'll expect you to help her."

"No problem. I'll wash your hands if you wash mine."

Teller reached over and hugged him again. Loop, there it was, the two things G disliked most about Teller happening simultaneously. Not only did she cut him off, but she also used slang nobody else understood, except for maybe that old geezer Polk. At least she was still wearing the same eye-scorching shade of chartreuse she'd been partial to ever since he'd known her. He imagined her closet filled, like a super hero's, with dozens of matching bright-green outfits.

"I'll show you out," Jonas offered.

"Don't bother."

G turned and ghosted the hatch, wondering what he would say to Florida. It looked as though Mere was involved somehow in Polk's transformation. Few in the city knew that the president was hundreds of years old and used the organiputer to clone himself new bodies. The name and the face changed slightly with each incarnation, but it was always the same Polk who emerged, those high cheekbones, curly black hair, and steel-gray eyes.

G hurried down the dimly lit hallway and found the stairs leading outside. From what Florida had told him, her husband was a scientist. Perhaps Polk needed this guy to help him transfer himself into a new body or else Mere had done something to thwart the president's plans. Either way, it looked like G had an interest in finding and safeguarding the husband of the woman he loved.

* * *

Mere charmed his way into the Xenon Plaza Business Center, utilizing a Kamchat accent he'd heard in the "Business of Laughter," a slapstick comedy starring holofilm heartthrob Vik Vlan. After fooling the hostess, he made his way to a row of unused comp ports. He took a leisurely pace, trying not to feel out of place in his outlandish nightwear. Don't worry, he told himself, they'll just think you're an out-of-town eccentric and spending your off-work time carousing with the locals. Mere hoped so. It had already been quite a morning for half-truths and brazen acts.

His troubles had started several hours ago as he'd waited in line at the Slice transit station. It hadn't occurred to him until he was nearly at the gravpod checkpoint that he no longer had his I-card. Without it, he couldn't use mass transit. Legally. He cased four or five Oldtown stops before finding one with lax security. He beat the revolving ghost at the North More Station, whisking in unnoticed behind a paying customer.

It was a rush to ride the lift without paying (something he hadn't done in years). After infiltrating Delta Row, a strip of Hightown hotels, casinos and restaurants catering to out-of-town businessmen, he'd talked his way into the compucenter of Four Kings, one of the best hotels in the city. Now, he kicked back in a revolving lounger and signed onto the net with one of his little used—and he hoped difficult to trace—pseudonyms. These terminals should be less closely monitored than Pyramid-based systems.

Careful not to tap into any research databases, he looked for alternate ways to delve into Polk's business and family matters. He was careful to route his searches through other systems as he hunted for references to The Twelve, Rainmakers, Teller, war games, and the Horsemen of the Apocalypse. Setting his comp alarm for fifty minutes, he dove into the local net and used generic gray-level clearance codes to access Pyramid files.

The searches were slow and, for the most part, unsuccessful. He hadn't pulled up anything more interesting than the standard PR spiel about Pyramid's success under the current administration and a breakdown of Polk's family tree. Most of the so-called historical documents were a familiar litany of folk tales starring hundreds of years of Polks. Mere scrolled through the biographies and inflated accomplishments. It wasn't until he tracked the family back to the city's founding that he discovered several interesting things.

First of all, family life was rarely ever highlighted. Marriages, divorces, and the births of children, other than the heir to the Polk line, were never mentioned. What in Usa's name did that mean? Were other family members disowned? Surely not, but then how come he had never heard about any of Polk's distant relatives? It was possible, he supposed, that they could be living far from the public eye in the plush comforts of Skytown.

None of this was that out of the ordinary. Ego alone could explain George Polk's narrow-minded "family" history. There was one trend, though, when added to other discrepancies that seemed significant. All the Polk heirs, including George, were born when their fathers were twenty and took over the title of president at the age of thirty. That meant mandatory retirement for the outgoing president at fifty. Strange. Mere backtracked and double-checked the stats on all the former heads of Pyramid. The lack of fluctuation was disturbing: twenty years difference in the age of each Polk who, in turn, assumed the office of president at age thirty.

The comp alarm beeped and Mere shut down his station. He wondered if the president and his ancestors were making creative and perhaps illegal use of the organiputer to help ensure such an exact dispersal of heirs. Why didn't he, or anyone else for that matter, know if Polk was married or had a concubine and children. Some execs were known to lead very private lives, but this lack of information on the city's leader was ridiculous. Besides, if history had any bearing, wouldn't it be time for him to retire soon?

So much for research. He had more questions now than when he started. He rose from his comfy chair, thanked the hostess for her hospitality, and made his way past security. Outside, the sky was already a rusty gray, approaching twilight. He must have gotten a later start today than he figured. So much the better. The night would be his ally in the weeks to come. He switched tracks toward the Pyramid administrative corridor— little used on weekends—to sneak on a gravpod back to Oldtown. There was someone he wanted to look up tonight, an old and dear friend of his parents, and the closest thing he'd ever had to family other than the clergy at the North Irony orphanage.

CYAN

18

Mere cased the eastside tract house for hours, waiting for the foot traffic to die down. Luckily, Carter Swen's apartment was on DuPont Circle in the heart of the Duke district, a mostly fenced-off residential neighborhood bordering New Heaven to the north and Bush to the south. Duke was a working class neighborhood, but more affluent than most. The majority of residents were homeowners and held Pyramid-affiliated jobs. Most Easters, as they were called in other parts of the city, tended to be conservative and religious, raising families away from high-crime districts like Irony and the Jungle.

After an inexpensive and filling dinner in a Mores diner, Mere spent half his remaining chits on a sycron overcoat with a hood to cover his outfit. The last thing he needed was for some skittish local to think he was cruising the neighborhood and call the white shirts on him.

Mere circled the block one last time and, after keeping a sharp lookout for passersby, hurried into a narrow space between two houses and crossed into a familiar backyard. Carter had known his parents before their demise and had let him spend quite a few weekends here when things got too depressing at the orphanage. He was a nice enough guy, if not a little strange. Carter was a devout Usan and his ultra-conservative views made his opinions even more radical that the oldage liberals in the Jungle. Carter firmly believed that Jesus was an alien who lived on a faraway star, waiting for the final battle between the wicked and the righteous before trekking back to earth and liberating the souls stuck in limbo beneath the city.

Still anxious about neighbors, Mere kept low to the ground and nestled in between an overgrown bush and Carter's tool shed. The yard looked uncharacteristically ill-kept and Mere found himself wondering how the old guy was getting along. Although pushing sixty, Carter had always seemed invincible, trim and fit from long hours of physical labor in the slag mines beneath the mostly un-settled Southeast quadrant of the city. Miners were an odd and earnest lot, and their lucrative jobs were usually passed down from father to son. At one point, Carter had suggested mining as a ca-reer choice and had been willing to put in a good word, but the prospect had never interested Mere who always thought he was fated for more important things.

Mere crouched and watched the lights flicker in the tiny two-story house. He was becoming suspicious by how often they were being shut off and on. Maybe Carter had moved out or passed on. It had, after all, been more than a year since he'd dropped by to pay his respects. Only one way to find out. He rose and wiped off one of the dusty shed windows. Standing on his tiptoes, he peered inside. It was difficult to see anything in the pre-moon dusk. As his eyes adjusted, he made out the familiar assortment of axes, picks, and shovels. He lowered himself back to the ground and kept a close watch on the back porch and the walkway leading to the kitchen.

A pair of shadows wavered in the corner of his eye. He froze in a half-crouch, craning his neck to the right. Through a branch of curling brown leaves, he made out a boy and his pet chimpan-zadog scuttling through the adjacent backyard to a small grove of miniatures. He waited for them to pass by and disappear into the stand. So much for being careful. He would have to make his move before being discovered.

He scampered over to the small hatch leading to the base-ment and punched in the alarm code. He worried that Carter had changed the numeric sequence or else he himself had forgotten the keycode, but then the thin metal sheet ghosted and he stepped down the short ramp into Carter's cluttered work room. Once in-side, Mere hurried toward the kitchen staircase, making it halfway across the treacherous walkway before the hatch whisked shut again, leaving him in total darkness. He edged forward, probing with the toe of his boot before putting down his weight. He almost tripped over a minivac and bumped his hip against a wobbly table, but managed to navigate his way to the staircase without making too much noise.

Mere rested on the bottom step and contemplated his next move. Regardless of how worried he was for his own safety, he didn't want to spring up out of the green on his friend and benefactor. Besides, Carter owned quite a few illegal firearms and would be more likely to blow him away than to keel over from a heart attack. Maybe it would have been better to have used the front hatch after all.

No sense drawing this out. He stood and tiptoed up the remaining steps, listening for sounds in the kitchen. He eased open the hatch, saying, "Carter, you here? It's Mere." He stepped out onto the checkerboard floor and peered into the kitchen. He took a breath to call out louder, imagining a crotchety old man loading flagettes into a pistol, but then he heard Carter say, "Mere," even as footsteps approached from the living room. "Get out of here!"

Mere crossed the kitchen toward the living room archway and was met by a pair of calloused hands on his chest pushing him backwards. "Carter, what the heaven?" he yelled, fighting to keep the old man from slamming him into the fridge.

Carter shot Mere a wild look. "Kid, I'm an informer. I never knew your folks." The old man glanced over his shoulder, whispering, "Get out of here."

Mere froze even as he heard another pair of footsteps hurrying toward them from the living room. He saw the shadow of a gun arm and twisted sideways as a shot rang out. He was nowhere near fast enough, however, as flagettes sprayed the cabinets by his head and exploded into Carter's back, flinging the old man into his arms. Reacting without thinking, Mere shoved the sagging body away from him straight into the wiry figure rounding the hatchway. The gunman was caught by surprised and reeled backwards, catching his hip on the corner of the counter by the sink.

Mere reached out and caught the gunman's wrist, twisting violently. The pistol clattered to the floor and he was tagged on the chin with a left cross. He growled and threw his shoulder into the skinny man's chest. The momentum carried him over Carter's body on top of his attacker. They crashed into the living room, Mere's weight driving his assailant hard into the floor, knocking the wind out of him. He placed an elbow across the man's neck and pressed with desperate strength.

Gray eyes bulged in their sockets as his would-be-killer wiggled beneath him. Mere pinned the right arm of his attacker to the carpeting as the man's left hand clawed at his face and eyes. He barely felt it. He just kept applying pressure. Outweighing his enemy by more than twenty kilos, Mere pushed harder into the man's windpipe. He pushed until he thought something might snap in himself.

* * *

G cursed himself even as he tracked the beat-up cab driving Jonas Grumby toward the eastside residential district. Normally, he would have enjoyed the challenge of following such a quick-moving auto, jumping from lanternhead to lanternhead to keep up with the knowledgeable driver zigzagging through lowtown. He wasn't in the mood to play tag, though. Since calling Varicose and discovering that Florida was late for work, he sensed danger surrounding everything and everyone, particularly her. She was probably just wrapping up the final details on her new rental. Still, he would have felt better if she had let him escort her back to Tampoca's instead of disappearing in a huff before he returned from his meeting with Teller.

Jonas's cab skirted the New Heaven expressway and turned south toward the Duke district. Since following Teller's bodyguard on foot to the Westend apartment of the short and balding cabbie who was now driving him around the city, G had spent hours tracking them. He'd jacked into the city's surveillance system and linked into more than a thousand lanternheads. His vision was starting to blur from using so many different eyes. The only places Jonas had stopped were an oldage hostel in the Jungle called Sierra Resort and a North Irony orphanage. G noted each location for later follow-up and thought about Mere Roosevelt, their mutual quarry, and what he had done to turn Florida into such a mess. He would have quite a bit to say to the man if he ever caught up with him.

The cab slowed in a Duke development called Lynn Circle and G noticed a small crowd congregating outside a two-story tract house further down the block. Jonas hurried out of the vehicle (which stopped well short of the assemblage), approached the throng, and said something to a woman on the outskirts who looked like she'd crawled out of bed, her long brown hair trussed in a lavender sleepnet. Jonas motioned for the crowd to disperse and sprinted up the porch steps.

What was going on? Just as Teller's surly assistant shouldered open the front hatch, G plugged out of his lanternlink. He woke up on a Westend bench, his body shivering from too many hours at a decreased heart rate. No time to worry about that. He remote-fed into his nearest underground base and, from there, into the city-web. He scanned through the Oldtown police frequencies, burrowing into the high-security system. He used a few of his patented shortcuts, circumventing the main information lines and linking into the Duke Police Station. If he was quick enough, he shouldn't have to worry about getting caught.

G scrolled through the crime log. He spooled through the list backwards, checking only the last few hours. There it was. Domestic disturbance: Lynn Circle. Possible gunfire. G didn't know if Jonas had caught up to Roosevelt yet, but it looked like he could use a hand. He inserted a report of banger activity outside the Clinton Manimall and broadcast it as a Priority 1 alert. Hopefully, any white shirts on their way to Lynn Circle would be diverted and give Jonas time to get out of there.

No time to play it safe. He hotlinked out of his remote hookup back into his old connection. Straight. His brain felt like it was on fire as he fought to refocus the eyes of his Lynn Circle lanternhead. To make things worse, Irena, the 153-years-deceased occupant of the lamp, picked now of all times to fight him for control. It probably meant that someone at the Duke Police Station was attempting to use this lanternhead to see if the potential crime scene needed immediate follow-up.

G jammed the incoming signal and overcame Irena in time to watch Jonas helping a stocky man into the back of the cab. Must be Mere. G focused through the pain, but to little avail. He swapped vantage points into a lanternhead further down the block to get a better view. Roosevelt looked out-of-it in the passenger's seat. He didn't even have the presence of mind to duck out of sight. Florida's husband had a medium Hightown complexion and curly black hair. His arms and head jerked occasionally from a series of spasms. What the loop was going on?

Several of the neighbors, although scared of Jonas, were moving down the block on the other side of the street to see if they could catch the ident on the cab. Tires squealing, the albino driver jacked the vehicle in reverse and kept it that way until after he turned the next corner. Smooth, but not as slick as G's next maneuver. He erased the short-term vid bank of his current lanternhead and backtracked along the cabbie's former route, destroying recordings as he went.

He knew that he was taking a gamble by not tracing the cab out of the neighborhood. He didn't know for certain they'd take Mere back to Teller's warehouse or the cabbie's apartment. Keeping Roosevelt's whereabouts a secret from the police took precedence, at least until G figured out what role Mere played in Teller's plan to wipe out Polk and, more importantly, if he knew anything about what was wrong with Florida.

***

Fingers. Prodding her. Poking her. Rubbing her belly. Caressing every centimeter of her skin. Ever since a rough hand had clamped over her mouth early that morning outside the Spring warehouse Florida had felt like dough being kneaded and patted for the oven. She'd lost consciousness hours before and lay now, without clothes, on a slick metal surface. A blindfold bound her eyes, filtering out all but the slightest suggestion of faint yellow light. Her hands and feet were manacled in restraints that pinched only when she struggled against them.

She'd had a bad feeling about the outing. Why had G dragged her to such a rundown section of the city in the first place? Nothing made sense anymore. She wondered if she was lying on her back in an abandoned building while some junker rounded up his buddies to have a go at her.

Footsteps clicked across a stone or tile floor. One pair. A man's confident, heavy tread. A hand settled on her stomach, swishing along the line of her belly button to the nape of her neck. With painstaking slowness, the smooth fingers slid up to her face, tickling her cheeks. She opened her mouth to speak, but thought better of it. The hand swiped her nose and tore into the fabric around her eyes, ripping off her blindfold. Her neck snapped forward and the rush of incoming light blinded her.

Florida realized her earlier mistake even as she blinked tears of pain and confusion from her eyes. This was no abandoned building. The ornate architecture, domed glass ceiling, lavish decorations and high-tech configuration of her surroundings made themselves immediately apparent. She was able to ID her captor even though his face was still a blurred blob. "Polk," she said without emotion or malice.

"Gail Roosevelt," came the equally humorless response. "Or should I say, Florida."

As the details of Polk's face sharpened into focus, she expected to see a smile or a smug look of superiority. What she saw instead was a grimace of surprise settling over the president's high cheekbones.

"So, you do recognize me," he said in disbelief. "I'm going to have to do something to make the procedure we use on our helpers more foolproof. Lina warned me that your memory of me was the reason why you left Roosevelt when you did."

"That's right," chirped a slightly clipped, competent female voice behind Polk. "Although who's to say she hasn't had contact with her husband since. Considering recent developments, I think we should proceed directly to the download."

"Yes, of course." Then came the smile and the smug look Florida had been waiting for. "Time for mother to do her duty." Polk glanced over his shoulder, asking his colleague, "You ever see a belly swell like this before?"

"No, it must be the food. Homegrown fruits and vegetables don't mix well with the alterations we made."

Florida raised her head and saw a tube leading from the crook of her elbow into an organiport. Brownish-red fluid slithered through the translucent funnel and she realized that it was fluid either being pumped into or out of her body. Either prospect was thoroughly disgusting, although she had a pretty strong notion that the rust-colored liquid was from her.

Polk turned back to face Florida and patted her belly in mock concern. "I bet, dear, that you're wondering just what alterations we're talking about. Don't worry. I won't let anything happen to you." He started laughing and Florida saw a short, thin woman with green-dyed hair approach from behind the president's barrel chest. She had cold cyan eyes and a mask of a face, one that did not smile often, her lips pursed in perpetual purposefulness. Polk reached out and held Florida's hand, rubbing her knuckles gently between his slick palms.

"I won't let anything hurt our baby," he said, a manic gleam fluttering in his gray eyes.

Mere sat next to Jonas in Teller's office, silent, as he had for the last hour. He felt dizzy from his latest bout of palsy. It was fortunate, in a way that he'd been struck by the fit after killing his would-be assassin. He'd come out of the spasms in the torn back seat of a fast-moving cab. His first memory was of a bald spot belonging to a now-familiar albino cabbie as Sax guided the yellow juggernaut with one hand and yammered away about a pack of strange hybrid animals that wandered the white light district in the wee morning hours. Mere ignored the chatter and tapped Jonas's shoulder. His friend smiled, then tensed, saying, "There was nothing we could do for Carter. He was already faded. Sorry, Mere."

Sorry. Yes, Mere was sorry. Jonas was sorry. The whole looping city of Collings was sorry, but that didn't change the fact that a kind old man was dead and the people around him kept dropping like an albino booted from Skytown, most by his own hands.

Now, he and Jonas shifted uncomfortably in the ancient lazy-chairs in Teller's headquarters, staring at the stark office walls or the warehouse floor, anything but at each other. The few attempts either of them had made at conversation ended in Jonas's claim that Teller was the only one who could explain what was going on. Mere asked several times why he should trust a woman he'd never met, but Jonas had no answer other than that she was a sworn enemy of Polk.

In the end, it was his friend's nervous mannerisms that convinced Mere to stay—pacing, wringing his hands, pulling strands of his hair out, and examining them like they were the fierce animals the albino cabbie had droned on about. Jonas's ticks made Mere feel better about waiting around the cold and impersonal warehouse. They were friends first and foremost. As teenagers they'd trusted each other with their lives more than once. Their history forged in the shadow of the North Irony orphanage and kept alive in an even wilder adolescence, made it difficult for Mere to understand how Gail had come so irrevocably between them. He himself shouldered much of the blame. He'd entered the scientific institute, switched gears, changed friends, and started a new life so quickly that Jonas never had a chance to complain. It wasn't that Gail and Jonas hadn't gotten along the few times they'd met. Neither was it their competition for his affection that killed his boyhood friendship. Marriage did. Work. Responsibility. And the upward move, a career.

These changes collided one into the other like buildings toppling in a cityquake and Mere never looked back. For years now he'd felt superior, imagining that he'd left his less-ambitious friend behind in North Irony. It was a simplistic and misguided view. Seeing Jonas watchdog him in the clandestine headquarters of a powerful underground figure like Teller made him rethink a number of assumptions and cast their rebellious childhood in a different light.

The hatch ghosted across the office and a stooped woman with long, straight gray hair whisked inside. Her face remained in shadows beneath the aquamarine cowls of a sycron hood. Before the hatch reformed, an odd-looking albino slipped in behind her, his movements more snake than human. The stranger reminded Mere of the Graylings, although there was little outward resemblance beyond skin tone between this tall gaunt specimen and the hunched-over creatures.

"What do you think you're doing here?" Jonas erupted, rising.

The albino held out his palms and said, "I figured you'd appreciate me showing up in person this time instead of just listening in."

"Yes," the woman agreed, her voice strangely familiar. "I asked G to give us a hand."

Gee? There was a name you didn't hear every day.

Jonas frowned, his nostrils flaring. "I don't like this."

"If it wasn't for me, the white shirts would have faded your ass in Lynn Circle."

"Who gave you the right to follow us?"

"Shut up, both of you," the old woman said, leaning against the edge of her desk, her face still shrouded by strips of folded-over cloth. "Mere is what matters here."

"Really? I'm sick of being talked about in the third person. You better tell me what in the starry hell is going on here. Why am I so important to you and, more importantly, why was I attacked?"

"Yes, why indeed. I'm sorry to say that I've had a small part to play with your difficulties."

"I'm all drums, lady."

Teller sighed and pushed herself up off her battered desk. "This isn't easy to explain. What do you think, Jonas, the truth?"

"Definitely."

"Can he take it?"

"We shouldn't expect him to risk his life for anything less."

Mere caught the albino looking him over and said, "Before you start letting me in on secrets who in Satan's sky is this guy?"

"You're asking the wrong question. You should be wondering how I happen to know your wife. She calls herself Florida these days."

"Florida...that IS something she would call herself. Where is she? Is she OJ?"

"There'll be time for gossip after our talk," Teller snapped.

"Gossip? The whereabouts of my wife is hardly—"

"As important as the mess you're in now." Teller paused and let silence punctuate the air. "Have you ever thought about what started the great war?"

"Of course," Mere answered, annoyed. "Who hasn't thought about what life was like before the city states?"

"True," Teller said, her voice husky with emotion or at least Mere imagined it was emotion spiraling out of the shadows where her head should be. "Only I was there and saw it firsthand. It was a race war, a genocide. Polk and I are the only two people alive who know what took place. We both helped to cause it, each in our own way."

"What's up, Teller? You almost sound forthcoming," G said.

"Believe me, this isn't easy. Originally, Polk and I were both scientists, part of a team that developed the organiputer."

"You?" a stunned G managed.

"Yes, it was an innocent-enough invention at the time, a way to make work easier and the company I was working for a lot of money. I was naive, I suppose. The project was my baby from the beginning and I saw hints of danger, but didn't act on them. There was another person on my team, however, who stole the device and used it in ways that only a madman could dream up."

"Polk," Mere said.

"Exactly. He discovered that the organiputer could do more than computations, that it had the ability to clone anything that it absorbed...and it could absorb anything."

A strange look washed over Jonas's face. "The meat vats, organic crops, the mines, all of them are part of the organiputer?"

"Yes, and practically everything that Pyramid exports is manufactured from it as well."

"That's sick."

"What did you think, that meat grew underground?"

"I don't know what I thought."

"To make a long story short, Polk stole my invention, sold it to some very bad men, and helped engineer a mindless army to eradicate all people of color."

"The Graylings," G said.

"Yes, the Graylings were that army."

Mere frowned, saying, "That's impossible. You said that people of color were killed. Dark-skinned people?"

"Yes."

"Then the war failed."

"Hardly. After the genocide was over, Polk discovered a way by which he could live forever. By cloning himself. Only the process darkened his pigmentation. To keep his body from aging, he needed to be crisped. Almost every day. He hid himself for a hundred years or more until people forgot their former hatreds. Then, slowly, Polk made dark skin desirable and albinos an aberration."

G burst out with a sound between a hiss and a giggle. "If that's true, then he must really hate himself."

"Yes," Teller agreed. "The son-of-a-bitch must really dislike looking in the mirror."

Mere and Jonas looked at each other blankly. "Bitch?" they said within a heartbeat of the other.

"Sorry, old slang. It means butch."

"What does all this have to do with me?"

"Everything, Mere. Polk clones a new body every twenty years and lets them age to thirty. He then takes over the new body and destroys the former one. Only one existing body of his can contain his memories at a time. His soul. Which brings us to you, Mere. You are his clone."

"Me...I...what about my parents?"

"Those aren't real memories you have bouncing around in your head."

G stumbled toward Teller's desk, almost colliding with the pacing Jonas. "None of this makes sense. If Mere is so important, then why wasn't he raised in Skytown?"

"It's funny, but it all has to do with Polk's ego. Even when I knew him centuries ago, he prided himself on being a self-made man. So every twenty years he clones himself twelve times and plants them at the ages of ten in different parts of Collings."

Mere didn't want to believe what Teller was saying and yet the clues were snapping into place. The twelve. The psychotic Conrad. The people trying to kill him. Straining to keep emotion from his voice, Mere asked, "So how come I didn't know anything about this and the other clones were in on it?"

"That is strange," Teller admitted. "After one or two incarnations, Polk started to make a game out of it. He pits his clones against one another and I think he plays favorites. He roots, usually, for the clone who reminds him most of himself. I think you were his chosen for awhile and he kept your existence a secret from the others."

"So you're telling me that my PRIZE for surviving this game is that I get to end up being Polk? You might as well kill me now and put me out of my misery."

"Easily done," G said, stepping toward him, his face twisted with rage.

"Stop it, right now. Mere's different. He's been altered from the others."

"Altered? What the jack are you talking about?"

"Have you ever wondered why you were always so sick as a kid?"

"Your palsy is a byproduct of this alteration," Jonas said.

"What? How long have you known about this, pal?" Mere grabbed Jonas's elbow and shook it. "What in Usa's name did Teller do to me?"

"It's not what you think, Mere. I'm on your side."

"We're all on your side," Teller said.

"Speak for yourself," G said. "I'm still waiting for a good reason why I shouldn't slag this dictator in the making."

"You shouldn't fade him because he isn't a dictator in the making. You'll appreciate this, G. I discovered, by accident, that Polk planted one of his clones in a North Irony orphanage. So I injected the clone, Mere, with a virus that will enable him to control Polk's memories after the transfer has been made. You, my boy," she said, pointing to Mere, "are a trap. Unfortunately, I was sloppy and Polk discovered that I was monitoring you. He has since gotten blood samples from you and he's a good enough scientist to have pieced together my plan. The fact that he's sending the other clones after you proves it."

"So your plan's a bust now anyway," G said.

"No, not if we can help Mere kill the remaining clones and then Polk before he can create any others."

"So it IS hopeless. Slagging Polk isn't that easy. What do you think I've been trying to do for the last hundred years?"

Jonas stopped his pacing mid-stride and said, "We've got operatives placed undercover throughout the city, even in Skytown. Our plan isn't hopeless. Now that we know Polk's using Mere's friends as bait, we can turn the tables and set a few traps of our own."

"I'm not sure I have many friends left," Mere said.

G nodded vehemently and said, "Teller, you can do whatever you want, but I don't think you're going to get the better of Polk on this one. I know what it is I'm going to do. Help Florida." G shot Mere an accusatory look. "Your wife."

G started toward the hatch.

"Wait a sec. I'll go with you. I think I have an apology or two to make."

"Suit yourself."

Jonas slipped between Mere and the hatch. "Take a deep breath and try to think this one through before running off and endangering—"

"Get out of the way," Mere said. "Or come with us. Your choice."

"Don't be stupid, Mere. The virus works. I injected it into myself and all the incarnations of Teller inside me are entirely within my control. It took me two lifetimes to perfect this!" Teller yelled, ripping the cowl from her eyes.

Mere gasped. It couldn't be, but it was. Teller was his landlady Helena. So the old witch had been watching over him for years, maybe his whole life. Controlling him. Using him as a pawn against Polk. Loop her! Loop Polk! It was time he took a few chances and did something for himself.

"Let's go," Mere told G. "I'll live and die on my own terms, Teller, not anyone else's."

"OJ," G said, brushing past the ancient scientist and bumping into Jonas before ghosting the hatch.

"You don't know what you're risking," Teller said. "You don't know shit. You haven't seen how beautiful a forest is in autumn or the colors of the sea...."

Mere followed the loping albino down the hallway to escape Teller's outburst. He looked over his shoulder once before hurrying down the staircase. His boyhood friend Jonas stared at him imploringly from the office hatchway, a deep pang furrowing his brow as though trying to figure out where his loyalties lay.

TURQUOISE
20

When Florida came to her senses, she was still groggy. Lina had stuck her arm with a scary-looking needle before ordering a gray-suited brute to escort her out of the lab. She was half-carried through a series of hallways cluttered with candelabras, hallway guards in lacy white uniforms, and copper urns spewing blue and green incense. The trip was a blur of smoke, distorted faces and bending colors as she felt her body slip into unconsciousness. She fought against the pull of drugs, but it wasn't long before even her desire to do so faded away.

Her last memory before drifting off was of being parked and locked inside a cozy cubicle with chameleon-glass windows and a high-domed ceiling. The room's mosaic-tiled walls were studded with sparkling turquoise and ruby triangles, and decorated with burning stakes and other icons of the Usa godhead. Three other hoverbeds hummed beside her, separated by bins of gleaming surgical equipment. It was a strange environment: part operating room, part cathedral...and did she imagine the breathing walls and chandeliers held up by tentacles?

Through the v-shaped skylight she could see occasional winks of stars in the overcast night sky. Three of the four walls were made of shutterglass whose triangular panes projected a dizzying display of city life. Colors, shapes, and people flickered on the glass in some deranged interior decorator's attempt to make the monotony of Collings seem more exotic than it actually was.

Florida was strapped to a hoverbed, although a bank of loungers lay vacant beside her. A pair of buxom twins came in to set up bar at an oval station in the middle of the spacious suite, ignoring her. Across the room a holohearth projected from the world's largest entertainment consol. A steady stream of fluid trickled behind her, draining from the tube leading into her arm.

The sound, she assumed, was an advanced form of torture.

It was the penthouse of an ozonodome, it had to be. She'd always wondered what one looked like. Now here she was, on top of the world. She looked wistfully between her strapped-in feet and wondered if she could get the two dark-skinned knockouts to fix her a stiff rom. Then it hit her—she could actually see between her toes. Her bloated belly was gone. So was her nausea, although it was difficult to tell because of the lingering numbness from her anesthesia.

A nervous man in his late twenties or early thirties, draped in layered blue fabric, entered and sat down at the bar, his back to Florida. The baristas fawned over him, their gravity-defying breasts swishing against his hands and arms. This blue shirt reminded her of Mere, although untold thousands had the same stocky build and curly black hair. Perhaps her husband came to mind because the man on the stool looked stiff and uncomfortable, like he didn't belong here or anywhere else, something Mere managed to project even when he tossed and moaned in his sleep. Her husband had never been able to grab more than four hours of shuteye at a stretch although he swore that he didn't have nightmares.

She was not surprised when Polk strode into the room, buttoning his shirt collar as though from an illicit rendezvous. He didn't condescend to look at her, but didn't go out of his way to ignore her either. It was almost as though she were one of the free-standing wall murals, gilded urns, pre-war paintings, or crystal chandeliers: a prop, a decoration, a machine. Polk snuck up behind the man at the bar like a naughty schoolboy and shook the visitor's shoulders while saying loudly, "Glad you could make it, son. Congratulations."

"Yeah, sure. Congratulations for what?"

"For killing Plague."

"Who?"

"That tricky bastard Oscar. I thought for sure he'd fade you."

"I got lucky. He got careless...and paid for it. How many does that leave now, three?"

"Yes, three." Polk said, anger and excitement rising in his voice, his grip tightening on the stranger's blue coat. "Soon to be two. I've got something to show you."

The visitor raised his arm as though to swipe Polk's hand off his shoulder, and then shrugged and slid off his stool. The blue suit turned and his wide jaw curled in a smile as Polk gestured toward Florida's table. The silhouette was unmistakable, as was the eerie coldness in those steel-gray eyes.

"Mere, you bastard," Florida spat out, baring her teeth. Of all the horrible and disgusting things she'd feared over the past few weeks, she never once imagined that her husband would be in cahoots with Polk. "How does it feel to be the world's biggest loser?"

Polk looked momentarily confused, then started laughing. Maniacally.

"The plot thickens. I thought you might appreciate this," Polk told her husband.

Mere giggled, then roared in laughter, finally gasping for air and saying, "I never really loved you, woman." He threw his arm around Polk's shoulder. "This is the guy I really love."

"You're righter than you know," Polk said, joining the blue-suited turncoat in a few chortles at her expense.

She slit her eyes, glared to kill and readied her nails in case Mere was stupid enough to bend down over her.

Mere seemed to sense her ire and turned to Polk. "So you got your hands on...who is this, his girlfriend?"

"His wife."

"Wife, it figures. Roosevelt looked like the domesticated type, not my style at all."

"Nor mine."

"What are you trying to pull?" Florida asked, unimpressed with his lame attempt at playing coy.

"I hate to be the one to tell you this, Mrs. Roosevelt, but this isn't your husband. He's the man who's going to kill your husband."

"I don't believe you."

"The resemblance between this man and Mere must be disconcerting to you. Normally, my clones end up looking different from one another. Conrad and Mere are an exception."

"Clone. That's impossible," Florida said, although now that she looked more closely, she could see subtle differences between the boyish face of the man beside her and Mere who'd always had a star-shaped scar above his right eye from an accident at the orphanage.

"Not for me," Polk said.

"How'd you get hold of her?" Conrad asked.

"That was easy. She was working for me all along."

"That's jack and you know it," Florida said.

"You didn't choose to do it, my dear, but you were my instrument all the same."

"Did you bug her?" Conrad asked.

"You could say that. I replaced parts of her brain and nervous system with duplicates from the organiputer."

"You can do that?"

"We don't like to advertise it, but yes."

"An abomination," Florida hissed.

"Every few months we dragged her in and downloaded everything she saw. More accurately, everything she remembered about what she saw. The hard part was not to leave her with too much of a time or memory lapse."

Conrad beamed so widely that Florida could see his canines. He elbowed Polk and said, "I can see how that would be hard, considering how thorough your investigation must have been."

"Yes, it was very thorough," Polk said, winking.

A litany of comebacks whirled through Florida's mind, but she decided not to bring herself down to their level.

"It's fortunate I'm paranoid. By using Roosevelt's wife for surveillance, I discovered an old enemy plotting against me. Her name's Teller and she's using Mere as an instrument to get back at me. She was managing his housing complex, but slipped away before I could set a trap for her." Polk's assistant emerged from a penthouse elevator, buttoning up an ankle-length dress that clung to her tall, angular body. "Fortunately, I got a bead on Teller again from the last download I took from Gail."

"That's not my name anymore."

"Whatever."

Lina approached the exuberant men, saying, "You want me to brief Conrad on the information we've gathered?"

"In a second. I was thinking about letting him see us raid Teller's warehouse." Polk snapped his fingers and motioned for one of his aides to swing over the nearest holoset.

"What should we do about her?" Lina asked, gesturing toward Florida with obvious disdain.

"Let her watch. We're going to give her to Conrad anyway as

bait. I don't imagine he's going to let her live through the experience."

"Got that right."

Florida gritted her teeth as Lina instructed Polk's aides to hook up the HV set and its complicated linkages into the organiputer. After a few harsh words, three more techs were called to the penthouse, the youngest of whom actually looked like he knew what he was doing. In a flurry of trial and error, the attending gray shirts finished hooking up the equipment and cleared the room in a stampede of arms, legs, and lab coats.

Polk fiddled with the remote on his belt as Lina and Conrad made themselves comfortable in loungers. They adjusted their seats and scooted up around Florida's bed like they were a family watching a holofilm: Polk and Lina the parents, Conrad the naughty child staying up late, and herself the decrepit distant relative. She'd spent little enough time lately thinking about her own family and was glad, at least, that she had kept her mother and brother out of her troubles. Polk's sculpted pinky nail punched commands into compressions on his belt and the HV snapped on, fluttering into a more-or-less steady focus.

The hologram displayed the outside of a dilapidated warehouse and, although it was early evening, Florida recognized the location immediately. It was the Spring district, the spot where she'd been nabbed.

"...works great. Led us straight to Teller's hideout," Florida overheard Polk say.

"Who is she? I've heard so many different stories that I thought she didn't exist."

"She exists in the same way you and I exist," Polk said. "Through science."

The crumbling facade of the warehouse swayed vertically, although the holovid projector soon stabilized it. Florida realized that the camera was really the eyes of a person, another cyborg creation like herself. A spy. Police were surrounding Teller's warehouse because of the memories they'd downloaded, making her responsible for what happened next. She found herself wondering when she had first been operated on and if this cameraman had agreed to be altered or was unaware of his role.

"Ready?" Lina asked.

Polk shook his head, rolled his shoulders, and settled back into his seat. Lina swung a thin silver filament from the crest of her green hair to her mouth. "Begin the sweep. Go slow and cover all the exits."

Before the cameraman followed his armed comrades through the warehouse hatchway, Florida glimpsed hoverpods circling on the periphery. Elbows and shoulders of marching police flanked the scene as the white shirts followed their leader into the brick construct, the transmitted image wavering in deep shadows.

"Infra," Polk said.

"Infra," Lina repeated into her headset.

A groan rose from the HV projector as the cameraman staggered, then straightened with a much-improved likeness of the warehouse.

"You're sick," Florida said, but no one noticed or cared. Just because you had the power to do something that didn't mean you should do it. Even with his faults and flaws, Florida found herself wishing her husband were with her now and wondering if she would ever see him again. Deep down, she knew that Mere cared about her, something she wouldn't have admitted to herself a month ago. If she had it to do over again she would have confided in him.

The human camera continued scouring the almost-empty building amidst the press of white shirts spreading out to scout the lower floor. The cop next to him swept the area with a hand-held metallic device and said, "They've got a fairly complicated security set-up."

"Have any alarms been tripped?" Lina asked.

"Hard to tell."

The squad leader swiveled a silver mouthpiece down from the bridge of his white helmet and said, "Move fast people. We have to assume that they know we're here."

The camera jiggled through a hatchway into a narrow hall spiked with disintegrating plaster and rotted beams of wood. Occasional pillars of organic steel dotted the passageway, shoring up the otherwise unsafe construct from the days when it was a factory. There was a flurry of movement ahead and the sound of a slamming hatch.

"Remember," the leader said. "Stun prods only, even if they're armed. "If you kill someone, Polk will have your hide."

"They know me so well," Polk whispered to Lina.

Several policemen lurched into the door of a loading bay and were greeted by a high-powered barrage of flagettes. The hologram blurred as bodies flew from the explosive shells. A tall, thin gunman fired away, shielded by the chassis of a delivery truck in what appeared to be a garage. The white shirts used toolboxes, crates, tires, and whatever scraps of metal were handy as cover, but they were dropping almost as quickly as they stormed into the loading area. The HV image whirled sideways and fell to a strange angle a few centimeters off the floor.

"Usa," Polk said. "Camera's down."

"Send everyone in. We need Teller alive," Lina ordered.

The police trickled through the archway until the gunman ran out of ammunition. A strange rasping was audible over the shouts and scrambling feet, and Florida realized that it was the wounded cameraman wheezing from his injuries. The truck's engine rumbled to life and lurched across the bay. A few uninjured white shirts dove headlong to avoid contact. The vehicle burst through a rusted garage hatch and skidded sideways into an alley, barreling over a few unsuspected police covering the exits outside.

"Come on," yelled the wiry gunman, jumping up from cover and reloading his pistol. This lanky desperado led what appeared to be Florida's ex-landlady Helena toward the opening provided by the truck. Helena was Teller? Strange, but no more so than what she saw next. Mere's childhood friend Jonas Grumby was ushering Polk's enemy toward the overturned truck and the Spring alleyway. Reinforcements poured in through the warehouse hatchway. Jonas reloaded and opened fire.

"Street view," Polk said, fumbling for the controls and Lina had to reach over and help him redirect the signal. They scrolled through a number of external vantage points shot by other cameramen until they found an observer holding a position on the second floor of a building across from the gaping hole in the warehouse garage.

A hovercraft dropped to rooftop level while a neighboring pod landed in an adjacent parking lot. Grumby fired down the alley with one hand while he gripped Teller's elbow with the other. Troops swarmed toward them from both sides, cutting off their escape, and Florida could hear her old landlady screaming, "Do it now," and placing Jonas's pistol to the side of her head.

Polk shouted, "No," and clambered to his feet as Jonas squeezed the trigger.

Nothing happened. The flagette chamber was empty. Jonas kept pulling the trigger anyway, to no avail.

"No," Teller yelled, echoing Polk.

The police broke from cover toward their quarry and Jonas patted his clothing for another magazine. Teller darted to the back of the truck, ripped open the back hatch, and pulled out a canister that she unscrewed, saying, "Fire it up."

Jonas fumbled for a lighter as Teller's shaking hands ripped off the top of the canister and a dark blue fluid flew skyward, dousing herself and her assistant from toe to head. The police closed in. Jonas sparked the miniature flame and pressed it to the sleeve of Teller's chartreuse robe.

Polk jumped out of his seat, momentarily blocking the HV grid. He bent over Lina, pinched her headset, and yelled, "Douse that fire, with your own bodies if need be."

The robe caught like a torch and Jonas stepped back from the spreading flames as Teller used her sleeve to set different parts of herself on fire. A tight wedge of white shirts threw themselves on top of Teller, knocking her to the ground. The police tried smothering the burning woman and, at first, only seemed to add fuel to the fire. Jonas dodged a squad of police approaching from the opposite direction and jumped into the driver's seat of the still-running truck.

The extra officers piling on Teller appeared to do the trick. Scores of them mashed the old woman, the smoke of the extinguished chemical blaze rising up between entwined limbs and writhing torsos along with cries of pain. Jonas floored the accelerator and the sounds of screeching metal added to the din as the truck barreled forward on four flat tires. He swerved toward the pile-up of officers and managed to roll over a third of the white mass. The sputtering truck bounced over the stack, swerved around the parked hoverpod and skidded out of the alleyway.

Polk told his troops, "The truck is secondary. Evacuate Teller immediately and get her to Skytown. Have a med team waiting. Time is of the essence."

Yes, time was of the essence and it looked like it had just run out on Teller, although Florida couldn't fathom why the woman had wanted to kill herself so badly. Could capture really be that bad? She wondered if she would feel a similar emotion later as Polk used and reused her for every purpose he could think of. Perhaps there were terrors worse than death. This revelation almost made her wish that she would not live long enough to see Conrad use her as bait. She would rather die than betray Mere, G, or anyone else. She was a person, no matter what parts of her body answered to the commands of another. A person.

Jonas Grumby's hands itched as he gripped the steering wheel and wrenched the damaged vehicle around the corner of a narrow alley. The walls of a former housing project kept the hoverpods from view and he counted himself lucky. He'd failed back at the warehouse. Utterly. Who knew if his mentor was really dead? Teller had pounded it into his head that she would rather be killed than letting Polk capture her. He had failed her in this mission.

Jonas accelerated and almost spun the truck up on two wheels on the next turn. He needed to ditch the lumbering beast and quick. He wouldn't be outrunning anyone on rims alone, especially hovercrafts. He braked and eased the vehicle under a mildewed awning that appeared at one time to have been the back entrance to a restaurant or store. He climbed out of the driver's seat, opened the back of the truck, snagged a handful of flagette magazines, and looked to make tracks. If he could put some distance between himself and the vehicle, he had a good shot at holing up in an abandoned building or finding an underground passage to the Rim.

He considered sending a few rounds into the truck to blow up Teller's files and the comp equipment they'd transferred into it, but figured it wasn't worth giving away his location. Covering his boss's tracks seemed a low priority now that she was captured. He was probably history himself, even if he managed to elude capture. If he weren't already identified, he would be soon. They'd been so close to clearing out of the warehouse, too. Teller had decided, quite correctly, that Mere and G constituted enough of a security breach to switch to a secondary location. He wondered if G had anything to do with the raid. Teller appeared to have trusted him and that should have been enough, but it wasn't. There was something about G that conjured images of chaos and destruction.

He hurried quietly past a crumbling brick building dappled

with rectangular openings that were once covered in glass. Staying out in the open was suicide. Time to get lost. He wove through a network of alleys and turned into an old industrial complex. He used the tail of his suede jacket to wipe the dark blue fluid from his hands, neck, and face. His skin itched and burned. He had no idea what the chemical was they'd used to torch Teller and if it was toxic.

He tiptoed to the edge of the building's foundation, peeked around a corner leading to a wider alley, and found himself face-to-face with G. Jonas reacted without thinking and swung at the albino's face, but ended up connecting only with air. Actually, he'd come close to tagging Mere, who was standing behind the quick-dodging G.

"Careful there," Mere said, grabbing Jonas's arm before he could swing again. "What in the jack do you have on you?" his old friend complained, dropping the damp sleeve and shaking blue liquid from his fingertips.

"Don't know. What are you doing here?" Jonas asked, relieved to see Mere, but also very much aware how Teller's plans had hinged on him staying in one piece. "You shouldn't be putting yourself in danger like this."

"You're one to talk."

"True."

"The police started pouring into the neighborhood on our way back to the Rim." Mere glanced over at G who was ignoring them. The albino's eyes were closed and he was muttering to himself, his palms sliding over the pitted surface of the building. "G snuck us down into the foundation of a building not far from the warehouse. We heard a crash and saw you tear away in the truck. Where's Teller?"

"On her way to Skytown," G mumbled, his eyes fluttering open. "She's badly burned, but it looks like she's going to pull through."

An invisible hand gripped Jonas's stomach and twisted. "How do you know...are you sure?"

G shook his head solemnly.

Mere grabbed a stunned Jonas and said, "I'll do what Teller wanted, only let's get out of here. Now."

"Yes," Jonas said numbly, realizing a lifetime of working for Teller had come to an end. She had shown him proof that his parents had been killed for political reasons and helped him believe he could make a difference. That wasn't to say that he hadn't committed acts over the years that made him question his morality, the worst of which was seeking out Mere's friendship. The funny thing was that it was no longer an act. Mere had become his best friend. Maybe they could still find a way to take the world on like they'd always dreamed of doing as boys. "You're right, let's go."

"Follow me," G said and they trailed after the albino as he picked his way through the rubble of Old Collings, looking for an opening into the underground.

* * *

After Teller was captured, Florida found herself ignored once again as Conrad wandered off for a briefing with Lina. Before leaving, her husband's lookalike had run his fingers through her hair and promised to "escort her away" after running a few errands. She hadn't been fed or given water, but assumed that there was something to the tubes funneling liquid into her body that kept her from becoming uncomfortable. Who knew, maybe with Polk's latest tampering she would no longer need food and would be able to subsist on machine oil and the crisping.

The crisping...there was something about the drug that wasn't what it seemed. It changed the people who took it—aside from skin color—in ways she couldn't fathom or explain. She thought about her last conversation with Mere when he'd been wiped out from the erotic hallucinogen. Lust, love, and shame had danced in his eyes, and she'd had to fight with herself in the early morning before leaving so as not to climb into his gravweb and sleep with him one final time. It was a shame that they'd never had children. It would have given Mere a chance to open up and learn to love someone unconditionally. For years she'd thought that she was the one who was infertile. Now she understood that it wasn't her fault, but Mere's. Cloned animals could not procreate and neither, seemingly, could humans.

She thought about what Polk had said at her bedside. Apparently, clones could also end up looking and acting very differently from the original. She could see traces of Polk's ego, self-centeredness, and rage in her husband, but only traces. Mere was a decent man underneath...or could be given the right circumstances.

"Bring her up. Next to the other prisoner is fine," Polk said, jolting Florida out of her reverie.

The president trailed behind a squad of policemen who pushed a hoverbed from the elevator into the penthouse. Several gray shirts scrambled ahead and cleared a row of loungers to make room for the prisoner or what was left of her. It was hard to believe that the charred body swaddled in bandages was once a vibrant woman. Teller—better known to Florida as Helena—looked like death cooled over. Her once bright green clothing was now burnt scraps, most of it pasted to her own rag flesh. Red and white blisters splotched skin that was cracked and oozing with abscesses. Her breathing was loud and uneven, but strong, and her limbs were bound to the table even more securely than Florida's.

Lina popped up out of nowhere and barked, "Everyone out. Now."

The sea of arms, legs, and necks around the patient swept toward the penthouse elevators, leaving what appeared to be a doctor hovering by Teller's bedside.

"Is she going to make it through the next few hours?" Polk asked.

"I think there's a good chance. We need to make a few tests, find out what chemical—"

"I didn't ask you about her long-term future, only if she would live a few hours."

The doctor took a half step back, holding up his hands as though to abdicate responsibility. "A few hours? Likely, unless the fluid that caused the fire is more—"

"Last chance. Yes or no, doc?"

"Yes," came the answer, several pitches higher than the previous explanation.

"For your sake, I hope you're right." Polk waved the physician away from the hoverbed.

"Hi, Gail, sorry to see you here," Teller whispered to Florida in a surprisingly clear and jovial voice. "See how much Polk enjoys making other people responsible for his decisions?"

"Sorry to see you, too...and yes, I'm living proof of that."

Polk ignored the chatter and focused his attention on Teller.

"Doctors haven't changed much since our day. Still as slippery as ever. Lawyers, however, I've had better luck muzzling. They're less greedy in my world."

"And the criminals are always guilty, too," Teller replied, her voice booming impossibly loud from her cracked lips.

"Yes, criminals do pay for their transgressions against me."

"What about transgressions against nature?"

"I'm surprised at you, Teller. Nature's something you reign in and control. Otherwise, you're at its mercy."

"I feel sorry for you if you think what goes on in this city is real. What makes you think you can control something you don't understand?"

Lina cleared her throat and frowned at the exchange, but Polk looked invigorated by the talk, almost as though he'd waited his entire life or a lifetime of lives to share his views with his old enemy.

"The power to impose your will over any situation makes up for a lot of shortsightedness. Besides, history has shown that you don't need to understand people to rule them. All you need is a governing system strong enough to stand against the opposition. A handful of city states around the globe are all that's left and I have them at my mercy."

"The organiputer's mercy, you mean."

"Yes, it's a fine tool. You should be proud."

"It will turn against you someday, I can promise you that."

Polk's supple lips curled in amusement. "If only it had free will, which it doesn't. I've been waiting to talk to you for centuries now and I expected much more from you than this. Your threats are as idle as your opinions, a product of an era long since past. Machines do not carry the souls of their creators, but of those who use them best. The organiputer has been fashioned in my image because I know how to squeeze every drop out of it. You wanted a thinking machine. I wanted something more."

"You didn't know what you wanted. You still don't. This is life, not a game."

"Don't tell me that life doesn't have winners and losers. Ask the carrier pigeons, the dinosaurs."

"What have you won, Andrew, beyond what other thieves and plunderers throughout the ages could claim?"

"The others failed, ultimately, while I'm immortal. I am history, Mona, alpha and omega, a god. Or, if you dislike the analogy, royalty."

Florida, already confused, reeled from the cascade of names. Andrew? Mona? Was that what these two were called before the war?

Teller's voice was resigned and tinged with sorrow, "You're a royal pain, all right. Even when we were close, I disliked your inability to see past what you wanted. Is life really that much better for you now than it was when we were together?"

"That's a joke, right?"

"Don't give me that snotty look, Andrew. Do you remember when you were excited about shaking things up? You always hated the establishment."

"Psychobabble didn't work on me when I was young. I have even less patience for it now."

"I don't have much patience myself these days," Teller admitted. "An outsider might find little difference in our methods if they were to look closely."

"We are becoming more alike. Remember what they used to say about pets and their owners?"

"Don't let what other people say bring you down, Andrew. You shouldn't think of yourself as an animal."

Polk guffawed. "I'm almost going to miss you when you're gone."

"Does that mean you're going to put me out of my misery?"

"No, I'm going to put you out of my misery."

"You owe me a clean death. I'm in a lot of pain."

"Pain isn't a worthwhile concept unless it has no end."

"Fortune cookie wisdom isn't like you, neither is beating around the bush."

Polk smiled. "It would almost be worth keeping you around as my fool."

"Or your conscience."

"Too late for that."

"Always the pessimist. Isn't drudging through the same life over and over getting pretty dull for you? I was so sick of being the same person that I took a chance and experimented the last incarnation. I'm a new woman, you might say."

"Could have fooled me. You sound like the same pain in the ass you always were."

"But I AM different. I'm not the Mona you knew. That's not to say that there aren't similarities. I do have SOME memories of when I was your boss, the war, the lifetimes after them. Only they pop into my head like an impression or intuition. Most of what I learned about you I read in Teller's journals after the transference. Surprisingly, I discovered that my former self didn't hate you so much as pitied you for your bigotry."

"Mona, there was a time when I might have listened to you. You were the only black woman I ever respected...or liked, but I'm not stupid enough to let you goad me into a trap. My best scientists have done tests on Mere and I suspect that what you say is true. If I allow him to become my successor, I have no idea if I'll be in control of him or not. I can't take that chance. I like who I am."

Florida watched her former landlady shake in laughter. Even though the convulsions appeared to bring her blistered body pain, Teller could not control herself. Lina drifted closer to Polk, shifting her weight from foot to foot.

"Mona, are you going to let me in on the joke?"

"It's hilarious that you of all people should talk about blacks. You're darker than any man I've ever seen."

"No, I'm a white person whose skin has changed colors. A big difference."

"It must be tough on you to be a shade of your former self."

"I'm not about to start hating myself now, Mona. I was right for what I did. The race war was inevitable and you know it."

"You're right, it IS inevitable in a society like this one. Think the people are happy?"

"We're talking in circles, Mona. I am the only power left in the world. There will be no more wars, no more destruction of the rain forests, or the ozone layer. The organiputer gives humanity every-thing it needs to survive...WITHOUT destroying the earth."

"Andrew Polk, humanitarian. It's too bad your subjects don't know how much you've done for them."

"Yes, a pity. I'm tiring of this conversation." Polk nodded at his assistant and muttered, "It's time," as he backpedaled from Teller's scarred visage. "You see, Mona, after I found out about your trap, I took steps to nullify it." As Lina took her cue and exited the pent-house, Polk seemed to pick up his assistant's characteristics, bounc-ing from leg to leg as though he had to pee. "I put a full-grown copy of my body into the organiputer as an insurance policy: alive, but without memories. If I were ever to die, this body—after Lina disposes of Mere and the other clones—will gain my consciousness and command the organiputer to carry it up to Skytown. I'm invincible now."

"Good for you." Teller coughed, her earlier exuberance having given way to grimaces of pain.

"But you haven't heard the best part. After I discovered that you could keep a body alive indefinitely in the organiputer, I thought what a perfect home it would be for you."

Polk paused and let his words sink in. Teller's face became even more horror stricken, if that were possible.

"You wouldn't dare."

"If I keep you alive in the organiputer, then you won't be able to clone yourself. Ever again."

"I'd tell you to go to hell but we're all living in it." Teller made a supreme effort to break her restraints and, for a moment, Florida thought that something, either the straps on her arms or her red-splotched limbs would surely break.

"I could imprison you in the mass and leave you to stew yourself into senility, but I thought how much more fitting it would be to use that mind of yours to my benefit in the very system you created. I have a space already reserved for you that was meant for a friend of yours."

"G," Teller muttered under her breath. Then she turned her head and whispered to Florida, "Kill me, please. Somehow, kill me."

"I can't," Florida found herself saying over and over as Lina arrived with a squad of gray shirts who fitted Teller with monitoring devices before pushing her to the backside of Florida's hoverbed. Florida tried to ignore the pleas for mercy as she heard the sucking sound behind her stop, only to be replaced by a loud slurp and the wheeze of suction. Then the impediment to the drain behind her was cleared and Teller was gone, fed to the organiputer. The slurping sound started up again. Florida clamped her lips together and tried very hard not to scream.

Jonas felt lost, adrift in a sea of names he did not know: Tampoca, Clight, Varicose. He sat at the front bar of the Rim Barter and kept his eye out for anyone suspicious, realizing that he must look that way himself. G leaned his long angular body over the front counter and spoke in hushed tones with the owner, a thick-wristed barista with zeb stripes on his arms and neck, and a thick mustache.

Mere stood upright at the bar, joking with one of the locals, but Jonas's old friend didn't seem like himself. He carried himself confidently but without swagger, like a man who'd overcome some inner demon and was no longer scared of death. G was that way naturally, but since they'd discovered that Florida hadn't shown up at her apartment or for work, the albino had become even more dangerous and intense.

"So why didn't you say so before?" G's voice rose, causing Clight to look around.

"You didn't ask," the Rim owner replied. "You seemed interested only in whether I saw her, not if some guy stopped by asking for her. Hold on." Clight bent over and rummaged through a box behind the front counter even as his free hand poured a double shot of rom for an inebriated customer. He stood, tugged on his mustache and wrinkled his face. Lost in thought, he stared up at a giant lizard hanging on strings above the crowd, then with an "Ah ha" reached up to the frame of the full-length bar mirror and pulled down an advertising holocard. "It was from some guy named Tyler, Doctor Philip Tyler. He was pretty anxious to catch up with her."

G examined the card a long time before passing it over to Jonas who had even less luck figuring out what it meant. The thin metal rectangle was handed to Mere who swilled his double rom with a wild look in his eyes. He flicked the holocard to live and ran his fingers over the three-dimensional blue letters: SR.

"Sierra Resort," Mere said, gnawing a triangle of ice between his front teeth. "Jack, it figures."

Jonas stared at his old friend blankly, waiting for an explanation.

Mere kneaded his fist into his forehead and examined the outside of the envelope. "Not this, too," he said.

"What?"

"Yeah, what are you talking about?" G shifted in his stool and bent over the crinkled paper.

"This is my handwriting."

Mere frowned and stared at the sloppy cursive scrawl. G shook his head as though it all made sense. Jonas examined the stream of people entering the establishment and wondered if they weren't all going insane.

Mere giggled.

Maybe the whole world was already that way and they were just catching up. Yes, insane.

***

Florida was getting sick of losing consciousness. When she woke this time, however, she recognized her surroundings. Sierra Resort. More exactly, she sat with her back to a tree in the building lobby, her hands fastened behind her with a rope or cloth. The lighting was dim, except for a bank of halogens above the entrances. The gnarled roots dug into her backside, but she was still numb enough from her latest injection not to feel much pain. Why did Conrad bring her here of all places? She'd overheard enough of his and Lina's conversation to know that he had gotten briefed on much of her life over the last few years as recorded through her own eyes. That meant her long-time friend Philip, the healing center's director, was exposed for his role in hiding her and likely in danger.

Philip had been an even better friend of her brother's before he died from UV poisoning. Her family seemed so distanced from her now, in every way. Maybe it was because her mother was naturally aloof and her father a loner. They were both good natured, but self-absorbed. Like Mere. Like G. Like everyone she'd ever loved.

What in heaven was her problem? She refused to spend what was probably her final moments feeling regret. There were worse places to be waiting for something terrible to happen. She'd always loved it inside the arboretum, even as a little girl. Philip's father had run the place before him and had allowed Florida and her brother to hang out at the retreat when it wasn't at full occupancy. She'd always found the resort a sanctuary from the hubbub surrounding it. A branch rustled above her and Florida tilted her neck, catching a glimpse of blue fabric in the boughs of the mammoth slake tree above her.

Of course. An ambush. Conrad was in hiding above, waiting for Mere to come looking for her. Great. Her chest tightened and she found herself short of breath. She closed her eyes and thought about anything that might calm her. Unfortunately, most of her comforting thoughts led her to think about the people she cared about, causing her even further anxiety.

To fight against it, she tried recounting one of the fairy tales her mother had told her as a child—the story of Florida, the girl who refused to grow up.

She opened her eyes and it seemed to work. She imagined herself as that other Florida who'd lived long ago with a tribe of ancient people who had trekked to the swamplands of the south to die. "Grow up," the elders would tell her when she wasted her energy on games or flights of fancy. They did not understand why she would want to live her life with reckless abandon or take grave risks just for fun. "Life is too short to squander needlessly," some would say and these were the ones who aged more quickly than the others. In fact, the entire tribe of old people would have soon died out if it were not for the continual hordes moving to warmer weather from the kingdoms to the north.

Florida was hiding the secret of her longevity. That's what the village elders believed when they tried to wheedle it out of her. They would not trust her when she told them that she stayed young because she viewed each day like it was the first one she'd ever lived. She was always recounting her daring exploits of stealing oranges from the rich landowners, traveling the dangerous mangroves for wildflowers, or walking the beaches unclothed, daring the sun to strip her golden skin from her back. She knew instinctively what it was that set her apart. She was a daughter of the moon and had nothing to fear except what was hidden inside her own heart.

The few ancients who managed to woo her for a night or two lived much longer than the others. This made her quite an object of admiration and flattery. Fortunately, she was much too fleet afoot to be caught unaware by the aging men and women who coveted her, except for those who struck her fancy and they were few enough indeed among the walking dead. Rumors of Florida's charms spread to the neighboring kingdom of Nasa and the aging king there became obsessed with finding her. He dreamed of skinning her and cloaking himself in her golden skin so that he might live forever.

The king's armies flocked to the southlands, searching for the girl-child. Although Florida did not care about her approaching doom, the elders hid their treasure from the marauders, cherishing her for what they themselves could never have. Florida didn't have the heart to tell them that she did not fear death. She actually relished the idea for she knew that it was the only way she would be able to return home to her mother and sisters on the moon.

The Nasa king became so distressed when his physicians proclaimed his approaching death that he set fire to the land of the ancients and burned their homes, trees, and gardens to the ground. The king gambled that the radiant Florida would live through the blaze. She did, of course. The southlands were razed to cinders and Florida was easy enough to find as she was the only thing left standing on the ashen plains and beaches.

Florida was taken back to Nasa and was surprised to discover how easily she fell in love with the silly old king, madman and murderer though he was, and he with her, although she felt sorry that so many people had to die for them to find each other. Perhaps it was because they were both creatures of extremes. The king coveted life almost as much as Florida did death, although he kept putting off the day he would flay her skin and use it for his own.

"Florida, I do not wish to kill you, but the day of my death approaches."

"I find it hard to believe that you who have killed so many would find it difficult to kill me if it meant that you could live forever." She said these words with the courage that marked all her actions, and yet, since finding love, she found herself regretting that she would one day have to leave him. She knew that it was wrong to love someone who was so selfish and terrible, and yet she did, with all her heart. They made love as no two other creatures ever had and a new rumor swept the land that to see them kiss was as though to see ice on fire.

As the king's health weakened, Florida could no longer stand the thought of losing him and decided to ask her mother for help. One night she cut off her locks and with them fashioned a pair of wings that carried her to the moon. Her mother was terribly disappointed when she discovered the reason for the visit. She and her sisters had been anxiously awaiting Florida's return. "You should be ashamed of yourself," her mother scolded, even as she hugged her.

Florida could not be swayed by emotion or logic and she told her mother, "I'll do anything to keep him. Anything." The moon goddess told her that there was a way that she and the king could be together, but it would mean the end of the world: the proud kingdoms of the earth would fall, many people would die, and those few who remained would bear the scars of her daughter's passion wrapped in shadows. It did not take Florida more that a single breath to say, "Yes."

That night her sisters wished her farewell and flew off into the night. Thus, the stars were born. Her mother was the last to depart and, after planting a kiss on her cheek, stole Florida's wings and flew away so fast that her hair unwound behind her and the former moon goddess became the greatest comet in the sky. Florida did not understand how her mother could betray her like this. She had now lost everything and was alone, without lover or family, fated to wander the pitted surface of the moon above a world she could no longer return to. Thinking herself abandoned, she cried as no one had ever cried before and her sapphire tears flooded the world. She stamped her feet in a tantrum and the moon wobbled in the night sky.

The earth shook with the fury of the resulting storms. People died. Tsunamis ravaged the coastlines and the ancient kingdoms crumbled from the fierce winds that sprang up with a childlike wail, "Why, why, why, why, why." Florida cried for so long that weeks went by before the sky was clear enough for her to see the sun or what she had unleashed upon the earth.

Finally, her grief was spent and all was ruin. She thought about throwing herself from the moon and falling to her doom. She was stayed from her rash course, however, by a voice booming from the surface of the sun. On the yellow orb, rode her beloved king with silver stirrups who, having seen his kingdom destroyed, sought to kill himself by piloting his flying ship into the sun. He was surprised to discover that his fury and will to survive had protected him from the flames.

The couple looked on each other with rapture, yet neither could find a way to reach across the sky to touch the other. Thus, it was as Florida's mother had promised. The lovers saw each other every day, but only for a few moments. They would be together forever, but at a distance. Only rarely did it ever come to pass that the sun and moon came together in the sky and they could touch. Such was the passion built up after so many decades that on earth it seemed that the day itself disappeared and became eclipsed by night.

Florida found herself smiling beneath the rustling tree, although the fairy tale didn't exactly have a happy ending. Love in real life was like that: messy, unpredictable, savage. The lights in the hatchway of Sierra Resort flickered and died, leaving her and her captor Conrad in the dark. For a moment she wondered if it was part of her jailor's planned ambush, but then heard her husband's look-alike muttering in his perch, "The electrical system is jacked. The hatch is open."

* * *

Jonas felt uneasy about waiting in the cab with Sax, but they only had one gun among them. To go ahead with their plan without better weaponry was suicide, but Mere and G felt the extra time would only put Gail (now called Florida) in harm's way. The disagreement over her name and the fights that it started between his two companions didn't bode well. Mere and G were both wild cards, dangerous in all senses of the word.

Mere had insisted on checking out the resort himself. He and G had argued about that, too, but Mere had made a strong case for himself after G explained that he could knock out power to the facility, but only from a lanternhead across the street. Both looked ready to come to blows until Mere argued that they wouldn't have the element of surprise long. Even G had to admit that it would take him some time to unhook himself from the light pole and make his way to the entrance.

The timing would be tricky and Jonas was tense about how many things could go wrong. Sax wasn't helping his nerves any with his endless chatter, "You ever notice how in some parts of Oldtown it's easier to walk than others. It's weird, almost like you're going uphill when you're really—"

"Shhh," Jonas said, peering over the cabbie's bald spot to where G was hooking a linkage from his wrist into the base of a headlamp. The albino bit his lip and grimaced, swaying from his efforts. After almost tumbling over, his eyes snapped back into focus and he faced the entrance of the nature retreat across the street. G flashed the agreed-upon hand signal and Mere hurried toward Sierra's front hatch. He clung to the side of the building archway and stuck out his foot, placing it on the automatic door. It whisked open, but Mere kept himself from looking inside until G managed to douse the lights. This was the most dangerous part of the plan, the few seconds where Mere would be totally exposed. Sax muttered under his breath and Jonas almost snapped at him, but realized how big a favor the cabbie—a longtime favorite of Teller's—was doing them.

G turned and gave the second hand signal. From his back seat vantage point, Jonas could see the lights inside the lobby flicker and die. Mere, brandishing his pistol, ducked down and snuck into the building. In the few seconds he was silhouetted in the moonlight, a shot rang out. Mere dove and rolled inside the lobby out of sight. A frenzied gun battle ensued. Jonas opened the cab door and crouched down behind it, using it as a shield against ricochets. G bounded through the light street traffic and leaned over the hood on the other side of the cab.

"I should have gone in. I can see better in the dark."

"We went over this, G. He'll be all right."

"I'm not worried about him. I'm worried about what might happen to her."

More shots rang out and G slammed his fist against the hood. He rose several times, as though to rush inside, but kept his composure until he heard a woman's scream followed by another flurry of flagettes, then silence. G pushed himself off the grill and sprinted toward the entrance. The albino moved so swiftly that he reached the hatchway before Jonas had taken three full steps. He followed the streaking albino to the automatic hatch and, taking a deep breath, plunged into the darkness.

"I got him I think," Mere called out.

"Who got who?"

"Conrad's down, G. I shot him."

"What about Florida, is she OJ?"

Mere's voice was shaky, "Gail? I'm not sure."

Jonas slid over to G's voice where he found the albino ripping wires out of the wall. "Stay back," he hissed. "I've almost got it."

The lights inside the facility snapped back on. G unlinked from a wall socket and, with a flick of a wrist, wires reeled back inside of him. Then he was off like a shot into the tree line. Jonas followed him carefully, zagging from tree to tree in the lobby, dreading how exposed he was. It wasn't long before he found a trembling Mere hunched over what appeared to be his twin, dressed in blue, whose upper chest and neck were lacerated with flagettes.

Beside them, G leaned over a woman's body face down in the brush, rope trailing from her wrists into a nearby bush. Her back and side were bleeding from multiple gunshot wounds. She was not moving, nor would she likely ever be again.

G stroked Florida's hair and held her head in his lap. It had gone exactly as he'd feared. The life of the only person he ever cared about was draining through his fingers. He monitored the ebbing electricity in her heart and cybernetic parts, and racked his brain for inspiration. The lights of the jungle resort were unnaturally bright, and it filled him with hopelessness. She was almost gone. He could hear her breath get shallower, then rasp, "Mere..." Her eyes opened. "Mere, I'm sorry. He was using me as a shield. I grabbed his gun and he shot me."

Mere rushed to her side and bent down on one knee. "Gail."

"Did you hear me, Mere, it wasn't your fault."

"Yes, it was. It's because of who I am inside. Who I'll become."

"You're a good person, Mere. That won't change unless you let it."

Florida turned and looked at G, her eyes moist, her pupils pinpricks. "G, I wish...."

Mere grabbed her hand and held on tightly. The light flickered around the edges of her eyes and her voice began to fade, "I love...."

"Gail, don't do this." Mere bent his head and began blubbering. Even so, G could hear her heart take its final beat and stop. Afterwards, he could sense a spark of electricity moving through her. It felt a bit like the signature of a lanternhead. Then it dawned on him—she still had some residual brain activity. She wasn't all-the-way dead. Not really. Her soul, or more accurately, the energy pattern that differentiated her from others hadn't left her body. He might be able to save her or part of her if he acted quickly enough.

G braced his legs and back, and scooped up Florida's limp body, making sure to cradle her head. Her thoughts would not decay right away. He turned and started toward the exit, but something held him back. He looked over his shoulder and bared his teeth. Mere would not give up his grip on Florida's arm.

"What are you doing, G?"

"Saving her."

Jonas moved in from the periphery, saying, "But she's dead, isn't she?"

"To you humans maybe."

"Humans, what are you talking about, you looping freak?" Mere rose and cocked his fists. "Put her down. Now. She's coming with me. She's my wife."

"Shut up, both of you. She's dead. The last thing any of us need is to be carting around a corpse."

"She's not a corpse," G insisted.

"You're going to be a corpse if you don't put her down right now."

"Mere, there's no time for this! The police are going to be here any sec."

G kept a close eye on Jonas in case he tried to flank him, but Teller's former bodyguard cradled his head in his hands and looked sick, his skin pasty in the crisscross of ceiling fluorescents.

"Put her down, G," Jonas pleaded. "Let's roll!"

"I'm going all right," G said, stepping forward smartly and dragging Mere behind him. "And you can't do a thing to stop me."

"OJ, you asked for it."

Mere spun and punched G in the nose. His head snapped back and brown fluid trickled out of both nostrils, but it hardly fazed him. These guys had no idea what two centuries of tortured existence could do to your pain threshold.

"Feel better?" G taunted. "Because of you, I'll never know if it was you or me she said she loved."

"What kind of monster are you?" Mere asked, staring at G's dark blood spackling his knuckles.

"A cybernetic freak and, yes, that's crisping on your hand. It's kind of in the blood, you might say. Not at all dangerous to you without electricity."

"Man, machine, whatever you are, I'm not going to ask again." Mere gripped the handle of the flagette pistol tucked in his waistband.

G was beyond caring. If this was the way Mere wanted to play it, so much the better. "Go ahead. Take her if you want her so bad."

Mere tilted his head in confusion and frowned. He loosened his grip on the gun and moved, trancelike, toward Florida.

G's thoughts surged with desperation and rage. The crisping's only dangerous with electricity, Mere. A little closer.

"Whatever you're going to do, do it now." Jonas watched the entrance anxiously and looked ready to jump out of his skin.

G smiled. Just a little closer. Come on, do it! Mere reached out and cupped his hands under Florida's body, his damp knuckles brushing G's forearms beneath her. Channeling the leftover charge from reconnecting the building's power, G shocked Mere. Not enough juice to kill him, but, when added to the crisping, more than enough to disable him.

"Pleasant dreams," G said and Mere dropped face first onto the synthetic grass. "Take care of him, Jonas."

"What did you do, is he...where are you going?" Jonas rushed to Mere's body and, for a moment, almost looked like he was going to snatch up the gun himself.

"Down," G said, cradling Florida gently and turning toward the hatch. "Straight to heaven."

***

Mere trudged across a barren plain into the teeth of a fierce wind. He shielded his eyes from dust swirls and breathed through the collar of his shirt. He gripped the handle of a leash tightly and looked back to see why they were moving so slowly. The exposed skin of his fist was chapped and fissured, a dreary white. Behind him crawled a Virgin Mary statue reanimated to life, her joints creaking with each swivel of elbow or knee. He found himself loathing the blemishes on the cobalt skin of the woman he'd once worshipped and yanked harder. She stumbled and spilled headlong into the parched field of grass. Her apocryphal face was smeared with the ochre of the earth and the gray of the air, but he could still see pity flash in her brown eyes. She arched her back and pushed herself up to her hands and knees. She lowered her head like a field animal and set her creaking limbs in a crawl so fast that he worried she might begin crumbling into dust.

Days, years, entire lifetimes seemed to pass before they reached the ruined outskirts of the village they'd once called home. The stooped inhabitants had changed as had the shabby constructs they lived in, pieced together from scraps of steel and cement. It had been a long time since they'd been back. Too long. Mere was reminded of a not-unhappy time when he believed in the divinity of the creature at his feet and loved her as a woman. That was before he had willed himself into a being more powerful than she who had given him life. And all like her. Women. Subservient. His to love and control.

They reached the garbage-strewn streets at twilight. It looked as though the rooftops and windowsills were smoldering, just as they had during the nightly raids so many years before. But the war was long since over, a psychotic's dream that someone, somewhere, must still be experiencing as reality.

"I can't face them after what we've done, even if their skin has peeled back from bone and their eyes have boiled into stars," the statue said. She stopped and rolled over onto her back. "You will not be allowed to return. The darkness will keep you from ever finding the love you crave or a home. It will emerge again tonight and every night. Your dreams will slip away."

Mary was really starting to piss him off. He jerked on her leash, knowing that there was some reason why they should hurry. He feared something would change or perhaps stay the same. He whipped her with the chain and bruised his fists on her metallic skin, but she would not budge. He hated her. He loved her. Something inside told him this must be a dream and the wind itself whispered, "No."

The sun was low in the horizon and storm clouds billowed to the west. In the fading light, he saw three fountainlike spurts arc and cascade into the beaten soil. She was bleeding brown from her belly and groin at an alarming rate. The light-blue color drained from her face and her armor disappeared into blanched flesh. He reached down and cupped her cheek. Nothing had ever felt so cold. His knees were seeped in crisping.

"A thief is all you'll ever be until you give me your heart," she said, smiling. He looked down and watched the greedy skin of his legs soak up the puddle of her blood and darken like the sky. "It's not over. I will never be enough."

* * *

What bothered Mere most when he woke was not that he'd been crisped again or that he'd slept on the stained cushions of a stranger's couch or even the horrific nightmare. No, these petty inconveniences were becoming commonplace in his life-on-the-run. What distressed him most was that he'd actually wanted to spend more time with the statue in his dream. She'd been trying to tell him something important. He was certain of it. For the first time in months he felt as though the answer to his misery was fluttering just beyond his flailing hands or skidding off the tip of his tongue. He was on the verge of understanding something important. Loop, it was maddening.

As much as he'd cared about Gail and the four people he killed (five if he ever saw G again), he realized that neither he nor they'd had any choice. Most of his life had been molded, shaped, and then controlled by a combination of Teller and Polk. He was everything and nothing in their eyes: a shadow man, a puppet costumed in razors, the blind fury of a cornered animal. He was the pain a madman becomes accustomed to, then craves, then swallows whole to feel even more pain and desire. Each day brought Mere either closer to death or eternal life, and he could not see how he would survive either option unless he could figure out a way to switch the sun and moon, and make the entire universe believe that the shadow was really a man, and the man who cast the shadow was nothing but a nightmare who sprouted legs.

Above all, he had to force himself to believe that he could survive this insane game he'd been dragged into with his soul intact. The hell with saving the world. It could take care of itself. If he could just keep himself alive and in control of his body and mind, Polk would not be able to win. It was that simple. To accomplish this he knew that he would have to take grave risks. He could no longer afford to be timid or second-guess himself. He would have to numb himself to the past and all the people hurt by the choices he'd made or, more accurately, had been made for him. The future was what counted. Every second of every day. Only by living well and choosing well could he make Gail's death mean something. She would want it that way.

"Good morning."

"Hello," Mere said, lifting his head from the lumpy bedroll and staring into the eyes of his host. Of course. It all made sense. He was once again indebted to a gibbering madman.

Sax extended a mammoth paw and Mere took it, fighting against his post-crisping fatigue. The cabbie pulled him upright and onto his feet.

"I wanted to wake you earlier, but she wouldn't let me."

"She? She who?"

"Cola."

"Cola's here?"

"On the second floor. Follow me."

Mere trailed the beefy albino through a maze of narrow walkways, skirting dead-ends of clutter placed almost strategically throughout the multilevel apartment. Sax's loft was almost as much a contradiction as he was. Topped by an ornate oval skylight and filled with flowers, potted vegetables and miniature fruit trees, the warehouse was also a garage, library, and home to displaced objects throughout time.

Mere was dizzy and out of breath by the time they climbed to a tiny bedroom whose door and walls were formed by hundreds of model cars hanging from the rafters on near-invisible wires. It was incredible. A rippling curtain of autos swayed from the cool night breeze blowing from an open balcony off the kitchen. Mere kept close watch where he put his feet. He didn't want to step on anything that might bring the room crashing down around his ears.

Sax looked back at him, as though to explain something, then turned his head with downcast eyes. Something was wrong. It had to be. Why else would the talkative cabbie be this quiet? Mere followed Sax's lead and spread several strands of cars to make a walkway. Cola looked up from the foot of a bed as they entered a small guest room. Wordlessly, she rose and hurried across the cluttered quarters, pulling him into her arms. "Sorry to hear about Gail."

"She died trying to save me. She didn't deserve to be dragged into this or," he added with a slight tremble in his voice, "to have a monster for a husband."

Cola slid her fingers up his back to his shoulders and shot him an intense look. No discernable emotion. Just intense. "I don't want to hear that jack from you. You're still the best hope people like me and Jonas have to lead a better life. You have the power to make a difference and you will if you set your mind to it."

"So you know then...about me and Polk?"

"What Jonas didn't tell me, I pieced together last night while he was in a fever. He was ranting all night, Mere, mostly about you. He's really sick. I don't know if he's going to...I don't know what to do. I was thinking about trying to find a doctor or a healer, someone who might be able to help."

For the first time, Mere noticed the mountain of multicolored fabric on a wide-frame steel bed. Jonas's chin poked out from the impressive stack of covers. His eyes were fiery red slits, his skin yellow. He was shivering, but seemed too out-of-it to feel much pain.

"Jonas...."

"Poison," Jonas moaned, huffing life a woman giving birth. "My brain's on fire, but my feet are like death."

Mere reached out a hand, but Jonas recoiled and burrowed his face into a pillow, pulling the covers up over him.

"See what I mean?" Cola asked.

"What's wrong?"

"He had some sort of chemical on his clothes and skin. And a couple of burns. I washed most of the goop off of him, but Usa if I know what it is or what it might have done to him."

"We would if we were at the lab," Mere said.

"I know, I thought about that, too. I just don't want to waste any time screwing around if he's in real danger."

"He's in too deep with the law just now to see a doctor. Every clinic will be alerted. Probably half the police in the city are after him."

"And you."

"Thanks for reminding me. You, however, shouldn't have that problem. Can you think of any reason why the white shirts would be after you, any way they can tie you to Jonas?"

"No, I don't think so. We were discreet."

"Good." Mere smiled despite himself.

"Besides, he was always so worried about me being dragged into his business with Teller. Aside from you, none of our friends even know we're going out."

"Then I don't see why you couldn't sneak up to the lab and

snag a med kit."

"I guess," she said, obviously reluctant. "You'll stay with him?"

"Every second."

She bent down over the bed and Sax swiveled gracefully out of her way.

"Jonas, hon, I'm going out for a little while."

He answered her with a muted groan. She tried lifting the bedding, but he rolled further into it, cocooning himself.

"I brought your electrar in case you feel up to it later." No answer. Cola turned to Mere. "He left it at my place a few days ago."

"When he comes out of it, I'll make sure he gets it," Mere promised, noting the hovercase in the far corner of the room.

"OJ, then I guess I'll be going."

She took one last look at Jonas, and turned to Sax. "Thanks for everything. For putting him up, for looking after him."

"It's nothing he wouldn't do for me or any of the other Tellers," the cabbie mumbled. Cola patted the albino's arm and leaned on Mere before departing.

"Wish me luck," she said.

"You'll be back before you know it. I promise if things get worse, I'll go out myself and find a doctor."

She nodded, and without looking back, slipped through the curtain of cars.

* * *

It wasn't even a half hour after Cola left that Jonas bolted upright in bed, seemingly his old self or at least a pale shade of it.

"It breathes again," Mere said in his best impression of the mad scientist in the holofilm *Cave Dwellers*.

Jonas smiled weakly, but his bloodshot eyes swam with panic. "Cola was here last night, wasn't she?"

"Yes."

"Where is she?"

"She went out to run an errand. She should be back soon though."

"I had a dream," he started, but trailed off. He looked at the yellow splotches on his arms and shoulders. "Usa, I feel horrible."

Jonas climbed out of bed and waved off Mere's efforts to help him stand. They moved his pillows and covers down to the living room and Sax put on some music, an ambient wash of keyboards and percussion. Mere went back upstairs for Jonas's electrar and the musician cradled his instrument in his arms and plucked an occasional note between intermittent sniffles and sighs. Despite Jonas's insistence that he was feeling better, he looked barely strong enough to keep the instrument balanced in his lap.

"I remember waking up last night and Cola was there, holding me," he told them. "She looked worried. It's probably nothing, the flu." Jonas's husky voice and glazed eyes told a different story. "Come on, Mere, quit looking at me like that. You're driving me nuts. I'm going to be fine."

"You were hardly fine to begin with."

Jonas's half-hearted chuckle spasmed into a cough. Sax, still unearthly quiet, sat cross-legged on the mottled camel carpeting and laid out a deck of Tara cards, the Collings version preferred by Jungle soothsayers and mystics. The cabbie muttered to himself and dealt out a wheel of cards, turning them over slowly. He grumbled, without moving his lips, and repeated the reading, sometimes with a few cards, and occasionally using intricate patterns that took up nearly half the deck.

Mere thought he might go mad between Sax's neurotic shuffling and Jonas's playing, but he closed his eyes and slowly felt himself relax. He let both sounds wash over him and mix with the music playing from the speakers on the floor and ceiling. He opened his eyes. Familiar images swept past on the cards: the Graylings, the organiputer, Polk, Teller. The cabbie's manic expression kept Mere from asking what he was trying to divine.

"The same, it keeps coming up the same," Sax mumbled under his breath. Mere got up to use the bathroom. He'd circled the couch and was about to climb the stairs, when he saw Cola slip in through the front hatch, followed by the last person in the world he thought he'd ever see again. His boss, Reed Bourne.

"Hi, Mere, happy to see me?"

"Hello, Reed, of course. Cola, what's going on?"

"I ran into Reed at the lab and he busted me on sneaking out with the med kit. I let him in on our problem. Don't forget he has a med degree and he said he'd help. No questions asked."

"No questions asked," Reed repeated, obviously amused.

Mere backed his way to the couch where Jonas sat upright, quivering in disbelief. Cola dropped the silver med kit onto the end table in front of Sax and the card of Polk flew off the table from a sudden breeze and fluttered to the floor.

"It's him," Sax said, rising, his high-pitched voice squeaking with fear. "He's come to pass judgment."

Reed laughed and pushed a button on his wrist comlink. An oval of gold light enveloped him from toe to head as he pulled a pistol out of the inner pocket of his gray jacket.

"It can't be," Mere said as he backed himself to the cushions next to Jonas. "You can't be one, too. No wonder people always thought we looked like brothers."

"I'm a lot of things, Mere," Reed said, clicking the safety on his pistol. "Tonight you can all just call me Death."

BLUE

24

A weary Jonas was adjusting the tuning on his electrar to play the blues when Reed Bourne accompanied Cola into the warehouse. He didn't like the look of his girlfriend's boss from the start. The guy carried himself with a cocky air of invincibility. Besides, Cola should have known better than to bring a stranger to a Teller safehouse. His fingers were still loosening the thick E string on his instrument when a golden light enveloped Cola's boss. It looked like some sort of body shield. As Reed drew his pistol and called himself "death," Jonas's bass string scrolled free from the top nut. The musician's fingers curled around the loose end and the string swam sideways against the imposed city gravity.

The room became deathly quiet. Mere backed up until he was almost in Jonas's lap and only just caught himself from falling. Cola's head and shoulders tilted toward the front hatch as though she were ready to bolt, but her eyes remained fixed on the drawn pistol. Sax slowly came up out of his crouch, his massive hands and tiny fingers held outward to show he wasn't a threat.

Reed rolled back a jacket sleeve and punched a sequence of nodules on what appeared to be an organiputer cufflink. The wrist communicator burped with static, then buzzed with the garbled whine of comlink. Reed lifted the silver band to his lips. "I've reached the location and found Roosevelt," he said in a sarcastic baritone filled with bravado. "It looks like I've cornered a few Tellers as well."

"Good," boomed the response from the metallic bracer. "I want those traitors alive."

"And Mere?" Reed tipped the barrel of his gun from person to person.

"Slag him."

"Great. I'm in the Westend. Follow my signal down and send in the clowns for the rest."

Reed clicked off his cufflink and tapped his pistol against his forearm. "As you've no doubt heard, the police will be down shortly. Run, don't run, I could care less. All I want is Mere."

"You heard him," Mere said. "Cola, Jonas, get out of here. You too, Sax."

"No way. He'll just shoot us in the back. I know it," the cabbie said, backpedaling into the stereo consol, his hip jiggling the control knob and raising the volume of the percussion-heavy music.

"This," Reed said, pointing at the drawn pistol with his free hand. "Is just for show."

Another of Polk's clones, Jonas thought. His fingers looped around his E string and he pulled it taut against the body of his instrument. He was slow on the uptake. The others must have already realized the danger they were in. Cola's boss clicked the safety on the pistol grip and reholstered the handgun. "Before any of you get any bright ideas, this light you see shimmering around me is a unishield. I suppose you've heard what it can do?"

"Standard police riot gear," Jonas said.

"Yes, only better. It was designed by the organiputer to repel any object, organic or inorganic, in Collings. Nothing can get through it. And since the organiputer has been fed molecules from every item manufactured in the city, including your skin, there's not a thing you can do to stop me."

Cola bent down, gripped the handle of the med kit and whirled. Her arms whipped around her body and the steel case exploded in Reed's face. The heavy kit ricocheted off the gold shield and flew out of her hand, opening. Sax whirled sideways to avoid the tiny missiles tumbling out as the case itself slammed into his stereo, silencing the overloud music.

Reed laughed and pushed Cola down into a chair.

"Just checking," she said. "It works, I guess."

Reed folded his arms and turned to Mere. "Let's see what you got, hero."

Jonas watched his friend curl his fingers into fists and stalk around the end table toward Reed. "More than you can handle, bossman."

"So do you like Polk's nickname for me?"

"Death? It suits you because that's what you're going to be when I'm through with you," Mere said, sliding his body in between

Reed and his friends. "Jonas, get everyone out of here. Now."

"Or stay and enjoy the show."

"Jack, I said leave!"

Reed waited for Mere to work his way into striking distance. "You know, I'm really going to enjoy killing you with my bare hands."

"OJ, tough guy, turn off the shield and let's see what you got."

"I'm afraid not, Mere. It took me months to gain Polk's confidence. I actually think he liked you best. At first. There was something about you that reminded him of his childhood."

"That creep was never a child."

Mere swiped halfheartedly with a roundhouse right and ducked back before Reed could counter.

"He is a child. An eternal child. I'm surprised you're fighting this so much. We're the only two clones left. If you'd kept your act together you might have been able to live forever."

"You're pathetic. I'd rather die my own person," Mere said, fainting with a left jab and whipping a wicked kick at Reed's groin. His foot bounced off the shield and the rebound sent him flying backwards over the end table.

"No," Sax howled, ripping the stereo unit from the wall and slamming the massive console on top of Reed's feet. The smile faded from Reed's lips when he realized that he was pinned.

"Jonas, grab Mere and run," the cabbie said, rushing forward.

Reed bent down to lift the bulky unit off his ankles. Mere stumbled to his feet, obviously shaken. Cola rose from her chair and screamed, "Come on, Jonas. Get a move on."

Her words knifed through his fever. One hand still gripping his guitar string, Jonas helped Mere to his feet and shoved him toward the hatch.

Reed pried his feet loose and fell backwards. Sax sprang onto the table and brought his massive torso down across Reed's chest. He bounced several times atop the shield, struggling to pin the intruder with his bulk. The still-seated Jonas was lost in thought. Nothing in the city could hurt this jerk. So be it. His electrar, smuggled in from the ruins of an ancient eastern city, had yet to be normalized to the city's gravity field. He'd gotten it through the Rainmakers for what had amounted to two years' salary.

With almost no effort, Reed twisted and shouldered Sax off of him. The mammoth cabbie crashed into the wall where the stereo had been and lay sprawled out, struggling to rise.

"Enough of this nonsense," Reed said, crossing toward Mere who was bleeding from his forehead and looked ready to topple without Cola's arm to support him. She ushered Mere toward the door, but Reed was faster, intercepting them at the stairs and cutting off their escape. Jonas ripped the E string from his electrar and struggled off the couch. Without his weight to steady it, the instruments swept sideways toward the stairs and picked up speed.

Reed pushed Cola away from his quarry onto the landing and flinched at the electrar whizzing toward him. "What the?" he said.

"My instrument was smuggled in," Jonas said, gripping the free end of his E string with his other hand. He could feel it wriggling in his grasp, laced with the gravity of the outside world, a place where Polk and the organiputer were nothing but stories to frighten children. Jonas sprinted toward Reed, saying, "As you'll discover were my strings."

Jonas crossed the living room as fast as his long legs could carry him. Reed reached for his pistol and took aim. Careful aim. He was history. Mere jerked up out of his crouch and snatched the electrar as it passed over his head. Growling like a man possessed, Mere swung the instrument down across Reed's arm. Jonas's electrar smashed in two. The pistol clattered to the floor. Reed fell to his knees, clutching his wrist. Mere reached for his former boss, but his hands slipped off the shield and he reeled sideways, stumbling to the floor.

Jonas leapt the final few meters over Mere's body and looped the string over Reed's neck. It sliced through the gold light and bit into skin. Jonas held on for dear life and fought to pull the string taut. His torso bounced against the shield whenever he pressed in too close, but he could find no other way to get leverage.

Reed bucked up and slammed the back of his head against Jonas's nose. The world reeled around him. Off balance, Reed fell back on top of him, driving the oxygen from his lungs. Jonas yanked the string harder and felt the shield spark against his body.

Anchored to Jonas by the loop around his throat, Reed no longer had room to use his shield as a weapon. Jonas pulled tighter and strained to keep from being lifted by Reed's efforts to raise himself up. His musician's hands strained with effort, the blues tune he was playing ripe for lyrics.

"Die death," Jonas howled as the writhing body on top of him began to go slack. "Die!"

***

Death swooped down on them from above, just as a different and much more real death ate away at his insides. Jonas would not be long for this world. He could feel the toxin raging in his blood, filling his lungs with poison. The poison of despair. Police hoverpods tracked the speeding cab and warning shots were fired. Sax veered half onto a sidewalk and scattered pedestrians, causing Mere and Cola to yell. It was an inspired piece of driving. Sax had managed to lead them along busy urban thoroughfares where patchwork buildings interconnected over the time-worn streets and made it difficult for the pursuing white shirts in hoverpods to draw a bead. An occasional warning shot was fired, but the police feared a full barrage in the densely populated Northwest end of the city.

The inside of the cab looked more like an ambulance than an escape vehicle. Everyone was bleeding from more than one place from their encounter with Reed. Jonas could see the matted blood on the back of Mere's head and a frightening gouge in Sax's shoulder. Fortunately, the fire ravaging his insides kept Jonas from mourning the damaged nerve endings in his musician's hands. It didn't matter. His electrar was destroyed. He would not be playing again.

Sax slalomed through a throng of school children and almost flipped the car up on two wheels trying to find cover in an open-to-the-sky traffic circle. He jerked the steering wheel one way, then the other. The tires squealed their complaint. They were headed toward the north industrial zone where Jonas had worked as a butcher since he'd gotten kicked out of school. He had a plan. A dangerous one.

"Which way?" Sax asked, his eyes moving from street to sky to street. "They're almost on top of us."

"Left, then right. We're almost there."

Mere pulled his head back in through the passenger window. "Almost where?"

Jonas felt Cola's fingers brushing his wrist before realizing she'd been holding his hand all along and he hadn't felt it.

"What do you have in mind?" she asked.

"I'll tell you, but not just yet. It's better that none of you know in case we're caught. This is one secret I can't let Polk find out about. The son-butch has too much of an edge already."

Jonas fought back a cough and decided he would tell Mere what he knew once they reached the underground tunnels beneath the organimeat vats. There would be no second chance. For any of them. He would have to trust that if and when Mere ever became Polk he would remember the sacrifices he'd made for him. The bigger the sacrifice, Jonas figured, the better. If he was going to die, he might as well give his best friend the guilt trip of his life, one that would keep him forever in his debt.

***

"Don't worry about me. I'll be fine. I have friends in low places," Sax said, slowing the cab to a crawl. They opened the hatches and jumped out of the taxi which accelerated and sped northward toward the Rim. Mere and Cola both managed to land on their feet. Jonas, meanwhile, could not seem to make his legs work and found himself contemplating the feel and texture of cement against his forehead. Mere helped him to his feet. Hoverpods whizzed past in the small patches of sky visible through the honeycombed buildings. The oblong orbs continued their pursuit of the possessed albino driver.

"I hope he'll be all right," Mere said and Jonas fought very hard not to snap back with, "He's going to die, just like I'm dying right now and it's all your fault," but instead he grunted and ushered them toward the meat mining facility.

"What in the Usavault of heaven is that?" Cola asked, twisting out from under his arm. Jonas almost tumbled without the support, but held onto Mere's shoulder with his good hand and followed the line of Cola's finger. A dozen or so black missiles streaked northward toward them, several meters off the ground. They were too slow to be weapons, too fast to be motopods.

They almost looked like...dogs.

"Looping doberhawks," Jonas spat, pushing Mere toward the

front hatch of his former workplace.

He'd never seen Cola move quite so fast. One second she was behind him, the next she was across the street and ghosting the hatch. The threesome whipsawed through security, followed by a horrible, inhuman baying. The hatch whisked shut behind them and several blue-shirt workers turned to stare at the commotion from a tunnel sloping down beneath the earth. The hatch would protect them, at least until the human handlers of those winged terrors caught up to them. Jonas waved off the lobby security, both of whom he'd chummed around with on occasion.

"You haven't seen us. Just buy us a few minutes," Jonas pleaded.

The confused men looked at each other and shrugged, then turned and strolled into a back room. A sudden surge of adrenaline coursed through Jonas as talons scratched and clawed at the outside hatch.

"Follow me," Jonas said. "We don't have a moment to lose."

$$* * *$$

Jonas pulled Reed's pistol out of his waistband and used it to clear a path through the blue shirts down into the mines. He tried not to look at any of their faces, as though that would somehow keep him from being recognized by his friends and numerous acquaintances in the small band of tight-knit workers. The whine of hand-held saws filled the fleshy caverns. Without his facemask the smell was almost enough to make him gag. He was used to it, however. Mere was chewing on the collar of his shirt and pinching his nose. Cola kept running ahead to try and clear the stench, disgust wrinkling her face. They'd cleared the beef, chicken, and pork levels, and were now navigating down to less-mined quadrants like lamb, turkey, and finger shrimp. The cavern walls were slick with condensation and writhed from the blood and oxygen pumped into it from the organiputer. Cola carried a flashbeam that Sax had snagged for them before fleeing the warehouse, but the cone of light provided barely more illumination that the glow radiating from the pulsating walls.

They cleared the lowest zones of the meat complex and descended into the tunnels beneath Oldtown where it was rumored that the higher functions of the organiputer were housed. By this time, Jonas had to stop every few meters. His brain felt like it was on fire and he was having trouble breathing. He had a cough he couldn't shake and had been spitting up yellowish-red phlegm the whole way down. He felt like he could keel over any second, but knew that he needed to hold on, at least until he guided them down as far as he himself had explored and could tell them his secret. He kept them pointed westward, tunneling beneath the Rim and, he hoped, toward the outer wall of the city.

Mere and Cola supported him on either side, propelling him forward. Burdened with his weight they could move no faster than a leisurely walk. He was really starting to impede their chances of escape. Although he hoped the smell of meat would keep the police hounds from following their trail, he knew there was little chance they'd dodge the pursuit. Mere was dangerous to Polk now, more dangerous than he'd ever been. Until the president managed to track down and kill his tainted clone, he would not be able to fashion a new body for himself. Jonas imagined that every white shirt in the city was mobilized and pouring down into the catacombs beneath North Oldtown.

He told Mere and Cola to keep a lookout for a marker scratched on the walls or floor, a tiny diamond left by the Rainmakers to tag their emergency escape route. As far as he knew, nobody had used this exit in decades. The Rainmakers used their considerable influence to infiltrate the pilot corps, preferring to smuggle their goods in under Polk's nose. He'd heard from Teller that this route ran westward from the north blue industrial zone. She herself had not used it in nearly a hundred years and two incarnations earlier.

"You have to rest," Cola said, but Jonas shook her off.

"I think we should slow down a sec and let you catch your breath."

"No, Mere, not until we see the markers."

Jonas leaned on the shoulders of his friends and barked out an occasional command whenever the tunnel forked. He had a good sense of direction. Always had. He kept them moving westward and down. The temperature had cooled considerably over the last stretch and the air felt stale. He wheezed and stumbled, unable to support his weight any longer. They'd reached a tiny alcove with three separate branches all running westward and the decision was too much for him to bear.

"Let me down," Jonas said and Mere lowered him gently onto a tiny outcrop of rocks. "Just need a sec," he said between gasps and coughs. Cola slid in next to him while Mere trailed ahead and began examining each of the three forks.

"You OJ?"

"I'm finished. You and Mere should go on."

"Here it is. A diamond, just like you said," Mere called out, his voice echoing loudly into the chamber, perhaps a bit too loudly considering there were hundreds of policemen on their tail.

"You hear that, we're going to make it," Cola said.

Jonas closed his eyes and said nothing, fighting against the unbearable pressure in his chest, fighting just to breathe.

Jagged crevices and water-shorn rocks enclosed the three-some. Jonas imagined them inside the toothless maw of a feeble, yet famished monster. The musician felt something slipping away but couldn't put it into words. He heard the distant trickle of an underground stream and fretted about the passage of time.

Mere and Cola had to lean in close in order to hear him whisper, "Teller told me that there's a pool of crisping not far from here in a huge storage vat. At the bottom of the cistern is a vent leading out of the city."

"Under the crisping?" Mere asked.

"Yes."

"Count me out then."

"It's the only way, Mere."

"You don't know what that jack does to me."

Jonas clutched Mere's collar and pulled him down, centimeters from his face. For some reason, he had a strong urge to bite his oldest friend on the tip of his nose. Mere could be an insufferable bastard sometimes.

"Grow up," Jonas forced through clenched teeth, ignoring the pain that he was sure signaled his demise. "The crisping's only dangerous to you when combined with electricity. I think so, at least. You have to do it, Mere, it's that simple. I'll stay behind with the gun and buy you some time."

Cola and Mere piped in with simultaneous "no's."

"I'm already dead. Can't you see that?"

"Then I'll stay with you," Cola said.

"Me too," Mere offered, although Jonas could hear the hesitation in his voice.

"Cola, I really wish you wouldn't."

"Just try and stop me. As far as my life goes it's mine to give as

I see fit and it really didn't amount to a whole lot until you came into it."

Mere backed away from the couple and leaned against a porous rock formation, his brow furrowed, his eyes sweeping the three untried passages.

"Cola, you shouldn't do this. This isn't your cause."

Jonas fumbled for the pistol in his jumpsuit pocket and pressed the barrel to his head, but Cola lowered his hand, saying, "Don't begrudge me even one second with you."

The baying of chimpanzadogs or some other canine trackers echoed faintly from the corridor they'd taken. Mere bounded up to them, his eyes panic stricken. "Come on, Jonas, I'll carry you."

Jonas nodded weakly. "If you don't leave right now, Mere, everything will have been for nothing. My death. Gail's." He coughed and barked, "Go! Now!"

"Get out of here, Mere," Cola commanded in a tone that Jonas imagined she might have used on their children if things had turned out differently.

"I love you both. I'm sorry," Mere said before darting away. He gripped the flashbeam like a weapon and plunged westward. Mere's shadow hung in the center fork for a moment, then Jonas found himself left alone with Cola in the dim yellow haze radiating from the cavern walls.

The barks and yelps grew slowly louder, intermingled with the encouraging cries of men.

"You know what they'll do if they capture you?"

"Yes, if they capture either of us," Cola said, cradling Jonas's head in her lap.

She gently pried the flagette pistol from his numb fingers and Jonas knew that she would kill them both before allowing them to be taken alive. Listening to the voices of the trackers sometimes get closer, at others recede, he found himself wishing that they would not be found. A vain hope. The labyrinths beneath the city, although vast, would not confuse their pursuers forever. Like life, these corridors too were finite.

Cola did not cheapen their final moments together with clumsy words of eternal devotion nor did she make small talk to ease the tension. She stared at him intently and her eyes said everything, that she loved him and was at peace with herself. He knew that he should try to be just as brave, but could not let go of his regrets, the most painful of which was the sacrifice Cola was making for Mere...for him.

"Let it go," she said. "We'll enter the next life together."

If there is one, Jonas thought, then realized how idiotic it was to be worrying at a time like this. He did not wish to meet his maker—if one existed—with so little courage. Jonas pushed aside his guilt and feelings of obligation, and let himself become as calm as the woman at his side, cherishing her smile and the touch of her palm caressing his forehead.

***

Mere rushed headlong through the twisting corridors and almost tripped several times on loose stones that had tumbled from the walls and ceiling. The tunnels were becoming narrower as the trail of diamonds took him deeper below ground. The air became substantially thinner and he could feel the walls closing in. Two shots rang out in the distance and he knew what they signified, the end of his friends. The death toll surrounding him was staggering. So many of the people he'd cared for had been sacrificed to Polk's contest and to his own survival.

Unworthy. He was unworthy. He took a corner too fast and clipped his forehead on a low-hanging archway. His eyes stung from the impact, blurring his vision. He forged ahead as fast as his legs could carry him, plunging recklessly through new forks, losing track of the markers. He could not keep the faces of Jonas and Cola out of his thoughts. The white shirt he'd slain and the bereaving family he imagined that the officer had left behind. Then there were the pieces of himself he'd lost—Polk's hapless clones which he'd dispatched without pity or remorse. He did not know how he would be able to live with himself any longer and found that he could not. Mere stumbled in exhaustion and threw himself onto a thin layer of silt covering the ground. He rolled onto his back and curled into a fetal ball for the deaths he would never be able to justify or avenge, even if he thwarted his baser instincts and brought Polk's reign of terror to an end.

***

When Mere came to his senses, he was standing in a subterranean cavern surrounded by dozens of the ghoulish Graylings. He
looked around anxiously and could find no entrance to the cave,
no means by which he could have possibly gotten here. A third of
the cavern inclined sharply and formed an immense oval depression brimming over with crisping. Fleshy stalactites spiked the ceiling above the rank-smelling pond and drops of dark fluid formed
on the ends of the low-hanging formations. They looked just like
teats. Mere's ears itched from the echo of crisping plopping into
the vat. He was shivering for some reason, although he had ceased
to be cold.

"They will not be able to find you here," the collective voice
of the amassed Graylings exploded in Mere's head. "You are under
our protection."

The lithe charcoal forms bobbed around him like jackmoths
drawn to neon. He could feel the displaced air brushing the hair
on his forearms, but the fluttering Graylings managed not to touch
him as they circled him.

"Tired, too tired," Mere said, weakened by grief and the outburst of tears he'd held in for months.

"We're here to help."

The Graylings, each in turn, altered the pattern of their movements and paused in front of him, running their fingers over his
scalp before making way for the next of their brethren. At first,
Mere could feel his emotions intensify from the contact and balloon into a fierce and overwhelming sorrow. He stared blankly into
the pool of crisping and became mesmerized by the concentric
rings formed by the droplets from the ceiling. He felt the pain
pouring from his chest like water squeezed from a rock. Then his
resolve returned and began to harden. Polk was to blame for Jonas's and the others' deaths as much or more than he was. Not to
mention the centuries of victims the president had eradicated and
dumped into the organiputer, increasing his power like a vampire
in fables of old.

Polk was not a man who would ever break down and cry for
the atrocities he committed, if, indeed, he had any feelings left in
that time-bitten soul of his. Hatred would do Mere no good against
such an enemy. He would have to be just as cold and calculating,

tapping a shadowy reserve in himself that would help him think in terms of power, domination, and winning at any cost.

He peered into the vat of crisping and could almost swear he saw his own reflection trapped deep within the pool. The final Grayling smoothed Mere's hair back over his bruised forehead and slid sideways, blocking his view of the dark liquid. Mere blinked the final tears from his eyes and stared into the emotionless gaze of the creature before him. The gray man moved his lips and spoke the first and last words he would ever hear from a Grayling, "Just as you created us, please destroy us. Show us mercy."

"Mercy," said the others in unison.

"What do you want from me?"

"All will be made clear in time."

Mere felt like any promise he would make the ancient creatures would only demean them. He shook his head solemnly and approached the beveled lip of the holding tank. He considered stripping his jacket and boots, but had no idea what would be waiting for him on the other side. Without a moment's hesitation or looking back toward the Graylings, he took a deep breath and dove into the muddy pool.

* * *

Mere knifed his way upward through the dark-colored muck and broke the surface, coughing and gasping for air. His arms windmilled and he fought to keep his head above the sluice of brown fluid encircling the city walls. As he choked and splashed his way toward the mud-coated base of the terra cliffwall, he tried to remember what he'd read about swimming. Something about not panicking. He lifted his head above the surface, took a breath, and kicked his legs frantically. His progress was slow and he could not help from swallowing crisping fluid, but luckily the moat was not that wide. Between strokes, he stretched his left arm toward the shore, willing himself forward. Finally, his fingers laced into soil and he pulled himself up onto a muddy bank. He wheezed and spat out a combination of crisping and rainwater, shivering from the cool autumn wind.

Outside...he was outside the city. There was not much to see, actually. The cliff intersected the west wall of the city at about a sixty degree angle and dropped past the intersection of the north wall several hundred meters further on. In fact, the steep incline continued below the other side of the city as well, far into the horizon. It was as though the entire surface of the earth was nothing but an unending cliff. Collings, by all accounts, should be at the base of the precipice. His eyes were not deceiving him, however. Somehow the city was fastened, on an angle, to the side of the terra cliffwall.

He wondered if it might not be easier to traverse the moat to the north edge of the city and climb down the cliff instead of scaling what seemed an insurmountable obstacle. Climbing down was harder than up, he imagined. Besides, he had no desire to try his hand at swimming again. His skin was sticky and he could not get the bitter taste of crisping out of his mouth.

Why would the Rainmakers' passage from the city be located here unless it was close to some village or mountain outpost? Steeling his nerves, he decided to scale the cliff while it was still light out and he could make out handholds and possible pitfalls. He scrambled up the slope and clamped his fingers onto a narrow shelf of grass, only it was growing in the wrong direction, to the side.

Using the tufts of vegetation to help him gain a purchase, he made steady progress up the incline. Luckily, unlike the name suggested, the terra cliffwall did not run vertically, and even the steeper stretches he could see ahead of time and find a way to maneuver around them. Still, he rapidly grew tired. By the time he reached another shelf about a third of the way up the city wall, his legs and arms were exhausted and already the moat of crisping below seemed like a fatal drop. His vertigo kicked in and he felt incredibly dizzy. From then on, he decided, he would only look up.

He lay on his back for a few minutes, admiring the tone and timbre of the unusually clear sky, and picked the route of his next ascent. Scanning the incline above, he thought he saw what appeared to be a ladder running up the side of the cliff, slightly to his right and about a hundred meters further up. He clambered to his feet and picked his way toward the unlikely apparition: thin parallel lines intersected by slats. The angle of his climb made it impossible to identify the object until he cleared a ridge almost on top of it.

It was a ladder, he surmised, although unusually wide with

rungs almost too far apart to be of much help in his climb. The sides of the ladder were metal, a primitive iron compound fastened to the hillside by thick wooden beams buried into rock and loose gravel that stuck to the hillside at an impossible angle. He kept close to one side and used the metal rail to help him scale. His progress soon doubled and he imagined the city wall behind him melting away.

Reach above, grab the rail, step up, and pull your weight onto a rung, then start the process over again. Inhale before stepping and exhale when you pause to rest. Mere lost himself in the rhythm of his climb. The landscape varied little, but it did vary. An occasional shrub and bed of wild flowers kept him from getting too bored, although he was disconcerted that all the plants grew sideways, perpendicular to the city behind him. He put all his ebbing energy into his efforts. The sun was swinging close to the top of the cliff and he imagined that, by now, he must be at or above the level of the ozonodomes that poked their mushroom heads above the city wall like mad sentries. He could almost feel Polk staring at him smugly from his penthouse even while aiming a weapon at him that would bring him crashing to a fiery death.

This paranoia made him scale more quickly, in a sprint, but it was a sprint without an end. The cliff stretched below and above as far as the eye could see. The late afternoon wind tore through him and he had long since lost feeling in his fingers. His legs were shaking from cold and exhaustion. He reached the limits of his endurance several times and pressed beyond them.

He caught himself from slipping by the tiniest fraction of luck and blunted reflexes, and knew that he would kill himself if he continued to climb. He tapped into a final reserve of energy and managed to keep scaling until he reached a slight relief in the incline where he could stop and rest in relative safety. Dusk was starting to settle over the precipice as he leaned into the ladder and prayed that his drained body would not slide off his purchase when he fell asleep.

He heard the rumble of an engine and a vibration thrummed through the metal railing by his ear. Hoverpod, Mere thought. Polk had seen him on his perch and had dispatched a pilot and crew to finish him off. He was helpless. Nowhere to run. He could not find it in himself to turn and watch his doom approach. Instead, he stared up into a bank of clouds bleeding sunset and waited, patiently, for night to fall.

Something else fell instead. A large metal projectile was hurtling down the cliffwall straight toward him. A missile of some sort? It was hard to tell. It appeared to be plummeting too slowly to be in free fall and hugged the cliff too closely to be a hovercraft. The small dot grew into a rectangle, but it wasn't until twin beams snapped on in front of the approaching object that Mere recognized what it was. A car or jeep of some kind, only it was driving down the cliff.

Mere dug his forearms into the thick wooden rung, holding on as best he could, hoping he would not be flattened. The headlights were blinding, but Mere could see the heads and shoulders of two shadowy silhouettes above the windshield. The vehicle skidded sideways and braked to a stop just to his right, glued to the side of the steep slope. A woman unbuckled herself and got out of the passenger seat. She stepped toward him cautiously, perpendicular to the cliff. Impossible. It must be a trick of the sun or a hallucination from the crisping in his system. He was more out of it than he thought or perhaps this was what an angel looked like close up. The wide sweep of the headlights illuminated one side of her body. She had a beautiful face, one he'd seen before.

"You OK, friend?" the woman asked. Her thick, guttural accent was like nothing Mere had ever heard.

"....careful," a man's voice called out above the roar of the engine.

Then Mere recognized her. It was the Virgin Mary, the statue of his dreams come to life, her smile set beneath brown eyes and the wind-blown bangs of her raven hair.

"You're beautiful," he said.

His dream woman knelt and reached a hand toward his brow. Her fingers touched his forehead and Mere felt a jolt of electricity course through him. The venom of crisping boiled up through his blood and paralyzed his body. He tried to hold on to the ladder, consciousness, reality, but his vision blurred. The woman's face splintered into a thousand miniatures that, one by one, bored deep into his skull. Every bodily fluid exploded at once, flooding the pits and ravines of the grieving earth. Mere feared his heart had burst. He lost himself in the eddies of his memories so fast and deep that he wondered how he could possibly keep from drowning.

Mere floundered in a whirlpool of crisping and blood, his mind boiling, his spirit unmoored from his body. He found himself propelled by shock-white rapids toward a cave whose entrance was spiked with the heads and torsos of men who, like boulders, threatened to capsize anyone passing through the treacherous channel. Despite flailing his arms in the icy foam to skirt the brooding men, he found himself tossed into the first and tallest obstacle, the muscular body of George Polk. Mere felt dizzy and disoriented, fighting to keep himself from drowning in the president's thoughts. A losing battle. He was flotsam in a current too fierce and cold to resist.

Mere sank into the rippling visage of Polk and lost himself in the sights, smells, and sensations of the man from whom he was cloned. He found himself atop the largest ozonodome in Collings, standing on the balcony of a private office just off his penthouse. He had sent his staff away hours before and was contemplating mortality for the first time in centuries. It was an unusually clear night and he leaned out over the railing to look over the mammoth city he'd created, all the while thinking of Teller—the woman he hated, the woman he loved—and the conflicting emotions raging inside him. Buffeted by contradictions, Mere reeled from vertigo inside his borrowed body. He strained to keep himself from being pulled into the depths, but could not keep himself from falling back in time to other bodies, other memories.

Foamy hands cradled him, raising him from the depths. Mere was whisked above the waves and tossed into the rocky facades of other Polk clones: David, Karl, Peter. He tumbled from incarnation to incarnation, bombarded by random thoughts, triumphs, and regrets. These personalities, while distinct, were but shades of men, their actions and personalities ruled by a hidden force, the mad scientist lurking within them who'd destroyed the world and emerged from the ashes a tyrant, a king.

Mere struggled to keep his head above water. He swirled past the final row of chiseled clones moored at the mouth of the cave and entered the dreamworld he'd denied for so long, a sorrow-filled life in a former age. Images of clones and broken men melted away like ice in blood and Mere found himself inhabiting the body of the original Polk, a troubled scientist haunted by demons, a man who had not yet dreamed of becoming a god.

His name was Andrew and he lived in a small two-bedroom house he'd recently rented in Mantou on the outskirts of Colorado Springs. He worked downtown in a mammoth complex of converted warehouses that were once a brewery, but now served as international headquarters for Live Wire, a high-tech firm funded by billionaire businessman Nicholas Sanders. Long derided by financial gurus and the media for sinking a fortune into organic computer technology, the company was poised on the verge of breakthroughs, major ones that would forever change the interaction between men and machines.

Much of the company's successes had been spearheaded by Andrew's supervisor Mona Teller, a brilliant scientist and a visionary thinker. She was also a talented mentor who knew how to get the most out of the people around her. Admiring Andrew's tenacity and ability to see the big picture, she was instrumental in promoting him onto her team over more qualified and accredited scientists. There was only one problem. Actually, two. Andrew had fallen in love with Mona, a black woman five years his senior. His passion for her went against his convictions. It wasn't just that he thought workplace romances were a doomed proposition. His turmoil went deeper, to the core of his being. He hated anyone who wasn't white and was certain that this feeling was mutual.

Tensions among races escalated, sometime wrapped in religion, other times from mistrust of people from other cultures. Although Andrew had grown up in a small town in central Washington where the only minorities he saw were the migrant workers who harvested the apple orchards, he didn't think he was any more bigoted than anyone else. Not really. He'd developed his hatred for people of color from years of city living. First in Seattle when he was putting himself through school at the University of

Washington and later in New York and Boston, where he did his graduate studies at MIT. Continually broke and working a variety of odd jobs to pay for his expensive education, he found himself in neighborhoods where the rent was cheap and he was invariably a minority.

He didn't have one of those horrible urban stories where he was beaten up or shot, although he was mugged twice in New York. He did, however, feel intimidated and harassed by the gang in his neighborhood. Once or twice he even tried to make friends with his neighbors, but it never panned out. He always felt put down, despised, the endless butt of jokes. After a time, he came to the realization that whites and blacks were enemies regardless of the actions of those on either side who tried to ease the tension. The hell with having to justify himself or apologize for the actions of his forefathers.

What was wrong with him? His desire for Mona was almost enough to make him want to kill himself. Because of his guilt, he found himself sharing his opinions about how races shouldn't mix and lost several friends because of it. He was a loner by nature anyway, but found himself more and more distanced from his family and the few acquaintances who put up with his anger.

He filled this void by getting involved in an organization of white supremacists called Blitzkrieg. At first, he logged on to their on-line conference and used it in an attempt to free himself of his attachment to Mona. If anything, it made things worse. He became a staple of the Blitzkrieg community and a supporter for their beliefs while his lovesickness only grew more intense.

Andrew was especially passionate about an idea that was at the heart of Blitzkrieg: the inevitability of a race war. Whites versus all non-whites. "The battle lines are drawn," he would find himself typing in the wee hours of the morning. "Forearmed is forewarned." Still, he was surprised several months later when he answered a knock on his front door and was met by the Blitzkrieg inner circle.

What amazed him most was that they weren't a bunch of crackpots as he'd feared ever since he discovered how obsessed the group was with women's breast sizes. In fact, the six men at his door were all older than he was: businessmen, middle-aged, and well-connected. Also, they had major cash to throw around.

On their first visit they slipped Andrew enough money to pay off his student loans and let him know that they could be generous to their friends and even more dangerous to their enemies. Andrew accepted the money and tried not to think too much about it.

Thinking back, he was a fool to put himself in the debt of a group of strangers, especially ones who were inclined to view the world in terms of good and evil, black and white. On their next surprise visit the Blitzkriegers initiated Andrew into their inner circle. The candles from the ceremony weren't even cold before their North American General Jeffrey told him that they were counting on him to make his scientific research at Live Wire of benefit to their cause. Andrew said something vague and positive sounding, trying to buy himself time and hoping he hadn't gotten in over his head. Fearing repercussions, he kept Jeffrey's suggestion in the forefront of his mind over the next few months at work.

Even Mona noticed how distant and preoccupied he'd become. Andrew shrugged off her concerns, trying to remain stoic and aloof. Besides, his work team soon had more important things on their minds when they made a breakthrough on their organiputer project. As is often the case in science, it wasn't one that he, Mona or anyone else on the team had been expecting. They met their project goals nearly a year ahead of schedule, but practically everyone was blind to the long-term implications of what they'd created.

He and Mona commiserated because they were the only ones who saw the full and frightening potential of their work. Parallel processing was the key to their new organic computer, unlike the linear approach used in even the fastest supercomputers of the day. They'd found a way to build a variety of "smart" cells that approximated the brain's own reasoning capacity. It had never seemed like a cost-effective way to build a computer as the creation of each cell was costly in terms of time and manpower.

Their breakthrough changed all that. They'd succeeded in creating a self-integrated organic system that could actually clone its own cells: a computer that could build itself. The implications went well beyond the mass production of superbrains envisioned by Nicholas Sanders and the other Live Wire board members. They could, potentially, replicate anything they introduced into the organic matrix. Andrew and Mona both saw how the abilities of their machine could revolutionize industry. Gold, gems, petrol, even uranium could be mass-produced by gigantic, city-sized incarnations of their creation. They kept their insights to themselves for awhile, however, as a frightening hypothesis formed between them—the potential to clone human beings.

Andrew and Mona began spending long hours together after work discussing their hopes and fears for the new technology and whether they were morally obligated to sabotage the project if they thought their work might be used as a weapon of war. They theorized how a perfect and endless supply of fighting men could be engineered, an idea that Andrew found both frightening and alluring. During one of these heated discussions, the event that Andrew had been dreading for so long actually occurred. Mona kissed him and he responded, leading to the most passionate sex of his life, the first he'd had in years.

After the initial glow died down, he realized that he would not be able to live with himself if he continued leading a double life. He knew that he would have to make a bold and irrevocable decision, one from which there would be no returning for himself or the world.

It was a miracle. The stranger had to be strapped to the jeep and later to the bed in the village infirmary to keep from sliding toward the walled city. Marin had grown up listening to ghost stories about the nearby metropolis that leaned westward like an overripe stalk of corn begging to be scythed. The city was alive much like a hive of bees, the village elders would say, bloated by the unimaginable bulk of a computer queen who feasted on the cells of the people born and fated to die within those forbidding walls. Marin never knew what to think about the legends and rumors. Even the ones that didn't contradict known facts were too fantastical for her taste. Now they had tangible scientific proof. One of the worker drones had escaped captivity and they would soon be able to hear the truth from the man's own lips.

Marin almost forgot to slip on her sandals in her rush to see the unconscious man as he tossed and turned in a fever that none of their healers could identify or treat. Her parents admonished her for leaving her breakfast half-finished and neglecting her studies, but she wouldn't be worthy of her princess reputation if she couldn't get her way when she wanted it. Besides, they weren't really her parents. The entire village was responsible for raising her, although she'd lived with Gary and Cheney ever since she'd graduated from the schoolhouse to their private tutoring of math, history, and hard sciences.

She was, after all, 'the chosen.' A title that had confused her ever since she was old enough to ask, "Chosen for what?" Subsequent years had done little to help her untangle the mystery aside from the promise made to her by the ruling elder Kalamazoo who told her that everything would be made clear before she left the village to embrace her destiny. Again, the obvious question was, "Leave for where?" but Kal wasn't about to give in and tell her what she wanted to know. He was one of the few adults in the village who stood up to her tantrums and she loved him all the more because of it. Still, the vagaries of her so-called destiny bothered her. She feared that she would end up like one of those idiotic virgins from bygone days sacrificed to a volcano God. That or some worse fate. Why else would everyone be so damn nice to her all the time?

Questions for another day. A much more interesting puzzle awaited her at the infirmary if only she could convince Charlotte and Missoula that the stranger's malady wasn't contagious. She picked her path carefully to the south side of town, making sure to avoid areas where she might be asked to pitch in and help. Harvest was pretty much over, but that didn't mean that there wasn't still plenty of work to do before winter. She'd spent most of the previous week at the dining hall mashing indigo corn into flour—one of the most tedious of all communal chores—which is why she figured Kal had caved in and consented to let her go on border patrol the day they found the stranger. That or the fact she was driving everyone at the kitchen around the bend.

It wasn't her fault that she wasn't suited for menial work. Her mind moved too quickly, like her body. She stopped in her tracks when she heard footsteps on the path ahead and circled to the backside of the nursery. Augustine, who ran the day care center, wasn't a bad sort, but was in the habit of asking her to watch the kids while she ran errands. Normally she wouldn't have minded, but not today. Marin hurried through the backyard past scattered children's toys and outside swings. She spotted her destination across the lawn and had to fight the urge to sprint to the entrance of the two-room infirmary.

Charlotte, as though sensing her arrival, stepped out from the empty waiting room onto the front steps. "And where do we think we're going?"

Marin wrinkled her nose. "We're not going anywhere. I'm going inside," she said with false bravado.

"I'd like to see you try," said the younger and more serious of the two female physicians who were rumored to be lovers.

Marin swallowed hard and lifted a foot. Charlotte's threatening look stopped her mid-step.

"What's going on out there?" Missoula hollered out the door.

"You're about to have another patient," Charlotte said, narrowing her eyes to slits, her lithe body tensed to pounce on Marin if she made another move.

"What?"

"Nothing," Marin called out. "It's just me, your neighborhood do-gooder, seeing if I can be of any help to the stranger."

She heard the waiting room door open and close, followed by wooden shoes clacking across the adobe floor. Marin put her foot down and smiled at Charlotte, trying to look as harmless as possible.

"Another patient?" Missoula asked, rushing over to Marin and placing a hand up to her forehead. "Offering to help? You must be sick."

The doctors both laughed, although Marin thought Charlotte put too much effort and energy into her cackles.

"You know, that really hurts," Marin said, pouting. If she puckered her face long enough she was sure she could actually begin to feel hurt, but then her exuberance got the better of her. "Has he woken?"

"In a way. He's conscious most of the time, but he hasn't said anything coherent yet," Missoula said, looking over at Charlotte before adding, "It does look like his fever's mostly gone."

"Then can I go in and see him? Please?"

Marin beamed at the two spinsters and watched the disapproval on Charlotte's face slowly melt away.

"All right, but only for a little while and if Missoula's in the room with you."

Marin hugged Charlotte and was on Missoula's heels all the way to the examination room. She knew that her exuberance would be seen as immaturity, but felt that it was important for her to speak with the stranger. Ever since she'd rescued him she had become more and more certain that he had something to do with her role as "the chosen." It was like she'd known him all her life and that they were meant to be together. Her irrational attachment to him scared her. Normally, she wasn't someone who succumbed to intuition or infatuation.

Missoula pushed the door ajar and gestured toward an empty chair next to the patient. At first, Marin thought he was asleep until the healer rolled back a corner of the sheet from his face. The patient's eyes blinked and he looked around the room with clouded eyes, mumbling to himself. His head—practically the only thing not in heavy restraints—rolled from side to side.

"We're starting to think he's having some sort of chemically based hallucinatory experience."

"Like a vision quest?"

Missoula's eyebrows arched toward her wrinkled brow. "I'm not sure city dwellers believe in that sort of thing."

"How can you judge a person or a group of people you've never met?"

"I know you may be a little young to appreciate this, but often when something sounds like a snake and looks like a snake...it really is a snake."

"We should give him every benefit of the doubt."

"And we will. Although, to be honest, I'm glad he's in restraints."

"Missoula, that's a horrible thing to say."

"Horrible," the stranger repeated, looking cross-eyed at Missoula as though he was looking right through her. His eyes swept the room, settling on Marin. "You," he said as though in recognition. "I've been looking for you. I'm sorry, Mona, for taking your project away from you. I'm sorry about everything."

It was then that Marin noticed the man's curly black hair standing on end, the follicles straining to return to the city from which he'd fled.

"But being sorry isn't enough," he said. "We're going to have to make things right...the two of us together."

"Yes, I'll help you," Marin said, rising and bending down over the stranger.

She could hear Missoula shuffling toward her. "Listen, he's delusional," the doctor advised.

"Then you'll forgive me?" he asked.

"No, she will not," Missoula said. "Marin, I think it's time for you to leave.

"But you don't understand, this has something to do with me. I knew it from the moment I found him."

"Charlotte," Missoula yelled, "Come in here."

"No need. I'll leave...for now." Marin directed these final words to the stranger whose muttering made more sense to her than the mundane concerns of her life in the village. She knew then that she would uncover the shroud of mystery surrounding the man's arrival and follow him to wherever their destiny together may lie.

* * *

George Polk knew that his only remaining clone would not be able to stay in hiding for long. Aside from the rage and guilt Mere must be feeling for the death of his two friends in the catacombs, he would not have the patience to lie low. He would want revenge for starters. This incarnation had an impetuous streak as well as a temper. Of course, the wisest thing for Mere to do would be to wait it out until George died of old age. Wisdom, however, wasn't a trait that came easily to anyone carrying the original DNA of Andrew Polk.

George's hands were tied. He did not want to chance cloning another version of himself—despite what he'd told Teller—until he found a way to eliminate Roosevelt. If something were to happen to him now, at least with Mere alive there was a chance that his personality would stay dominant after his spirit transferred itself into his clone.

Loop Teller and her meddling! She'd been a thorn in his side for centuries now, always a step too fast, too cagey, until last week when he managed to capture her alive. Now he couldn't figure out why his victory was leaving such a bad taste in his mouth. He imagined her kicking and screaming his name, snared in a webbing of gray tendrils as a conduit in the organiputer. Their organiputer. Once or twice he considered contacting her, but knew that it was a torture that neither of them deserved. He'd made his choices and would stick to them. Love did not exist, after all. There was only love of self, something humankind had proved him right about during the war. In the end, the worst atrocities had not been committed by him. At least he could find solace in that.

"No sign of him," Lina whispered in George's ear, almost making him jump out of his skin. She'd snuck into his private office and Usa only knew how long she'd been standing behind him, watching. He whirled and bared his teeth.

"Don't look at me that way, George. You've spent too much time cooped up in here lately. Your staff is starting to worry."

George rolled his eyes and sighed. Lina was looking out for his interests, as usual. She was the perfect administrator and advisor for someone as temperamental as himself.

"You're right, of course. I'll be out shortly to take charge of the search myself."

Lina beamed her approval and rubbed his shoulders with her soft academic's hands. "That's the George I know and love."

"Any leads?"

"Aside from the two bodies we found in the tunnels below the north industrial zone, we haven't found a trace of him. No tracks. No scent."

"What about the albino driver?"

Lina grimaced. "My team has told me that it's a dead-end to question him. His thinking's too erratic. We downloaded his memories into an organiport and verified that Roosevelt entered the catacombs at the meat vat with his two friends."

George mulled over the news and came to the same realization as Lina who muttered, "I think your pets helped him to escape."

"They're not my pets," George snapped.

"If they're not, then why do you allow them to live? They're subversive and openly hostile to your policies."

"I suppose you'd recommend killing them."

"Isn't that what you do to your enemies?" she asked, then, with a warm lilt of admiration, added, "It isn't like you to show mercy."

"Trust me, Lina, I'm not showing the Graylings any mercy. Just the opposite. Their lives are an exquisite brand of torture."

"You know best."

Lina stopped kneading his shoulders and drew herself up to her full, regal height. She turned on her heels and slipped from the room as swiftly and silently as she had arrived.

More perturbed than angry, George wiggled his bare toes in the thick brown shag before rising from his seat. He crossed his den and bolted the ghost on his office door. He hated it when Lina called him on his shortcomings. Contrary to what he claimed, he'd given freedom to the Graylings—those deadly instruments of war—out of the guilt and sorrow he felt for what he'd done to them and through them the world.

Although he'd never openly admit it, he hoped that the Graylings would be able to find absolution for their crimes, something he was incapable of ever seeking or receiving. If he could not make amends to Teller, the woman he owed it to most, he was beyond redemption. He thought back to those days after he'd stolen the organiputer from Mona and relocated to an abandoned warehouse in Colorado Springs with the help of Blitzkrieg. He'd convinced them of his unparalleled knowledge in genetic engineering and used the rapidly growing intellect of the organic computer to help him test his theories—first on animal subjects, later on the DNA of humans.

The organiputer soon surpassed all human knowledge in several fields and it became a relatively simple process to create and program the Graylings. While the Blitzkriegers used their connections and influence to ship out the cloned soldiers to their clients, George remembered how alone and empty he'd felt. He spent a lot of time fixating on what he could do to alleviate his misery. On their last evening together, he'd injected Mona with a knockout drug and stolen samples of her skin and blood. What would it be like to clone an actual human instead of building soulless creatures from scratch? He fantasized about how great it would feel to spend his life with Mona, only this time with her skin bleached to an angelic shade of white.

* * *

G had been putting this moment off for days. He'd moved much of the equipment from his safe areas scattered throughout the underground to a cavern below the religious neighborhood of Jazz. He figured the heavy patrols and troops snooping around to the north must have something to do with Mere. Florida's husband was no longer his problem, if indeed he ever was. He could care less about Mere's troubles with Polk or even his own childish desire for revenge. Before he met Florida, he'd lived an empty existence. Polk had stolen away his humanity and she had helped him to restore it. He'd lived far too long in the shadows of death and killing, and would do everything in his power to bring his lover back to life.

"*She's dead,*" the organiputer had told him when he first informed her of his plans.

"Clone her a new body. We might still be able to save her mind, her memories."

"That's crazy. Besides, you know it isn't right."

As if he needed a lesson in sanity or morality from a flawed and erratic machine. In the end, G had used every trick of persuasion and guilt he could muster until he convinced the organiputer to follow his wishes. "Mother," he'd called her. "My only friend."

Now it was time to see how his plan had worked.

He lowered himself down a tiny shaft leading to a direct link with Collings where he had been monitoring the progress of Florida's newly formed body. It was a tricky situation. He wanted her to progress past puberty, but realized that there was a danger of her losing what little memory she retained to the organiputer. After several restless days of watching and waiting, he was ready to bring her back into the world in the body of an eighteen-year-old woman.

He reached the bottom of the shaft and sat cross-legged on the squishy membrane of Collings' outer layer. He'd removed his clothes before his descent to minimize the possibility of infecting his former lover. He thrust his elbows into the brown fluid seeping from the gray mass and attempted to make contact with the organiputer.

Although he'd chosen a down time in the system—the beginning of Indigo shift—it still took him hours and a good deal of concentration before he got Collings' attention. It took him even longer to break through her gibberish and remind her of the clone she was carrying inside of her. G was nearing exhaustion by the time Collings started giving birth. The extraction was not easy. He had to continually channel his thoughts to keep her focused on the task at hand and to soothe her nerves. The organiputer kept fearing what Polk would do to her if he ever found out that she'd cloned a human without his permission.

G was considering calling the extraction off when a head and shoulders pushed through the artificial womb. Florida was certainly no bawling child. As soon as she got one arm clear, she began pulling herself up out of the tight gray tunnel, clawing and rending at the fleshy floor. Her hair and body was slick from crisping fluid, easing her passage. G bent down and slipped his hands beneath her shoulders, pulling her torso and hips through the opening.

G felt the words, *"I'm a mom,"* bubble up through the sticky floor, but he had no thoughts for anyone but Florida. He eased her onto her back and wiped the viscous fluid from her mouth and eyes. He felt a strong sensation course through his lover's body, an angry and confused current similar to the one he'd felt emanating from Collings just before the last time she lost control and made the city shake.

Florida slapped his hands away from her face and crawled backwards until she bumped into the wall beneath the shaft to his cavern.

"Who the jack are you?" she asked, glancing from side to side for an avenue of escape.

"I'm your...friend," he replied and, in that moment, their relationship was defined.

She flashed him a smile that hinted of mischief and said, "Good, I'm hungry."

She held out a hand. Wordlessly, he pulled her to her feet and slipped her arms over his back, lifting her onto his left shoulder. He staggered and almost fell because of the warmth coursing through him. He fought against his shaking knees and quivering stomach, and purchased a handhold on the rocky incline above. He hauled her up the shaft toward his new home...and he hoped their new home.

PLUM

28

It took more than a week, but Marin got permission to take the stranger...Mere...for a picnic. She'd pestered her step-mom Cheney to convince the healers that some fresh air would do their patient's recovery some good. Meanwhile, she'd badgered Gary to convert one of the run-down tractors by the mill into a wheelchair heavy enough to keep Mere from sliding back to the walled city. The physicians agreed to the outing with a little grumbling, but it took Marin several days to convince her step-dad to help her build the device.

The roller chair was a success...more or less. It took Mere a lot of effort to move himself in the contraption—even with her help—and almost an hour for them to reach the sparse woods north of the village. Now that they were outside, Marin didn't know what to say or do. Mere had been withdrawn and moody since he snapped out of his stupor. They sat across from one another, silently, in a small field spackled with yellow grass and autumn leaves. The only hint of summer that remained was the wrinkled plums bending the boughs of a small grove of trees to the west. Just a few months ago they would have found blooming wild flowers and ripe blueberries in the glade, but Mere seemed content to stare at the clouds sweeping past the mid-afternoon sun.

"The food makes me feel sick," was all she got out of him for quite some time. "Most of what we ate in Collings was grown by the city."

Marin stopped eating to make him feel more at ease. Cheney had teased her about how much time she'd spent in the kitchen the day before and if she'd known where the cooking utensils were.

"I'm sorry, I must not be very good company," he said.

"Hardly. I was thinking the same about myself. You must be tired of me hanging around you so much."

"No," he said, rolling his chair over the parched field grass and next to the blanket she'd put down for their picnic. He reached down and held her hand. "If it wasn't for you, I'd be going nuts in this place."

"Thanks. I was wondering if you thought...."

"Thought what?"

"Forget it," she said, knowing that if she continued her line of thought that she would only end up sounding pathetic.

Mere stared up again at the slightly overcast sky. An occasional brown or orange leaf fluttered down from mostly bare trees.

"Being out here has only made it easier for me to make up my mind," he said.

"About what?"

"About going back to the city."

"But you told me it was horrible there."

"It is and that needs to change."

"And you think you can change things?"

Mere sighed and brushed several leaves from his lap. "There's a chance I might be able to do something. At the very least, I doubt I'll be able to make things worse."

"I'll go with you...if you need my help."

Mere nodded slowly, staring off into the horizon. "I do need your help, although you've done so much for me already. Do you think you can get me a meeting with your leader...what's his name?"

"Kalamazoo."

"Yes, Kalamazoo. Think you can do that for me?"

"It shouldn't be a problem. I wonder why he hasn't introduced himself to you already."

"Maybe it's because he knows I'm trouble."

Mere's mood brightened momentarily. A thin smile arched his lips, his gray eyes laughing even though he was not.

"You saved me," he said. "I've dreamed about you my whole life. If there's anything I can do for you, please tell me."

Marin tried to fight the fluttering in her stomach and an urge to pour out her heart to him.

"I'll let you know," she said, pulling her hair back from her face. She'd always thought that made her look older.

***

"You're pathetic," Florida complained. "Why you choose to live down here I can't possibly imagine."

G grimaced and told her, "I'm a wanted man, just as you'll be if the authorities ever find out that you're alive."

"I can't breathe down here," she said, kicking her feet child-ishly from her brand-new lounger and flipping channels on their illegal HV hookup.

The Jazz cavern, as spacious and homey as G had tried to make it, felt claustrophobic with the clothes and luxury items he'd pil-fered to make Florida feel at home. They were both losing patience with the arrangement. G had yet to find any trace of the woman he'd once known and Florida had only his word to go on about the nature of their past relationship. She was filled with the fire and exuberance of youth...and something more. She could be mean spirited and petty when it suited her, and she took his affection for granted.

"And can't we get some real food down here instead of this packaged jack you keep pushing off on me?"

The HV wasn't doing Florida any good, G realized. The pulp she tended to watch was giving her an unreal view of male/female relationships. Not to mention the world. She could still be nice to him when she wanted something, but G feared that his capacity to give her the things she coveted was finite. He worried that as soon as he finished teaching her everything she needed to know about the city above that she wouldn't feel guilty about leaving him behind.

She would stop her ears with her fingers if he even brought up the subject of their past relationship. The pain, which he hoped would go away by bringing Florida back to life, had only become heightened, unbearable. She was a ghost of the woman he once knew. Sometimes, an expression or mannerism would remind him of her former self. Her personality, however, had changed radically from the cloning.

"I'm going up to watch the street," she said, rising and depart-ing the living area without waiting for him to respond. She slipped on a pair of shoes he'd stolen the day before from the Jungle ba-zaar and started up a tunnel leading to a grate that overlooked a residential Jazz neighborhood. She'd spent a lot of time up there

recently, ignoring him and watching the sleepy surban neighborhood. She knew that it hurt his feelings to be up there so often, but
something else was bothering him. This morning, while Florida
slept well into the early afternoon, he'd checked the bolts on the
metal cover at the top of the tunnel ladder and discovered that
they'd been taken off and put back haphazardly.

Trouble was brewing on the horizon. She'd been out in the
neighborhood at night without telling him.

***

Mere could not keep his thoughts from wandering as he waited
for Kalamazoo in the largest structure in the village, a combination
city hall and church. He was feeling guilty about how he'd acted
on his picnic with Marin. He knew that she was infatuated with
him and should keep her at arm's length, but she was his only ally
in an otherwise unfathomable world. It wasn't that he didn't have
feelings for her. Just the opposite. It was uncanny how much she
looked like the statue of the Virgin Mary from his dreams. Besides,
there was something about her that affected him. Deeply. Like the
way she stared at him with an impish grin and wore endless matching outfits of bright-green clothing. He was glad that he'd convinced her to wait outside until after he spoke with Kalamazoo.
She would have been a distraction and he needed to keep his attention focused on finding a way back into the city.

He readjusted the heavy strap around his chest and made sure
the brake was set on his wheelchair. Every day he felt the eastward
tug of gravity lessen. He wondered if it would disappear altogether
if he remained in the village. Not that he would be staying long
enough to find out. If Kalamazoo decided not to help him, he
would find a way to escape and sneak back into Collings.

There it was again. Out of the corner of his eye he saw the
apparitions who had been haunting him since he'd climbed the
cliffwall: Graylings emerging from a warehouse assembly line. This
was no time for the crisping to be dragging him out of the present
and into the cauldron of his fears and doubts. He closed his eyes
and tried to keep himself from being carried into the nightmare
that was his past and, quite possibly, his future.

He breathed in the country air and tried to place the smells from a world so much unlike the one he'd known. The scent of pine intermixed with the aroma of bread baking in the adobe oven outside the dining hall. He was in control of himself, he mumbled to himself. He continued breathing in through his nose and out through his mouth like the doctors had taught him to do as a child to keep his palsy in check.

A hinge creaked and Mere cracked his lids. A tall man entered the hall with heavy footsteps from a rough-hewn door beside the raised stage. He walked with an air of someone wearing a lot of clothes, although thick laborer's muscles bulged beneath a short-sleeved shirt and mud-splattered shorts.

"Sorry to keep you waiting," he said, sitting in one of the dozens of wooden chairs scattered throughout the hall. "I had work to do in the lab."

"Lab?"

"Yes, we have a small one," he said, his voice rising in anger. "You probably think we're a bunch of uneducated farmers."

"To be honest, everything here is so alien, I'm not sure what to think about anything."

"I'm sorry, that was rude of me. Long day."

"No offense taken."

"Kalamazoo," the man said, offering his hand.

"Mere Roosevelt."

Mere reached out and squeezed Kalamazoo's outstretched palm. The village elder loomed over him from what to Mere still seemed uphill. The edges of his vision wavered, before settling into the flickering shadows thrown by the ringlet of torches mounted on the walls.

"I'm sorry that it's taken so long for us to meet."

"Marin told me you've been busy with the end of harvest and... your lab?"

"Yes," Kalamazoo said, refusing to take Mere's bait to talk about the village's scientific facilities.

Mere figured that his research probably had something to do with fertilizers, pesticides, perhaps even plant hybrids. It didn't matter. Nothing mattered other than his plan to return and face Polk.

"Do you ever have any dealings with Collings?" Mere asked.

"Dealings?"

"Do you sell or trade anything with them?"

"No, they don't seem much interested in importing food, our main commodity. Most of their trade is with the other Usan cities. Why do you want to know?"

"I'm thinking about going back there and I was wondering if I couldn't sneak in on a transport."

"What's wrong with the way you left?"

"I'm not sure I can get back that way. It's too risky."

It was, too, more than even the harsh descent would demand of him. He didn't relish another attempt at swimming or submerging himself in crisping. He still hadn't recovered from his last encounter. Although he hadn't told the healers or Marin, he was not at all well. He was still seeing glimpses of his past life worm their way into his waking hours. These bouts were becoming less pronounced, although Mere still found the intrusion of people and events from long-ago Colorado Springs disturbing.

Kalamazoo stroked his short-cropped black beard. "We can find a way to radio the authorities in the city. It shouldn't be too hard to get someone to come out and get you."

"I really wish you wouldn't do that."

"It's just as I thought. We're harboring a fugitive from justice."

"I don't know how much you know about Collings City?"

"Enough," the elder interrupted.

"Then you must know that there's no justice to be found there."

"Maybe you're right," Kalamazoo said, "but we've survived as close as we have to the city by not making enemies of any of the Polks."

Mere's hands clutched the wheels of his chair, readying himself to bolt if the conversation continued in this vein.

"So you're going to turn me in?"

"If I decide your actions warrant it."

"Listen, you can't possibly understand how high the stakes are."

"Try me," Kalamazoo said.

Mere nodded vehemently and ran his fingers through his thick, curly hair. "Great, now I'm supposed to trust a man I don't even know."

"You have to give trust to get trust, Mere. Besides, if what you say has merit, I know some people who might be able to help smuggle you in. For the right price."

Mere felt trapped in the bulky chair. He was having a hard time gauging the intent of the man across from him. He thought about the few interactions he'd had with the locals. Aside from Marin, everyone he'd met had been wary, but ultimately fair. If the village had chosen this man to represent them, then Mere would have to assume that he held the same values.

Mere wiggled in his seat, loosening his grip on the wheels. He cleared his throat and began, "Not long ago, right around the end of summer, I was invited up to a party put on by the president of the city, George Polk...."

PURPLE

29

G plodded through a network of familiar tunnels, veering north toward the patrols, amazed that he'd yet to be discovered. He was making no effort to be quiet and chose branches that had signs and of recent activity. He wanted to be captured. He had nothing to lose and even less to live for. His arms and legs were dotted with purple bruises from where he'd pinched them in his frustration. He was a fool for believing that he could ever be a normal person with a home and wife. Florida had taken to going and coming whenever she pleased and was openly hostile to him the brief stretches she spent in the Jazz cavern. She still counted on G for an occasional meal and a place to crash when she didn't get lucky at one of the lowtown clubs and bars she frequented.

He could not believe that decades of hiding, planning, and plotting revenge had come to this. He'd been undone by love and an obsession that was tearing him apart. G could not bear to think about Florida carousing the city without him and spending sleepless nights with interchangeable men or, as he feared, selling her body for the funds she needed to move out on him. It was easier to live as a machine than it was a human being. Unfortunately, there was no returning to the stilted voyeur he'd once been. He wanted no part of a machine half-life and yet could not imagine giving his heart or trust to another person again. Let Polk capture him. It was better than waiting for Florida to finish breaking his heart. Besides, there was a chance Polk would let down his guard once G was back in the fold and he'd unseat the old tyrant yet.

"Hello, anyone down here?" G called out.

His voice rang through the tunnels, echoing into the dank corridors ahead. He stopped and listened for a response: voices, hounds, rustling, but heard nothing. This was maddening. Spit on a street corner and six policemen will appear out of nowhere to hand you a citation. Stroll out into the middle of a gigantic man-hunt screaming to be hauled off and there wasn't a white shirt to be seen. Maybe they were on a break. He paused and leaned against the slightly moist concrete wall, watching a yellowish glow stream through his fingers. He was getting tired of this charade. Maybe Florida would come around in time. He felt his resolve to do him-self in falter and considered trekking back home, but just then he heard the frantic clacking of footsteps along the right fork of the juncture ahead.

He hurried toward the patter, shouting, "Come and get me, I'm the man you're looking for. I'm not getting any younger, you know."

He veered right and accelerated, but the frantic footsteps ap-peared to be receding. He followed in an elongated sprint, panting and hoarse from his calls for surrender. He started to close the gap, hot on the trail of what sounded like a scampering horde of fleet-footed ghosts. What was making that racket? Perhaps a stream of starved rodents or a pack of once-domesticated hybrid dogs or cats. He'd seen more than his share of strange creatures haunting the tunnels over the years.

G pressed on, the thrumming of tiny feet pounding in his ears. He could no longer get his bearings. The footsteps seemed to come from the floor, the ceiling, inside his own head. He was surrounded by clicks and stomps and whirs. He plugged his ears with his fingers, but the chattering only grew louder. G dropped to his knees and tried to shout away the onslaught. A fear of the unknown assailed him and a voice inside his head was telling him to flee. The archway in front of him transformed inexplicably to stone while the wall beside him melted into a yawning chasm.

G bared his teeth and tried to focus. Someone or something was altering his senses, trying to frighten him. These hallucinations might work fine on a human, but G had resources most people couldn't comprehend. He adjusted the frequencies of light and sound he was receiving, dampening the sensory overload and slowing the avalanche of sensations to a trickle of their former strength.

The identities of the creatures he was encountering struck him just before he made out the stooped figures surrounding him in a slow, yet graceful dance. It was the Graylings. He hadn't run across them in quite some time, thirty years or more. There was little chance that this was a coincidence. The creatures must have wanted him to find them.

"Quite right," a tiny, though insistent voice registered in his head. "We've come to teach you a lesson, G. A lesson in death."

The illusions shimmered and faded. The walls pulsed with an unearthly purple gleam. The Graylings closed in on him in a ring with feral eyes and outstretched arms.

* * *

Mere was wheeled like so much useless baggage across a frozen field toward a hovercraft shimmering in the distance. It was morning, early morning, and he was shivering from the brisk air. He was unused to both the wind and the cold. The air inside the city had been warmed by the organiputer and circulated inside the steep walls that encircled all but the tallest ozonodomes in a protective ring. He would soon be returning to that stilted city, but whether it was as a riotous inmate setting prisoners free or as the new warden, only time and luck would tell. He hoped he had not made a mistake in trusting Kalamazoo, but there was no time for him to formulate another avenue of escape.

The village elder had not let Mere in on the specifics of his plan—supposedly to protect them both if something went wrong—aside from when he could expect to be picked up. Kalamazoo had come in person to free him from the clinic just before dawn to keep Charlotte and Missoula from asking questions. He also suspected it was to keep Marin from trying to tag along. Her step-father Gary had shown up at his bedside with Kalamazoo, roller chair in tow, looking none too pleased about whatever it was that the elder had asked of him.

They'd buckled Mere in, carted him outside, lifted him onto the back of a wagon, and hitched a pair of horses to the cart. Gary drove the team north past the field where Mere had picnicked with Marin while Kalamazoo lounged with him in back, talking half-heartedly about the weather: the humid summers and the severity of winters past. Mere didn't have much to say other than to ask why the village didn't have a name.

After that, Kalamazoo stroked his short beard and muttered,

"Maybe we're not really a village," before quieting and staring placidly at groves of trees interspersed with open fields.

The only sounds for the remainder of the trip were of the swirling wind, creaking floorboards, and the clopping of horses' hooves. Carried by the snorting beasts into uncharted terrain that was even more beautiful than the paintings of nature coveted by Pyramid elite, Mere could almost imagine himself freed of obligations and wandering the world for the remainder of his life. The boundless expanse of land and sky was intoxicating. The city would have to die. He knew that now. He'd tear down the walls stone by stone if necessary. Polk was not the only thing wrong with Collings. The people who lived there believed that everything, including themselves, could be controlled. An hour outside in this vast and terrible beauty would be enough to show them that the world was bigger than the people who tried to control it.

Kalamazoo leaned over and said to his partner, "We better not be late."

Marin's step-dad grumbled and urged the horses into a trot. They soon reached the end of a dirt trail where a mammoth hovercraft rested in a field of grass.

"Looks deserted," Gary said, his fingers looped around the jangling reins.

"The boys must be on the far side, I guess. Go around."

Mere was about to ask the village elder who "the boys" were. However as the cart looped around the field, he saw two gangly farm hands shoveling grain from a larger wagon into the back of the city transport.

"Sorry to do this," Kalamazoo said, reaching into a weather-worn pouch at his side. "But the people smuggling you in are nervous."

Before he could protest, the maudlin chief withdrew a cloth sack and pulled it over Mere's head. Kalamazoo tightened the thick woven material in the front and fastened it with a drawstring, blocking out all but the tiniest glimmer of light.

"The people we're dealing with are very particular," Kalamazoo continued. "They wanted cargo for taking you on-board as an alibi for stopping here. Some of my people are going to go hungry this winter because of it. I hope whatever you're going back for is worth it."

"It is," Mere said and everything became a blur. Several men exchanged coarse whispers as he was lifted off the wagon and rolled up a ramp into what he assumed was the hovercraft. Almost immediately, he felt the sideways tug of gravity lessen. Footsteps retreated and he heard the whir of a hatch ghosting shut, sealing him in. The darkness and silence were overwhelming. He hoped he hadn't been set up.

While waiting for what seemed an eternity for the engine to start up, images started to form inside his hood, the apparitions of his former life. Why bother to fight it any longer? Besides, it didn't look like he was going anywhere yet and anything was better than worrying about what he could not control and turning into a neurotic mess. He let his mind wander and allowed a sprawling room to take shape around him, the studio apartment above the warehouse where Andrew's experiments with the Graylings were taking place.

Mere was shocked by how easily he could now enter the memories of his progenitor. He wondered if Andrew Polk could sense him seeing through his eyes as he paced his cluttered apartment, unhappy with the way things were going. Aside from the skylight above the bank of upper level generators, Andrew had not seen sunlight in nearly two months. What cable channels that remained on the air charted the disturbances and uprisings sweeping Europe, the Middle East, and Asia.

The worry on everyone's minds was that America was next. The country had armed itself to the teeth while calmer heads were calling for no rash actions to be taken. A vain hope. Hundreds of Graylings had been set loose in major metropolitan areas armed with military hardware and with orders to target minority neighborhoods. These creatures had been cloned with no defects and possessed advanced strength and intelligence. Something else had triggered in these clones as well: the ability to manipulate the nature of reality. The cities were now in flames. The people there tried to protect themselves but the Graylings were ghosts. Factions developed. Anger rose against the police who did nothing. Bloodshed is an odd and terrible thing. Once the border of savagery is crossed it is difficult to ever return to the way things were. It wasn't difficult to hate others. Real bravery is learning to love those you don't know.

He'd been wrong to set these forces of war and chaos into motion. It was only a matter of time before someone used a nuke for a better and more irrevocable genocide, forcing other superpowers to follow suit. China was massing for war on all its borders. Russia was threatening armageddon. It wasn't hard to see why America was staying out of the carnage as long as possible. The graylings wiped out anyone with impurities, programmed for this mission by the white supremacists who, it ended up, hated nearly everyone.

Andrew didn't want to die alone. His only human contact over the past few months had been the low-level Blitzkriegers who arrived to pick up the latest batch of his soulless soldiers of fortune. His most recent experiment in cloning hadn't helped his loneliness much either. He jingled a small copper bell on his coffee table and his new servant rushed in. Lily white and without a single opinion to call her own, Mona's clone whisked into the living room and set down his lunch. She hovered just at his elbow, waiting for a command, but he brushed her away, and she scurried back into the kitchen.

He couldn't stand to look at her. It wasn't just the small patches of brown bleeding through her skin from an imperfection that the organic computer hadn't yet been able to fix. This Mona had no spunk or spark, nothing that set her apart from a chair or a lamp or the television. Her conversation was banal and he couldn't bring himself to sleep with her, although she was more than willing to fulfill his desires. He thought he'd be happy to have Mona humbled and at his beck and call, but it only made him sad for what he'd lost, for what the world was losing.

The news got progressively worse as the weeks passed. Biological and chemical warfare, border skirmishes. When it looked like Europe would be overrun by the sheer force of anti-white sentiment against it, France and Great Britain threatened nuclear attack. Africa was in flames. Chaos ruled American metropolises and many non-whites found themselves relocating to Mexico until things quieted down. No border was enough protection in the madness overtaking the globe. The genie of hatred had been unleashed and craved blood.

Then the news reports stopped altogether and Andrew had no idea what was happening outside his prison. The deliverymen who picked up the batches of Graylings he created couldn't provide any answers either. The world was turning into a wasteland and he was its architect. He remained in seclusion, following Jeffrey's orders, until one chilly November morning when he woke beneath his mound of blankets and discovered the cloned Mona standing above him. Something was different about her, though. A look of stark fury dominated her face, and Andrew noticed the kitchen knife she had pressed against his groin.

"How dare you?" she hissed.

"Mona, is that really you?"

"Yes, it's me or what's left of me. I was shot in the chest when my safe house was discovered. Next thing I know I found myself here, in this warehouse, only in this aberration of a body. What the hell is this all about?"

"I made a clone of you, Mona. I think you died and afterwards your spirit transferred itself into this clone of you I made."

"I have the memories of everything you've done to this body. It's strange, like being two people."

"You know what this means? We can live forever. You and I, together, if only you'll give me a second chance."

"You can't lie to me about the role you've played in all this. You're a sick man to use my creation to kill people. The war is your fault. I'll never forgive you for that."

The knife in Mona's hand swiped forward and rested on Andrew's throat before she pulled it away and ran from the room. "I was really starting to fall for you, too. I wish I'd never met you."

With that, Mona Teller was gone from his life....

"Mere?"

...only to appear in different incarnations over the centuries.

"Mere Roosevelt?"

Currently, she was imprisoned in the organiputer and would never be able to clone herself again unless he willed it to happen.

"It's me, Blitzen."

Only he wasn't Polk, he was Mere Roosevelt, and the decision about Teller was not his to make, although it might be someday.

"Roosevelt, are you OJ?"

Mere blinked and looked into the fierce eyes of Blitzen, the smuggler and pilot he'd befriended in the brief moments before the Rainmakers had handed him over to the Graylings. The behemoth's fingers curled into Mere's shoulders, shaking him gently.

"Yeah, I'm fine."

"You were out of it for a long time. I almost had Kalamazoo send for a doctor." Blitzen paused and smiled. "I'm glad to see you lived through your experience with the Graylings, although I doubt the other Rainmakers will feel the same way."

"Thanks," Mere said even as his head throbbed dully from his vision, dream, memory, whatever it was. If what he'd seen during the last few weeks of his crisping-induced hallucinations were true, Polk...and the part of him that was Polk had been responsible for billions of deaths. Mere now knew what he'd do once he found Polk. He would find a way to kill the bastard and then himself before he could turn into that mad scientist. Maybe Blitzen would help him.

"Listen, I'm going to go up front to help with the take-off, but I'll be back. My co-pilot's a good guy, but he wants to stay clear of whatever you're planning. Me, I'm half crazy anyway, so I figure I'll try to help you sneak away from the dock when we land. In the meantime, put this on." Blitzen tossed a violet jumpsuit, similar to the one the pilot himself wore, onto the floor next to Kalamazoo's discarded sack. "After take-off I'll come back and we can discuss our plan of attack."

The pilot turned to leave, but Mere's words stopped him mid-step, "I may ask you to do something you're uncomfortable with."

Blitzen winked, saying, "There's very little I won't do for the right cause," before ghosting the hatch to the cockpit.

G's under-earth apartment looked like a ravenous beast had been set loose in it. Fist-sized chunks were missing from the floor, walls, furniture, and appliances, giving the cavern the appearance of a war-ravaged bunker. It was easy enough to figure out, of course. The beast was him. G flexed and unflexed his fingers, whisking his hand over the clothes he'd swiped for Florida and absorbing the synthetic cloth through his skin and into his body. There the sycron would join the rock and metal from his apartment as well as the molecules of the Graylings swirling inside his cells.

His encounter with the arcane band of creatures was fresh in his thoughts, even if its aftermath remained murky within him. The ancient clones had done something to his body with an odd humming and, one by one, had stepped inside of him, melding their knowledge and memories with his own, changing his cybernetic parts into a receptor for their forms. He imbibed their bodies and thoughts into his cells where they would remain for as long as he lived. The Graylings had tinkered with Polk's manipulations and reformed G into something more than the coupling of human and machine, in some ways greater than Collings herself. They'd turned him into a black hole of a man, the opposite of an organic computer.

Instead of being able to process information and endlessly clone and manufacture raw ore and consumer goods, he now had the ability to absorb organically generated material. Anything that Collings had ever created, he could suck into the jail of his own body.

His new powers were difficult to control. Nothing within the walled city could harm him now, nothing but his own emotions. Florida lay on her back in a tiny alcove off the main living area that served as her room, but she wasn't alone. His metamorphosis had both heightened and distorted his senses. He could feel two life forces flickering behind her pulled drapes, intertwined in carnal exploits that he had once cared about and enjoyed. Never again. Never would he have cause to think that he was human enough to please another person or be pleased. His hands had only one function now—destruction.

G rolled his lounger forward, reached over to the entertainment center, and absorbed the holovision into his body, dividing the chemicals from the console into its primary components and undoing the processes that Collings had used to create the device. With each passing minute it became easier for him to imbibe and digest the diverse elements of the city. Nothing would escape him if he put his mind to it. He was the great equalizer, an exterminator. This was the role that the Graylings had envisioned for him. He could sense the ghosts of their thoughts on the matter. Why they chose now of all times to give him this power he couldn't fathom.

Florida strolled out from her room trailed by a husky middle-aged man. Both of them were naked with skin slicked with lovemaking. Florida carried herself erect and unabashed, but her partner took a wary look at G and turned back for his clothes.

"Don't worry, hon, it's just my dad. Aren't you my daddy, G?" Venom dripped from Florida's voice like white sugar, the memory of which the Graylings had imparted to him along with other pre-war tidbits.

Florida looked awfully pleased with herself. She shimmied toward him, rolling her shoulders and hips in a primal dance, swaying to an internal rhythm. She was in rare form. Even with the complete disregard she'd shown recently for his feelings, G never imagined that she would openly flaunt her sexual encounters with other men.

Florida laughed at the look on his face, a feral, mocking exhalation of air. There was nothing human in that beautiful body that jiggled toward him. She was a disease without a host, a body without a soul. He should never have brought her back to life, a mistake he could now rectify.

G didn't stand as much as he assimilated the lounger beneath him. He bent up out of his crouch and smiled. Florida either didn't notice or care about the disappearance of the furniture, lost as she was in her gyrations. G held out his arms and waited patiently for their bodies to collide. Florida teased him for awhile, feinting forward and slipping back, long enough for her lover to emerge from the back room. Darting to her left and right, she scissored forward into G's embrace.

"Florida, how long do you want to hang out here? I'm starved."

It was a funny thing for the man to say because G felt the same way. Florida could not answer as her tongue and windpipe were the first things he absorbed into him. He did not want to hear her beg for respite or mercy. The warm body in his arms disappeared inside him in seconds, very much unlike the difficult birth that brought her to life. The space where flesh once writhed was replaced by vapor and air as G's arms swept through nothingness into the folds of his own body.

Florida was inside him now. He would never forget her.

G thought he heard a man's shriek followed by the patter of racing footsteps, but it might very well have been the breeze moaning from the grate above and swirling down into the cave. He could sense the flickering of the thoughts and emotions of his former lover within him, ones he had not been able to see or touch in the flawed incarnation that he and Collings had cloned. He lowered himself and lay back on the floor, allowing himself to sink into the synthetic cement.

Particle by particle, he feasted on the chemical stew below, plunging through the layers of Collings' skin. He would soon submerge into the depths and join his surrogate mother and friend. He would ease the organiputer's suffering. The whole world's suffering. He eased back and let his body devour the floor, wondering if he had any limits or if the entire city would not be enough to sate him.

*   *   *

Marin checked to see if her knife had fallen out of the scabbard at her side before lifting her head above the pile of wheat in the cargo hatch of the hovercraft. It had been relatively easy for her to sneak past Boise and Toledo—the two farmhands Kalamazoo had corralled to load grain onto the ship. It had been much harder, by far, to be devious enough not to be left behind by Mere.

She'd snuck up onto the eaves of the town hall and had eaves-dropped on his conversation with Kalamazoo.

Now she was on a vessel hurtling toward Collings, the city she'd watched from afar and dreamed of one day visiting. Mere would not shed her as easily as he thought. He would need her help, she was sure of it. Besides, any risk or danger was better than staying another minute in her village without the ability to control her own fate. The hell with being the chosen. She'd never asked for the honor or responsibility. Let them pick a new victim for their plans. She had better things to do than living at the beck and call of others.

Marin wished the tiny windows in the cargo bay looked down as well as out. Even though she'd waded through the grain to the glass by the back hatch, she could not make out anything other than a series of tall spires above the city walls, the ones she'd stared at and monitored her whole life. The ship approached the tower of the tallest domed building and circled to the far side. It hovered momentarily then descended toward a series of docks not far from the top of the structure. A small squad of men waited for the craft to land as the vessel turned in mid-air and backed into an empty berth.

Worried about being spotted, Marin submerged herself in the wheat, leaving only her forehead peeking above the tan mound. She had no idea if the patrol at the docks was dangerous so she fought the urge to race toward Mere until after he emerged from the ship and dealt with the armed men. Patience had never been one of her strong suits and the dried grain itched like hell, but she struggled to keep her composure and remain still. She would be out of the hold soon enough, long before the oxygen ran out, at least that's what she kept telling herself. She was probably just imagining the air getting thin anyway.

Before she could work herself into a paranoid freak-out about the lack of ventilation, Mere appeared. He walked around the side of the transport next to the bearded pilot. Both wore slate-colored jumpsuits, bordering on violet in the deep shadows cast by the building looming above the loading platform. Several armed men in white shirts approached the pair and Mere's husky companion did the talking. What Marin expected to be a tense scene was miti-gated by the pilot's smile and easy gestures. Whatever Mere's friend said seemed to work. Weapons were holstered and the patrol followed the twosome into the building.

Marin counted to a hundred, readying herself to follow after Mere. She didn't want to take too long in case workers had been dispatched to unload the cargo. At thirty she thought she might go insane from her itching skin; at forty-five another man left the hovercraft and snuck past the building checkpoint, presumably another pilot; at eighty Marin lost her patience and crawled up on top of the grain, flipping a toggle that she hoped would open the back door to the vessel.

A metal ramp descended and clattered against the paved floor of the docking bay, and her world turned upside down. The realization of what she'd done came to her in the short amount of time it took her feet to slide out from under her. The gravity inside the ship had been regulated. Without it, she was affected much like Mere had been in her village. Her perspective of the world changed in a heartbeat. The ground became a wall that she slid along—the side of the mushroom-domed building became her floor. She tucked and rolled down the incline, crashing to a stop against a strange-looking glass window that refracted the light inside like a prism.

Her spine ached and her knees and elbows bled from several spots, but she was more worried about the clatter she'd made while falling—not to mention her inadvertent shrieks. She should have foreseen the shift in gravity. It was a miracle that the ship had landed on this side of the building and she hadn't plummeted to her death.

Marin heard several men's voices approaching. She staggered to her feet, perched on the side of the building which to her was the ground, only inclined thirty or so degrees. She raced along the glass windows above the archway and saw several white shirts scurry out onto the docks below her, rushing toward the open grain compartment.

"Stowaway?" she heard one ask, before their voices were lost to the wind. She hurried up the slope toward the top of the dome, figuring she was safe from being spotted. Still, she didn't want to chance one of the men looking up and seeing her. It was an odd feeling. Exhilarating. She felt like a fly or a spider as she scaled the glass spire.

Mere's destination must lie at the top of the building. She felt certain of it. She didn't understand how she'd come to rely so heavily on her intuition, but who was she to question fate? Careful to plant her sandals on the slick surface before taking her next step, she walked toward the curved underside of the oval dome feeling very much like a god.

* * *

G swam in the memories of the Graylings—gunfire, chaos and bloodshed—as he sank beneath the foundation of the city, lower than he'd ever been before. He had no idea that Collings was so immense. The organiputer was at least the mass of the city above, having pushed herself down hundreds, perhaps thousands of meters into the earth like a bundle of tree roots. If she were to suddenly disappear the city would cave in on itself in a cataclysmic quake.

Millions would die, like they had during the war. The city's destruction was a difficult decision for G to make, but one he was willing to shoulder. Humankind was ill-equipped to see itself as the virus it was or to grieve the thousands of species it had slain during its industrial revolutions. The parts of Collings he'd absorbed in his downward spiral made his vision clearer, his decision easier.

He stopped his descent and sent his consciousness swirling through the organiputer to experience the city one last time before wiping it from the face of the earth. It was an odd feeling. He found himself encompassing the metropolis from bottom to top, end to end. Many of the structures, particularly the lightscrapers, had been constructed by the organiputer. They would not be immune to his hunger. Other cities weren't safe from him either. He could sense linkages leading from Collings to smaller segments of the organic computer housed in other ports around the globe. He would draw these portions into his body as well. Chaos and change would once again dominate the world.

He now knew what it was like to be Polk, impotent and omnipotent both, with the pulse of the planet at his fingertips. He understood that this kind of power was too exhilarating not to use and that he'd spent unnecessary energy despising his longtime nemesis. Polk was to be pitied almost as much as G himself was. He could also sense Teller's body deep within the organiputer, straining against her fetters to even the slate against her long-time foe. She would not be immune from his wrath either. He would bring the long war of these two bitter enemies to a fitting, apocalyptic end.

VIOLET

31

Mere had an intense feeling of deja vu. He was manacled by thick metal bracers to a combination gurney and organiport in Polk's penthouse. He was not far from where he'd brooded by the bar months before during the Skytown party when he was first crisped and his former life had been wrested from him. Blitzen lay beside him on a similar contraption. The additional strap gagging the Rainmaker's mouth did not seem to rattle the pilot's composure or affect his capacity for mirth. The pilot's eyes darted, not from fear, but in anticipation of what was probably the final scene in the tragedy of Mere's life.

It was all so anticlimactic. Donning the pilot's violet jumpsuit and striding into Polk's stronghold, Mere had felt almost heroic. He and Blitzen had been discovered by a security patrol, cordoned off, and captured before they could even agree on a sensible plan to sneak up to the upper levels of the lightscraper. What was wrong with him? Had he thought his decision to return to the city and confront Polk was an end onto itself? Without a rigorous plan of attack, he hadn't had the ghost of a chance to succeed. His incompetence shouldn't surprise him. Throughout his battle with the other clones, Mere had survived through dumb luck and the sacrifices of his friends.

It was miracle he'd lived as long as he had.

At least he and Blitzen didn't have long to wait. Polk, shadowed by a tall thin woman with green-tinted hair and a permanent scowl, entered the penthouse and ushered away the detachment of guards and gray shirts who'd accompanied the prisoners. Polk paused and whispered something in his companion's ear. Mere tilted his head and craned his neck as he watched the hushed conversation heat up. He had spent many hours like this growing up, lifting his head above the level of his bed reading novelights. His neck muscles were thick and he could keep this position for hours.

The woman nodded vehemently and asked, "What if something goes wrong?"

"I'll be fine, Lina. Besides, this is one of those times a man needs to be alone. Mere and I have a lot to discuss and I think it's only right that I give him the dignity of dispatching him myself."

"Here then," the woman said, slapping a small bag in Polk's hands. "Just administer the solution into an artery. I'd recommend the neck."

"I know how to do this. I've killed clones of mine before."

Lina shrugged and stomped over to Blitzen's table. Switching it to hover mode, she eased the gurney across the penthouse and over to the elevator which she took down to a lower level, leaving Mere alone with Polk.

"I wasn't trying to frighten you by the way."

"What then?" Mere asked.

"I killed those other clones because I thought they were flawed, unworthy of becoming president."

"Becoming you, you mean."

"That too. The transference isn't so bad. I still have the memories this body had before I took it over, as I do the lives of my other hosts. Some of them are quite strong."

"Sounds like you're trying to convince yourself, not me."

Polk looked genuinely perplexed. "Brave words considering the position you're in. It's a shame that Teller had to interfere. I would have enjoyed getting to know you."

"What do you have to lose?" Mere asked.

"What do you mean?"

"Why not chance letting me be your next incarnation. Aren't you getting bored being the same person decade after decade?"

Polk laughed. "Let me put it this way—are you eager to die, Mere?"

"No."

"Have you ever thought about killing yourself?"

"No, never."

"That feeling doesn't change whether you live thirty years or three thousand. As a matter of fact, the longer you live the more you understand how precious life is."

"Quite the philosopher, aren't we?"

"Actually WE are quite dense about some things. I'm sure you've seen it in yourself. Self-absorbed. Unappreciative of the people who care about you."

Mere didn't know what was more insufferable. Being killed or getting a lecture from an obvious hypocrite.

"OJ, fine, Polk. I admit I've made a lot of mistakes, but what have you done that's any different? Where are all the people in your life with whom you share quality relationships? That woman in here earlier, is she your girlfriend?"

"Not exactly."

"And friends, who are your friends, Polk?"

"You don't understand. I never claimed to be a wise man. I do think, however, that I understand my limitations. I'm not destined to have any close relationships. It's not in me. It's not in you."

"I'm not sure what happened during the war to screw you up, but the person you're talking about isn't me. If I have a chance to live past today, I'll devote myself to helping other people."

"I find that difficult to believe."

"That's because you don't believe in anything. You're pathetic, Polk. Looking at you now only convinces me that being at the top is the sickest kind of dream. How many people have you killed so that you wouldn't feel uncomfortable?"

"More than you can imagine. Including you."

"Why did you change your name to George? When your skin changed color from so many clonings you couldn't handle it. You're a coward."

"Maybe I just hated my father and the name he gave me. At least I had a father."

Silence settled on the penthouse after that for quite a few minutes. Polk sank into a lounger, zipping and unzipping the small white bag like a possessed violist. Occasionally, he fondled a needle and a vial of clear liquid inside the case. Polk did not look up and Mere couldn't stare at him without feeling sympathy, an emotion he didn't want to have for his murderer or for himself.

He peered across the room to the banks of shutterglass that did not distort light or reflect images as magnificently as they had during the evening hours. Ghostly traces of an overcast sky gave a milky sheen to the city while Polk sighed and muttered, "It's all about the spectrum, isn't it? Perspective is a moving target."

Outside the window opposite him, Mere swore that he saw Marin clinging to an ozonodome window dressed in chartreuse shorts and a long-sleeve shirt. She was positioned at an odd angle, almost as though she were standing on the side of the building, the undersides of her worn sandals clearly visible.

Mere took it as an omen and a final hallucination from the crisping. He was just seeing a hint of those things he professed to Polk that he would miss: friendship, a relationship, perhaps even a marriage with a young woman who had yet to be beaten down by might-have-beens.

Polk came out of his stupor. "Do you think black's a beautiful color?"

"As a scientist you should know that it's the absence of color," Mere said, distracted by how surreal Marin's form was up among the clouds.

"It's funny. When I was younger I had beliefs about people based on the color of their skin. In the end, the most important color is red. The color of blood."

"You've certainly spilled enough of it to know," Mere said.

Polk rose, closing the bag and dropping it onto his lounger. With a sweeping gesture, he motioned toward the ceiling to the company logo, an immense red pyramid hanging on wires above him, casting a triangular shadow over his grim features. "Is this worth worshipping? Am I? What if I told you that this pyramid wasn't red, but violet. If I tortured you long enough you would believe it."

The building trembled as though in response. A transmission blinked on Polk's comlink, but he ignored it, saying, "When you define the world for everyone else, it has no meaning for yourself."

"Cry me a river of tears," Mere said, pulling the saying from inside of him through his connectivity to Polk's past lives.

Polk smiled and it was horrifying, the building vibrating behind him. Mere squirmed in his restraints. This was no hallucination, but a cityquake, a mammoth one. The room swayed and buckled. The wires mooring the pyramid above Polk's head snapped, sending the massive sculpture plummeting toward the president who had time to say only, "A miracle," before being crushed beneath the massive corporate symbol.

Mere felt like he'd been kicked in the stomach. The world

swirled and his eyes could find no place to focus that was not in frenzied motion. The floor buckled and cracked from where the pyramid had fallen, but nothing of Polk remained except for one of his hands reaching out from under the triangular base, the lighter skin of his palm bordering the darker curls of his fingers. The supports of the canopied bar toppled and fell. Paintings shook loose from the walls. Vases tumbled into shards. A knife shattered the shutterglass across the room and Marin tumbled through the opening toward him.

She whisked across the floor as though it were a slide, trying to slow her descent by grasping onto pieces of rubble, the destroyed bar and, finally, the pyramid. She crashed into the organiport next to his hoverbed and scrambled up the wall. She looked a fright: bloodied, bruised, and beautiful. She sliced through his thick restraints with an odd-looking knife. Once his hands were freed, Mere helped her loosen the braces around his feet, gripping her waist to keep her from sliding away. He held her tightly to his chest as panes of shutterglass shattered and the see-sawing lightscraper sent them ricocheting across the room.

Marin holstered her knife and clung to him as they reeled and skidded in the maelstrom. Although they shouted warnings of falling debris and flying glass to each other, no words could be made out over the rumbling of the earth. Mere fought to navigate himself and Marin through the deadly obstacle course of a building shaking apart, but her sideways gravity and the swaying tower kept smashing them into the wall by where he had been imprisoned. Luckily, this section of the penthouse held organiports and very little metal and glass. Mere took the brunt of the collisions with his back.

He had to get them away from the raining mortar and shattered panes or they wouldn't stand a chance. He aimed them toward the balcony off of Polk's private office. He knew where it was from his dream or perhaps it had actually become a memory now. Something strange was tearing at his insides much like the vibrations destroying the ozonodome.

Flashes of Polk's thoughts, regrets, triumphs, and previous incarnations flooded over him as he struggled to maneuver them toward the room in the northwest corner of the building. The skylight burst into shards of death above as Mere fought against the tides of Polk's memories. It was obvious now that the president was dead and his spirit had moved on to attack Mere. Fear swelled inside of him in a fevered pitch and he felt the immediacy of another presence. Drop the girl and save yourself, a voice said. You must survive. WE must survive.

It would be so easy for him to push away Marin and stagger toward his office, unencumbered. It was his only real chance to survive.

Cowardice. Heroism. Denial. Despair. Victory. Hope. He would not give in to fear. The bastard would not overcome him. Not now, not ever. He would not leave behind the woman who had risked her life to save him, even if it meant his own death. Mere redoubled his efforts and forced his way over mounds of rubble and broken furniture to the private office. The roar of the quake was deafening. A portion of the penthouse splintered off and slid away where the banks of elevators had once stood. The lights snapped off and the hatch to Polk's office ghosted.

Mere muscled his way through the wreckage of the room. He aimed for the balcony archway and saw the cliffwall swaying toward them. Marin's off-kilter gravity and the tilted room whisked them toward the shattered glass doors. A loud crackle, as though the spine of the building had snapped, rattled in his ear drums. The ozonodome swung closer to the cliffwall which Mere now knew was really the ground outside the city. They slid across the broken glass, through the archway and slammed into the balcony. With his free arm, Mere gripped the steel railing and held on for dear life as the dome of the lightscraper seemed poised to swing into the earth.

The building slowed just before crashing and an equilibrium was reached. The mooring of the building shrieked and Mere could sense the dome poised to catapult itself the other way, all the way to outer space for all he knew. He leapt, pushing himself and Marin off the railing, which clipped his feet as it whipsawed back toward the city.

He wrapped his arms around Marin as their conflicting gravities dragged them eastward and down like a sickly bird shrieking toward a crash landing. But it was flying, nevertheless. They were, perhaps, the first people ever to be blessed with this feeling without the assistance of metallic wings or high-tech machines even though they would soon collide with the unforgiving earth. No better way to go. In these final moments, he even lost his fear of heights. *You've earned a good death, Polk,* Mere found himself thinking, *better than you deserve.*

* * *

Marin groaned and slowly raised herself up on her elbows atop a hillside choked with yellow grass, her battered body shivering in a cool breeze that hinted at the unforgiving winter to come. She looked around the rugged slope, but Mere was nowhere to be seen. She must have been unconscious for quite some time. It was twilight over the walled city that was no longer walled, but rubble as far as the eye could see. Not a single ozonodome remained standing in the carnage of what was once Collings. The fading sun cast a blood-red hue on the newly formed ruins, although she swore she could see thin violet strips shimmer and intermingle with the red. Perhaps her eyesight had been damaged in the fall or else the sunset, one of those that layered the colors of the rainbow one atop the other, was playing tricks on her.

Nothing seemed broken, but every movement brought her a diverse sensation of pain. Moving her neck, her toes throbbed. Leaning on her elbow to climb to her hands and knees, her temple burned. Every nerve ending felt punctured and dislocated. Her mind was little better. For better or worse, she understood now what it was to be "the chosen." She had chosen herself, after all. She was a clone of Teller, she knew that now. The memories and former lives of the ancient scientist filled her head with confusion and triumph. Triumph because Collings and the organiputer that Polk had used to trap Teller's previous incarnation was now destroyed. She wasn't sure how it had happened, but suspected that G had something to do with it.

Was this really the end of Polk? She was certain that no one could have survived the impact of the sculpture that had fallen on him. He must have died almost instantly. If so, Mere must have already been under Polk's influence when he saved her. If only she could be sure.

She staggered to her feet and stared toward the flattened city. All her previous inclination toward logic and science was heightened and supported by centuries of observations. It was strange to possess knowledge that she herself hadn't learned. Marin limped toward the edge of the ridge and glimpsed a figure that she had both hoped and feared to discover. Mere lay spread eagle at the foot of the slope not far from the shattered city wall. He must have kept tumbling after he hit the ground. His skewed gravity from the destruction of the organiputer must have reverted back to normal there.

His violet jumpsuit was in shreds from the waist up and he wasn't moving. As much as she desired to know if he was all right, she couldn't bring herself to hurry toward him. Each possibility—his life or death—would be reason to celebrate or mourn.

She eased her battered body down the incline, weaving her way along a less rugged portion of the hillside toward the fallen clone. Mere's face was poised directly skyward. For the first time in his life, his gravity was normal, the organiputer's spell broken. She dipped down below the level of the fading sun onto a shady slope and her younger self won out. She rushed toward him with all the speed her aching body could muster.

She threw herself down next to him and placed an ear against his mouth. At first, it was difficult to tell if he was breathing because of the swirling gusts, but she felt a warm stream nip at her lobes and a tickling in her drums. She shivered. He was alive.

But who exactly was alive? Polk or Mere? After everything Teller's former selves had gone through, how could she trust that no remnant of the tyrant remained trapped beneath Mere's skin. She drew her knife and held it to his throat just as the first clone of herself had done before escaping from Andrew's laboratory without getting her revenge. How many centuries had she...part of herself rued the day that she had not slit his throat while he slept.

Marin pressed the blade into the soft skin of his adam's apple and drew a bead of blood that welled and trickled down his neck. She was a child. She was ancient. She would have her revenge. She would not let her actions be controlled by a bitter woman who had destroyed more than a few innocents to further her own ends. She was Marin and Teller both, but who would win out in the end? It was the same dilemma facing Mere, a mobius of admiration and revenge.

She noticed how stark the pale skin of her knife hand was

against Mere's blackness. He had darkened considerably since he'd fallen from the ozonodome, almost to the shade that Polk had been. She found it handsome on him and fitting. That which you hate you will always turn into in the end.

She shifted onto her knees, trying to stay comfortable until Mere woke. She had no idea what decision she would make. Perhaps it would be best to kill him, then herself. That way the knowledge they had of Pandora's Box would forever remain with them.

Feeling the cold wind bite through her hasty choice of clothing, Marin lay on her side and burrowed in next to Mere so that they could share each other's warmth. She kept the knife blade pressed close to his throat, waiting for night to fall.

ULTRAVIOLET
Epilogue

Greek bent over the crackling fire, which bled smoke up to the jagged hole in his cavern's ceiling. He huddled from the winter gusts that managed, despite his best efforts, to invade every corner of his domain. He snapped twigs, like the brittle bones of the residents buried in the rubble outside his cave, and dropped them into the sputtering flames. He had scavenged for food in the ruins of Collings many times that winter, but his former self, G, had done much too good a job drawing all the organiputer-generated objects inside of him, including packaged food. The pain in his sunken stomach went well beyond the usual rumbling from hunger. A feral quake shook his insides from neck to waste, a collision of tectonic plates from where man and machine intersected.

He was going to die. Not even the crisping could help sustain him now. He had swilled all the vials of the drug weeks before, hoping to either overdose or lose himself in the memories of Collings City, Colorado Springs, and the hunting lodges of the long-forgotten tribes whose shades lingered on these steppes. There were some things you were better off not knowing. Humanity was blessed that way.

It was a dark age outside his cave. The scattered bands of nomads wandering the land after Polk's fall had no way of knowing their past and he was convinced that new legends would arise to explain the world, perhaps even a few about himself.

Greek recalled the first and last time he left the ruins of the city—just after he'd destroyed it. He was insane at the time, but could sense another small organiputer housed in a farming village outside the city walls. The villagers had tried reasoning with him, but seeing the mad look in his eyes, they let him storm into a primitive, yet functional scientific lab and draw the fledgling organic computer into his body. It was Teller's personal creation, the one by which she'd used to fuel her long battle with Polk.

No one would ever live beyond the span of a natural lifetime again, except for himself. Now death looked ready, finally, to claim him.

Even a few weeks earlier, Greek would have stood a good chance of surviving the journey to New Springs, a community of several thousand situated some distance to the south. Standing up was a colossal enough undertaking these days let alone such a rigorous winter trek. He hadn't been outside at all since yesterday, at about the same time, when he'd dragged himself out to watch the sunset, one of the two things that occurred outside his memories that still gave him pleasure. That and the appearance of the unfamiliar rodent-like creature that had wandered into his hearth a dozen times all told since winter began. The curious animal had pointed ears like a dog or cat and its mottled patches of black and white fur hinted at some previous hybrid mutation.

Greek had wrestled with his conscience for days now, trying to decide whether or not to lay a trap to catch the beast. The meat would provide him with a week more of life at most, even with the low needs of his supercharged metabolism. His reticence in the matter was ridiculous. The man who had devoured a city full of people had qualms about fading some insignificant rodent with a brain the size of his little finger.

"He was a noble man in his declining years, that's what you hope they'll say about you."

I'm not in the mood.

Some—very few actually—traveled long distances to ask the advice of the world's wisest man and all they got in response was the incoherent rambling of a drug addict.

"Not any longer. There's no more crisping. I'm free of it."

Hardly. I bet you're smart enough to create an organiputer and distil your own crisping.

"I'll kill myself first."

If you're so hot to kill something then why don't you slag that nasty rodent so you can live longer.

"Go to hell."

We're already there.

Greek's stomach cramped and he could swear he felt his spine touch the underside of his belly button. So hungry. The pain, at least, quieted the voices inside him. He crawled away from the dense smoke and crackling flames that spoke in ancient and indecipherable tongues. He dragged himself toward the entrance of his cave and peered westward onto the rolling hills that led to a range of mountains that had gone almost unnoticed inside Collings and had been seen merely as ridges on the terra cliffwall. It was funny how the earth, when seen at a strange angle, distance or perspective, could erase the greatest of landmarks. Greek struggled the last few meters to the cavern mouth and eased into a sitting position with his legs dangling out over a small ridge leading down from the ruined ozonodome.

Greek could not tell yet if the sunset would be dazzling or not. So often it was blunted by the crests of the mountain peaks before it could burn from orange to fiery red. Not important. It was the mysteries that hovered just outside the spectrum of colors that interested him most. The machine part of him sensed a greater swathe of colors than the human eye and sometimes he could discern the sounds and static caused by the winds and the continually shifting earth. After all, colors had the capacity to bewitch and confuse the weak spirited, those who did not understand that shades are nothing but a trick of tumbling light.

Sight was the most misleading of all senses. A crutch by which women and men could order and define the mysteries of mountains, sky and rivers that would otherwise make them feel small. Greek closed his eyes to the trickeries of twilight and searched for the secrets of the land and air with his skin, nose, ears, and tongue.

He did not want to die without gleaning what was beyond the senses of the living. He could understand why people turned to religion in their fading years. It was comforting to believe that something of you could survive beyond the shell of your body. This hope, like most faith, spurned people to dazzling heights of creation as well as frightening acts of cruelty and barbarism. To believe in something, you have to know it to be true and to know something is to lose yourself to the possibilities of the present.

Loose rocks cascaded down the slope below him. Greek opened his eyes and discovered a young woman, burdened with a backpack, deerskin coat, and fur boots, scrambling up the rise to his cave. To the south and west, he made out a half dozen figures unloading a dog-drawn sled and setting up camp for the night.

Were these emissaries from New Springs or marauders searching for plunder in the ruins?

The long-legged woman reached the small shelf next to him and took off a snow-spackled hat, shaking long brown curls away from her gray eyes. High cheekbones and supple lips highlighted a long jaw line. Her skin was brown and her otherwise youthful face was creased with worry lines around her mouth and eyes. Bending to his level, she said, "Are you the man called G?"

"My name is Greek now."

"My grandparents told me that you might be calling yourself something different these days. We brought food and medicine from New Springs. We're sorry it took so long, but we've had some difficulties. The coalition of city states have mobilized troops to cut off our trade routes and isolate us from our allies."

"Your troubles are no concern of mine."

The woman dropped to her knees and said, "I didn't mean to offend you. My name's Florida. I've come to ask your help."

Florida. Why did she have to be called that of all things?

"I believe you know my grandparents: Mere Polk and Marin Teller. They told me to tell you their last names, although I've never heard them use those before."

Just when he thought he no longer had the capacity to be surprised, he was faced with the descendant of mortal enemies. Polk and Teller's grand-daughter was named after the woman he'd loved, almost as though to torture him. He wanted to deny such a thawing of hate could ever happen, but he could see traces of both scientists in Florida's face and in the confident way she carried herself.

"They wanted me to ask you to accompany us back. They said you might be able to help us stop the war that's brewing between the cities and plain dwellers. They told me that you know a great many things that others have forgotten."

Greek felt too drained to laugh and too bitter to feel pride from the compliment. Did he really want to live among other people again? All he could do was prolong the inevitable. Humanity seemed destined to destroy itself. Yet, Florida was living proof that new beginnings could spring from despair. If Polk and Teller could overcome their hatred and fears, perhaps he, too, could change.

"I'll come with you, but I'm not sure what help I'll be. Can you help me up?"

Greek reached out with an unsteady hand. Florida took off her gloves and pulled him to his feet.

"You don't look so good. Are you well?" she asked.

"I'm fine, never better."

"My friends should be starting dinner soon down below, if you're hungry."

Greek laughed and his stomach twisted in anticipation. "Why don't you go and ask everyone up. I have a fire started and I think you'll find my cave more comfortable than sleeping outdoors."

Florida squeezed his shoulder like an old travelling companion and said, "I'm glad you'll be joining us. Be right back."

The young woman bounded down the incline and raced toward her waiting friends. Greek took in his final sunset from the cavern archway and strode back inside his home with more energy than he'd had in eons. He halted at his wood pile and selected several meaty logs to make a worthy fire for the night's festivities.

A small, squat figure looked up from its berth next to the fire pit and tore off down a hallway into the bowels of the ozonodome. The rodent was nimble and well fed, with a healthy black and white coat. It had found a way to survive the winter without him. It was a survivor. As he was. As Polk and Teller were. As people were.

Perhaps Greek had maligned hope unfairly. He had to admit that his insides were burning with anticipation for the future. Maybe humanity could finally overcome its destructive nature. Maybe they could learn. There was nothing to lose by trying.